even
when
you
lie
to
me

even when you lie to me

JESSICA ALCOTT

 Published in the United States by Ember, an imprint of Random House Children's Books, a division of Penguin Random House LLC, New York. Originally published in hardcover in the United States by Crown Books for Young Readers, New York, in 2015.

Ember and the E colophon are registered trademarks of Penguin Random House LLC.

Visit us on the Web! randomhouseteens.com

Educators and librarians, for a variety of teaching tools, visit us at RHTeachersLibrarians.com

The Library of Congress has cataloged the hardcover edition of this work as follows:
Alcott, Jessica.
Even when you lie to me / Jessica Alcott. — First edition.
pages cm.
Summary: Because she sees herself as ugly and a misfit, tolerated only because of her friendship with pretty and popular Lila, Charlie dreads her senior year but a crush on the new charismatic English teacher, Mr. Drummond, makes school bearable until her eighteenth birthday, when boundaries are crossed.
ISBN 978-0-385-39116-0 (trade)
ISBN 978-0-385-39117-7 (lib. bdg.)
ISBN 978-0-385-39118-4 (ebook)
[1. Self-perception—Fiction. 2. Teacher-student relationships—Fiction. 3. High schools—Fiction. 4. Schools—Fiction. 5. Best friends—Fiction. 6. Friendship—Fiction.] I. Title.
PZ7.A3349Eve 2015 [Fic]—dc23 2014006648
ISBN 978-0-385-39119-1 (tr. pbk.)

Printed in the United States of America
10 9 8 7 6 5 4 3 2 1
First Ember Edition 2016

Random House Children's Books supports the First Amendment and celebrates the right to read.

To John

For the tagline,
and for everything else

even
when
you
lie
to
me

The day after I turned eighteen was the day Mr. Drummond left for good.

I was never a pretty girl. I knew it more from people's silences than from anything they said. They didn't call me beautiful. They didn't say I was winsome or sexy or gorgeous. They told me I was smart. They told me I could write. On the subject of my looks there was dead air, like a space in a cracked tooth waiting for a cap that never came. There was something complicit in it, as if they were waiting for me to duck my head and apologize.

Drummond was the only one who ever made me feel any different. And I was the reason he left.

august

chapter 1

It was my last day of summer, and even though I hated summer, I was dreading the end of it. I stretched out on my bed, annoyed and hot. In summer I was always too hot. Clothes stuck to my skin like a greasy coat of paint. The sheets had twined themselves around my legs during the night, and I kicked them off impatiently. I'd woken up early, nervous about the first day of school, and now my mind wouldn't slow down. The longer I lay there, the more I thought about it.

My phone rang; it was Lila. "Pool?" She had been lobbying for the pool all summer.

"Ugh, really? Do we have to?"

"It's our final day of freedom and you've come to the pool *once*. Yes, we have to."

"But it's hot outside."

"That's the genius of it, Charlie. You go to the pool when it's hot and the water cools you down."

"Or—follow me here—you stay inside, in the air-conditioning, and never get hot in the first place."

"I am not letting you go to the library again. You're frightening the librarians. You're supposed to leave at night."

"They have free books and comfortable chairs and no limit on how long you're allowed to stay, all right? I checked."

Lila sighed.

"Fine," I said, though my pulse sped up.

"Thank you. You could bring Frida."

"To the pool? I don't think she's allowed."

"We could tie her up outside the gates and let her out in the park after. Good guy bait."

"I'm not using my dog as some kind of man lure."

"I'll be outside in twenty minutes," she said.

I took a quick shower, blasting water at my knotted hair and finally scraping it back in defeat. It was just going to get wet again anyway. Frida, who'd been sleeping in my room, woofed softly as I left. She was a big dog, a malamute—my dad liked to call her a husky enlarged by 150 percent—but she had the temperament of a semiconscious pillow.

"Bye, Dad," I called. "Frida's upstairs if you need her for . . . napping."

He appeared in the front hallway. "Off with Lila?"

"Unfortunately," I said. "You sure you don't want any help today?"

"Yeah, I'll be fine," he said. "You should not have to spend your last free day working in the basement with me."

I had been his assistant over the summer: he was an artist, and he sold most of his work over the Internet. My mother had helped him for years, but just before the summer she'd gotten a new job—she was some kind of bank manager now; I could never remember the exact title—and she'd been working late nearly every day since.

I sighed. “Mom got to you too, then?”

“What did Mom get to Dad about?” My mother came in from the kitchen with her hair in a sun-yellow slick of ponytail, wearing workout clothes that skimmed her body like a tongue. I had on some paint-spattered terry cloth shorts and a faded floral bathing suit with one sagging paralytic strap. I was suddenly aware of how tight the suit was against my stomach.

“Oh,” I said. “I thought you’d left for work already.”

“No, you didn’t get quite that lucky, Charlotte,” she said. “You want to come running with me? Get your energy up for your last day?”

“That’s funny,” I said.

“I’ll take it slow,” she said. I could feel her looking at me like she was assessing a used car for damages. “You can change first if you want.”

I could feel my neck flushing. I turned to my dad. “Why don’t you ever get asked to go running?”

“Your mom gave up on me before you were even born,” he said.

“You’ve still got the short shorts, though, don’t you?” I said. “I saw you wearing some while you mowed the lawn last weekend.”

“That was a laundry emergency,” he said. “But I apologize if I caused any permanent retinal damage.”

My mother watched us like we were playing a game with rules she couldn’t follow. “Okay, well, if that means you’ve decided you’re not coming, I need to get a move on,” she said. She pulled my dad to her for a kiss. I looked away.

"Bye, Charlotte," she said. "I hope you have a good last day."

I waited until she left to say, "I'm changing."

When I came downstairs again, my dad was getting ready to take Frida for a walk. He was silent for a moment as I pulled my shoes on. Finally he said, "Kiddo, I know it's hard sometimes, but she loves you."

"She could show it a little better," I said. "Those clothes were something, huh? She looked like she got hit with a cannon full of Nike products."

He ran his hand through his graying hair and tried not to smile. "Don't start."

"I'm not," I said. I stood up. "You definitely don't need me?"

"No, I don't," he said. "Now please leave. Frida and I have a busy napping schedule to adhere to."

I gave him a hug. As always, he smelled faintly of the cigarettes he pretended not to smoke. "I'll be back," I said.

"I hope so," he said.

Lila honked outside. "Okay see you later byeeee," I said all in a rush, then slammed the door and sprinted down the front steps. We lived in the thick of the suburbs; most of the houses in our neighborhood were restored old colonials, repainted in tasteful pastels. Our house was the smallest on the street, crammed in like it was jostling for its place. It felt like our limbs stuck out the windows when we tried to stretch.

Lila's car was as cool and dry as a cave. She looked annoyingly pretty that day: big brown eyes and a wide warm slash of a mouth. A pair of oversized white sunglasses barely pinned down her long dark hair, and she'd kicked off her flip-flops already. Her bare foot rested casually on the accelerator.

"Where's Frito?" she asked as I shut the door with the satisfying *whump* of an expensive car. Lila's parents were comfortable.

"Told you, she's not man bait. My dad needs the company, anyway."

Lila attempted a three-point turn that eventually became a nine-point turn. "This stupid car's too big," she muttered.

"They say girls don't have a good sense of spatial relations but I think that's a myth."

She glared at me. "Sexist."

"Curb!" I shouted as the front tires reared up.

Lila swore, then said, "I'm testing the bumper's resilience."

"Is it working?"

"Considering the number of times I've tested it, yes."

"And the neighbors' mailbox?"

"The neighbors' . . . oh." She squinted at it. "It's shaped like a cow. I did them a favor."

She grinned in a way I resented: it was so warm and flirtatious that I couldn't help smiling back, but when I saw her use it on other people I hated them for being drawn in by it. When we were younger, we were both outsiders—she was too loud and too brash, and I was too quiet and too shy: a flimsy negative of her. But as we got older, she began to tame herself into someone people liked; she kept her smile but learned not to lean in too close. And I—I watched.

When I was with Lila, I saw how much attention it was possible not to get. The waiter would bring her free drinks, or the cashier would write his number on her receipt, or the guy at the stoplight would roll down his window and lick the empty space between the V of his outstretched fingers. They acted like she owed them something just because they thought she was pretty. Watching it happen made it impossible for me to pretend that I was attractive. I could feel people's eyes slide off me as if I were coated with Vaseline.

She seemed to inhabit a different universe than I did, where even the most mundane interaction throbbed with sexual energy. It seemed exhausting. But I was interested in her stories of making out with random guys at the movies both because I was jealous and because I was curious. It wasn't like I had any of my own to occupy myself with.

Lila turned on the radio and twisted the knob, scrolling through station after station, only glancing at the road occasionally to ensure we hadn't drifted into oncoming traffic.

I pushed her fingers away. "Is driving boring for you? I take my life in my hands every time I get in this car." A DJ I liked came on and I settled back, satisfied.

"The greatest soft-rock hits of the eighties, nineties, and today," Lila said. "This is why we're so popular." But she didn't change the station.

By the time we got to the pool it was already crowded. Acid fizzed in my stomach.

"Come on, you're not going to melt." Lila opened the passenger door and I stepped outside. The heat pressed down on me like an iron.

"Blurgh," I muttered. "If I die, tell my mother I'm glad I didn't waste my last day of vacation by going on a run with her so we could talk about stride rates."

"I'm sure she'll be happy to hear that." Lila hooked her arm around mine. I hesitated. I never knew what to do with myself when people touched me, even people I knew as well as Lila. It felt like they were going to take something I wasn't willing to give. But Lila gripped me firmly, pulling me toward her, and I let her.

"I would be if I were her," I said. "Let's get this over with."

When we got to the changing room, I sat on a bench as Lila changed into a bikini.

"You're going to be boiling in those clothes," she said, nodding toward my black shirt and dark jeans. "Why did you wear your disgusting old sneakers to a pool?"

"Better boiling than burned. And I wore them because I like them and they are impeccably fashionable."

Lila sighed. She stripped off her shorts in one swift movement and turned her back as she lifted her shirt up. I couldn't help looking. Her body was beautifully simple, an unbroken sine wave of curves. My skin didn't fit the same way; it puckered and spilled out in places as if whoever had engineered me hadn't bought enough fabric.

Lila glanced at me, caught my eye, and quickly turned

away again. I stood up and started to pace. Just then, a group of girls' voices crashed into the room ahead of them, ricocheting off the tiles like bullets. I stiffened, but I didn't recognize any of them. I watched as they collided with one another, screeching and cackling and squealing and teasing.

"I'm ready, dude," Lila said. She saw me watching the girls and looked over at them too. "Charming. Come on, let's go boil."

We'd entered through the changing room, and even though I knew how busy the pool was, the noise and the crowd hit me with the force of a punch. A tinny radio was blasting a Top 40 station, and toddlers were screeching as they splashed each other with water. The sun was so white that the people crowding around the lip of the pool looked spectral. I couldn't help scanning the place for kids we knew, but I didn't see anyone yet. My T-shirt and jeans felt huge and ridiculous. I hesitated at the door, trying to think of some excuse to stay inside.

Lila spotted a couple of vacant sun loungers and sprinted over, her towel billowing behind her like a flag. When she noticed I wasn't following, she shouted, "Charlie! I found some *chairs*!"

The lifeguard twisted to look at her and then at me. "Goddammit, Lila," I muttered as I moved back into the shade. It was all too much. I hated the creaking, rusted loungers with their loose rubber slats that felt like a child's damp palm on your skin. I hated walking in the oil-slicked puddles on the concrete, hated the noise and the heat and the blinding sun. I couldn't go out there.

"*Charlie!* Get your ass on this *chair*!"

Now more people were looking, though when I didn't move they lost interest, used to teenagers shouting at each other.

Lila waved at me and raised her hands in a *what the hell?* gesture. I made myself walk toward her, keeping my eyes on the lounger. When I got to her she said, "Sudden-onset agoraphobia?"

"Something like that," I said, settling myself as the chair shrieked underneath me. "This thing's a safety hazard."

"It's fine," Lila said. She stretched out; her towel slipped lower to expose her smooth belly. She pulled her giant insectile pair of sunglasses down and adjusted them on her forehead.

"Are we playing canasta later?" I said, gesturing at them.

"Screw you, denim. They're trendy." She lowered them to the bridge of her nose and gave me the finger.

They looked good on her, but I never would have admitted it. I settled back and closed my eyes against the white glare of the sun.

"Boorman! What the hell are you doing here?"

My eyes flicked open. It was Jason Tierney, a guy from our class. Great.

He was eyeing Lila, trapping her under a leer. His plaid shirt was open, and I could see a shell necklace around his throat, resting on a smattering of curly golden chest hair. He held a pair of mirrored sunglasses in one hand and flicked them restlessly against his thigh.

I was horrified to see Lila give him her most flirtatious

smile. "Hey, Jase! Just trying to relax a little before the shitstorm tomorrow."

"I hear ya, I hear ya," he said, nodding too vigorously. "I tried to do a few laps, but with all the freaking kids here I could barely get through."

Lila laughed with the deep, throaty chuckle that she only ever used around guys. "This pool is probably half piss. So where've you been? Haven't seen you around much this summer."

"Been working at my dad's office in the city. The money sucks, but I got to go to a lot of gigs for free."

"Oh yeah? Like who?"

He reeled off a list of names I'd never heard of, but Lila nodded appreciatively. Jason hadn't glanced at me once.

Two other guys appeared behind him. I vaguely recognized them from school; they were a year behind us. One was bare-chested, with faintly outlined abs but enough pudginess at the edges that you could tell he would run to fat in a few years. The other was wearing a striped polo shirt, khaki shorts, and flip-flops; his body was as well maintained as an expensive racehorse's. He surveyed the landscape like he was looking for flaws in it, with the kind of casual authority that suggested long summers at his family's vacation house upstate. They both had on shell necklaces. Maybe they'd bought them together as a douchey alternative to friendship bracelets.

I became aware of my heartbeat, pulsing into my fingertips. It wouldn't be long before they noticed me; they were watching Lila, but they knew Jason had claimed her already. And sure enough, polo shirt was looking at me now, up and down, not in appreciation but with something that seemed like amusement. I felt naked despite my clothes. He was bored, clearly, but I was less boring than staring off into space.

"Nice outfit," he said. "You can't afford a bathing suit?"

A hot flush spread on my face like a stain. "Guess not," I managed to say eventually.

"Seriously? Are you poor or something?" He was interested now. He leaned forward slightly and smirked.

"No, I'm not poor. I just don't like swimming."

"You don't like swimming? Who doesn't like swimming?" His pudgy friend's head swiveled in my direction. "Did you hear this, Mike? She doesn't like swimming." He laughed.

My throat was so dry that the words stuck there until I coughed them up. "No, I don't. What does it matter?"

My defiance was a mistake; it only piqued his interest. He sat down on the edge of my lounger, his straight white teeth bared in a grin.

"Why would you come here wearing that?" he said. He laughed again when I didn't answer. "You got a boyfriend?"

My heart was pounding so hard I could feel it in my teeth. I trained my eyes on my hands, hoping that if I didn't look at him he'd disappear. My skin was almost blue, and I could see every line on my knuckles.

"Guess that means no?" He tapped my leg with his sunglasses. "You know, Mike's single. I'm not making any suggestions here, but maybe you two could help each other out."

I didn't look up. He had to go away eventually. Had to. Had to.

"Austin . . . ," Mike said. He glanced at me and then away again before he had to meet my eyes. He turned toward the pool and ran his hand through his hair.

"Sorry if you're gay or something. I mean, with Lila as a friend I wouldn't blame you. But there's not much substitute for, you know"—he lowered his voice—"for dick, is there?" I flinched. "Mike knows a little something about that, don't you, Mike?"

"Fuck off, Austin." Mike raised one leg and kicked him awkwardly in the back.

Austin grinned with all his big white teeth. "I think he's into it."

"Come on, man," Mike said.

I couldn't look up. They had to leave, didn't they? What was Lila doing? I was sure everyone was watching us.

"No?" Austin said. "The girl's got a lot of pent-up feelings that I bet she'd be willing to express for you." He leaned in so far I could see his shadow on my legs. "What do you say? I think he'd even buy you a bikini."

I was too terrified to feel the anger I knew would come later. The only way I'd learned to deal with guys like him was to play dead until they left.

"Talk to you tomorrow, then, Lila?" Jason's voice broke through the static like an orchestra coming into tune. "You ready, guys?"

Austin rapped his knuckles on my shin. "Consider my proposal, okay? See you in school."

I didn't breathe until they'd gone through the gate, huddled together and laughing.

Lila settled back on her lounger. "Jason got hot. Shame he thinks Nickelback is the cutting edge of music." She'd missed the entire thing. I was almost grateful.

I looked at her. "Take me home. Now."

chapter 2

That night my mother knocked on my bedroom door, which I'd accidentally left ajar.

She peered through the gap when I didn't respond. "Can I come in?"

"Mm," I said. I turned back to the page I'd been staring at. I was lying facedown on my bed, my feet on the pillow, my face hidden behind my hair.

"Got another new book?" she said. "Is it good?"

I shrugged. The words had been swarming in front of me like a cloud of gnats.

She stepped inside, still in her work suit. Even after a full day she was perfectly made up, her skirt freshly pressed, her hair lying flat in its neat curtain. She was forever moisturizing and touching up and reapplying, as if her skin were a mask that concealed some clawing deformity and only her constant vigilance kept it in place. When I was young I thought one day I'd want to learn her rituals myself, but I never did (what difference would it make?) and now I knew I was disappointing. She wanted a daughter whose hair she could braid while they lay entwined on the couch, who'd go shopping with her and clap at her new top, who'd trade hair straighteners and boyfriend anecdotes. The more she wanted me to be that girl, the more I felt the shadow of the daughter she wanted pressing up against me, crowding me out.

She sat down on the edge of my bed, barely dimpling the sheets. We were silent for a few moments as she absent-mindedly stroked my hair.

"I wish you'd let me cut this," she murmured, and I pulled away and said, "I like it like this." She held her hands up and then sank them into her lap as if to stop them from wandering into more trouble.

"So what did you get up to today?" she said finally. She glanced away as she asked, as if she was afraid I wouldn't answer if she looked at me directly.

I shrugged. I felt like any answer would expose me—I'd start crying and wouldn't be able to stop. I hated the thought of her seeing me like that.

"You went out with Lila, right?"

"Yeah."

She paused and then tried again. "And how was that?"

"Fine."

"Can you give me an answer longer than one word?"

"Nope."

"I walked into that, didn't I?" she said.

I sighed and turned toward her a little. "Going out with Lila is just . . ."

"Just what?"

"It's just . . . I don't know. Anyway, she was happy. She found a new boy to pursue."

"Did she?" She shuffled her feet, which were still bound in panty hose. With her shoes off they looked like mannequin feet, the toes all fused together, the seam in the fabric the edge of her plastic mold. "And what about you? And boys?"

I shook my head. I didn't trust myself to speak.

"You know—" she started carefully.

"No," I said. "Please don't." Tears welled in my eyes.

"Oh, sweetheart, what's wrong? Did something happen today?"

"No, I'm just . . . I just hate going back to school," I said. I sat up to distract myself from crying, and as I did, I cracked my head on the shelf of books that hung on the wall above my bed.

"Ouch," my mother said, wincing as if she'd done it herself, and her hand went to my head again, and then I was crying, hard. I leaned into her lap and she smoothed my hair down as I sobbed.

"It's okay if you're nervous," she said after a minute. "It's nothing to be ashamed of."

When I didn't respond, she said, "I remember the day I took you to preschool for the first time. You were fine until I tried to leave, but I looked back just as I got to the door, and you were staring at me with this look of absolute betrayal. You started sobbing and tried to run to me, but your teacher picked you up and waved me away. When I got to the car I sat there and cried for I don't know how long. It felt like hours."

I couldn't remember any of it. "What did I do when you picked me up?"

"You begged me not to take you back there."

"Did you?"

She hesitated. "Yes."

"Why would you do that?"

She shook her head. "I thought I had to."

We were silent again. I let her massage my scalp, and I

relaxed slightly, though my eyelids were puffy with tears. I felt pleasantly hollowed out from crying.

"Charlie," she said finally, in such a way that I knew she was bracing herself for my reaction, "your dad and I want you to start an extracurricular activity this year."

"What? Like what?" I twisted around so I could see her better. Her nostrils looked sinister.

"Well, I know not to hope for a sport"—her lips curved up slightly—"but what about the band? You liked the clarinet. Or an academic club?"

I sat up; my head throbbed. "You know how I feel about marching bands."

"For one, high school marching bands do not look like Hitler Youth—"

"Is this because of your job? You think I need to achieve more or something?"

"No, of course not," she said. She looked down at her nails. "I know you and your dad enjoy having your little club down there—"

"Our little club? What's that supposed to mean?"

She stopped, looked away, and started again. "Your dad has everything under control. The truth is I should be pushing you harder. I think it would help if I did."

"You mean for college? I thought we agreed I'm going to apply early to Oberlin, so it's not going to make much difference now."

"I know. It's not that." She looked at me, almost defiantly. "Charlotte, I just think you'd benefit from having a few more friends."

"I have Lila," I said.

"Lila's not exactly— Okay, but don't you think you'd like to have more than one?"

"Wow," I said. "Thanks."

"No," she said, "I didn't mean to— You just depend on your dad so—"

"I love how every time you say something you make me feel worse."

"It's wonderful that you two are so close," she said, "but if you'd just . . ."

"Do you think I need a boyfriend or something?"

"Of course not," she said, but I was sure I could hear different in her voice.

"Ah," I said. Tears smudged my vision again and I bit my tongue, hard, to clamp them inside. "Did Dad actually have something to do with this? I'm going to talk to him."

I started to get up, but she held my arm.

"Don't," she said. "I haven't discussed it with him yet, but I know he'll support it."

"You mean you thought I'd do it if you said he was behind it."

She smiled a little as if she knew she'd been caught, but she didn't say anything.

"You think you can force me to make friends?" I said.

"I certainly can't force anyone to *like* you." Her eyes widened, as if she was surprised she'd said it. When she spoke again, her voice was softer. "But . . . but I think it's never a bad idea to meet new people and be in new situations."

"I already know everyone at my school," I said. "There's no one new to meet. New *situations* aren't going to make us friends if we're not friends already. Weren't you just telling me you regretted making me go to preschool when I wasn't ready?"

She looked down again. "I did regret it at first. But after a week you were fine. Better, in fact, than you'd been when you were at home."

I sat back. "Well, I don't remember that. And maybe things are a bit different now, since I'm not four years old anymore."

"Of course they are. But I think I need to push you when you don't want to be pushed sometimes."

My head was throbbing again, but not from the bruise. "You know what? *I* think *you* need to *back off.*"

Her eyes took on the hard, glittering cast I dreaded. "You need to join an extracurricular activity this year," she said. "You can have a week from tomorrow to decide which one."

"And what if I don't?"

"Then you'll be grounded until you find one. And Lila can't drive you to school. You'll have to take the bus."

There was no point in arguing with her; she'd increase the punishment the more I fought her. Of course she wouldn't understand how horrible school was. She'd been popular and pretty; I'd seen her yearbook picture, all straight white teeth and high blond ponytail. We'd have hated each other. Or at least, she would have hated me.

She stood up. "Good night, Charlie. I'm sorry it had to happen this way. I think you'll come to thank me in the end."

"I'm sure," I muttered. She pretended not to hear as she closed the door behind her.

september

chapter 3

"It's BS, I agree," Lila said the next morning as I rested my throbbing head against my chair. There was a knot where I'd banged it the night before. "Just freak her out and join the cheerleading squad."

"Are you kidding? She'd be delighted." I clutched my backpack to my chest. "What will take the least amount of effort and social interaction?"

"You could work in the school library but I think they're just as afraid of you as the one in town is," Lila said. "I'm not saying you should be proud, but . . ."

"They are *not* af— Just because you're illiterate, you don't have to mock people who can read."

"*Cosmo* comes out once a month; that is more than enough reading material for me," she said. "But listen, we have to concentrate on my goals for the year. I need something other than worrying about college. And do not tell me that Chatham Valley is always looking for fresh blood." Chatham Valley was the local community college, a place her parents' money ensured she'd never go, even if her grades hadn't been as good as they were. She played down her academic achievements, but she was one of the top students in our class.

"Number one is not getting me killed when you're searching for a hairbrush while going seventy on the interstate."

"Realistic goals." She was tapping in letters now, her fingernails clicking against the glass.

"Who are you texting?" I asked, glancing at the wall clock. Two minutes till the morning bell. I pressed my hand against the bump on my head as if I were trying to stop it from spreading.

"What?" Lila said, looking up. "Oh, just some dudebro I gave my number to at ShopRite."

This always happened to Lila. We didn't talk about the fact that it didn't happen to me.

"Classy. What's he saying?"

"Ugh, some come-on involving numbers and abbreviations. I'm just blowing him off." The bell sounded. Lila fell back in her chair and groaned. "Calculus first period. Stanford is not going to be pleased with my grade. Which will be a D."

"I've got Math for Stupids with Gorgon. She already hates me from study hall with *someone* who wouldn't shut up half the time."

Lila narrowed her eyes at me. "We'll discuss my awful influence on you in English, okay? I have things to cosine."

I got up, steeling myself for the long walk to my classroom. The first day back was risky—I might see people I recognized, or ones I could quickly smile at, but I might also run into people who'd mutter things I couldn't quite hear or nudge their friends and laugh. I wasn't one of the worst outcasts—the ones who wore sweatpants to class, the ones who were glazed with religious fervor, the ones who grasped your arm and wouldn't let go when they talked to you. It was mostly because I had Lila. But there was always a threat bubbling underneath my time at school, that someone might say something cruel and collapse the ordinary day I'd been having. Sometimes I wished I lived in a place where no one would know who I was or care, and I could walk without my head dipped low, always glancing behind me.

Lila opened the door into a burst of noise; she waved and grimaced and then she was gone. Someone bumped me from behind and made a halfhearted gesture of apology. People stopped suddenly and yelled to each other and glanced at me, then looked away again. A couple stuck to some lockers like tree roots twined together. A boy shoved past me and turned, and when he saw me, his eyes lit up. "Hey, Porter," he said, and I wondered where I knew him from. His smile looked genuine, but his eyes glittered in a way that worried me. My heart sped up and the knot on my head throbbed with it.

Finally I made it up the stairs and into my classroom. I was the third person to arrive; Will van der Hoff was at the front, reading a paperback, and Eric Bastian was off to the side, texting someone. I knew Mrs. Morgan didn't assign seating, so I had my pick. I chose a desk at the edge of the room with the word *Boobies* etched into the surface next to a peace sign.

A few kids shuffled in as I drew aimlessly in my notebook. I avoided eye contact with most of them; the majority were juniors, so I didn't know how many would end up being a problem. Mrs. Morgan still hadn't arrived, which was unusual. I'd had her for Algebra II the year before, and before class she'd always been behind her desk, sitting ruler straight, her milky eyes focused on the distance, her hair pinned into a bun the color of a weathered seashell.

The bell rang and the last stragglers leapt to their seats. A small, slight bird of a woman with bad skin and short black hair came through the door and ignored us as she walked toward the desk. The class quieted briefly, but when she continued to pay us no attention, everyone quickly resumed talking. She shuffled some papers, grabbed a binder, and then stepped out in front of us again.

"Can you all please settle down?" she said in a high, tentative voice. She looked young, and like she was already out of her depth. The noise dipped again, but a girl I didn't know was still on the phone with someone, and a boy, Stephen Williams, was facing backward, slapping his hands on his chair and laughing. The woman paused, then said again, "Settle down, please, class."

Class was her first mistake. They didn't like being addressed as *class*.

"Where's Morgan?" someone called out. Sean Varniska—he was obviously thrilled at the chance to unsettle her.

"Mrs. Morgan is on extended medical leave. I'm Ms. Anders and I'll be your trigonometry teacher for the foreseeable future." She seemed to gain confidence as she spoke, but her eyes darted around the room, never settling on anyone.

"What's wrong with her?" Sean asked. He was sitting on top of his chair, his legs splayed like his balls needed ventilation.

"That's not really important, is it?" Ms. Anders still wouldn't look at Sean. "Let's just get started with what we have to learn this year. We've got a lot to cover."

"Well, I want to know and I think most of *the class* does too." Sean looked around at a few other amused faces, silently massing them against her. I kept my head down and drew circles in my notebook. If I made eye contact with her, I'd only confirm her humiliation. I hated her for being so stupid, for not being able to pull herself out of this.

Ms. Anders gripped the binder. "What's your name?" she asked, finally looking at Sean.

He considered her for a moment, clearly deciding whether to lie. "Sean Varniska," he said finally, straightening up.

"Sean, if you're really interested, can I suggest that you ask Principal Crowley in your free time?"

Sean sucked in a breath. A soft "ooh" went up from the class. "Are you saying you don't care about my teacher's health? Her health is very important to me and, I think, to the rest of *the class*."

Ms. Anders looked at the floor, then the wall. She stepped back as if she'd been rocked by a wave and then turned and began writing on the board. "Okay, let's get started with some fundamentals. Who can explain the Pythagorean theorem?"

But the class was murmuring again, and Sean was laughing now. "Um, Ms. Anders, is there a reason you don't want to answer my question? Is Mrs. Morgan having private lady problems?"

The dam broke and the class burst into giddy laughter.

A few kids still sat looking down at their desks, not meeting Ms. Anders's suddenly desperate gaze.

"Sean, please settle down and take your seat," she said, but her voice was shaky again. "We need to move on from this."

Sean grinned. "I guess I will take this up with the principal."

"Sean," she said again, but it was more of a defeated sigh.

He slithered down into his seat, satisfied. The class buzzed with noise again. Ms. Anders went back to the board, but by then it was too late: she'd lost us and she wasn't going to get us back.

I looked at the wall clock. Only six hours left.

I found Lila in the hallway as we each made our way to our new English class.

"How'd the morning go?" I asked, dodging another entwined couple by the lockers.

"The usual," she said as she hitched up the books on her arm. "On the plus side, I think I learned a few nuclear codes. What about you?"

"Study hall and history were fine. Trig was terrible. We had a sub. Sean nearly made her cry."

"Ouch," Lila said. "What happened?"

We'd reached the door of our classroom; Lila led the way in. It looked different than it had the last time I'd seen it. The walls were bare, and our seats were arranged behind a horseshoe of tables rather than desks. There was a bank of computers against one wall, all of which were grimy and gray with coughs and fingerprints. Lila grabbed a chair in the corner and I slid down next to her.

"General anarchy," I said. "She lost control a few minutes in and no one paid attention after that. I wanted to tell her to stop arguing with them, but obviously . . ."

"Obviously," Lila said. "That's a shame."

"It was. On the other hand, I didn't have to learn any math."

"Bonus."

"Yeah. I guess trigonometry was the real loser today," I said, cocking an eyebrow at her.

"Quite," she said, stroking her chin.

I heard someone huff and looked toward the battered desk at the front of the room. I'd thought we were the first people to arrive, but the new lit teacher was there already, leaning over a sheaf of papers. He was smiling, clearly listening to us, but he didn't look up.

I exchanged another raised eyebrow with Lila.

Katie McManus arrived, and Frank Gowser, and—oh, fantastic—Sean from my math class, as well as a couple of new kids we'd been introduced to on our induction day: Asha Madhani and her twin brother, Dev. I smiled at them, and Asha sat down a few seats away and smiled back. The bell rang, and more kids wandered in, and then after a minute our teacher stood up, shut the door, and settled himself on the edge of his desk. A couple of people were still chatting, but they stopped when they realized that everyone else had turned their attention to him.

"Hi, guys," he said when everyone had gone silent. "I'm

Mr. Drummond, and I'm your AP English Lit teacher. First I'm just going to check that everyone's showed up here and we don't have a bunch of people desperately attempting to take this class without permission. Let me know if you like being called by your given name or a nickname." His voice sounded confident, but the paper he was holding vibrated slightly.

When he reached my name, he called out, "Charlotte Porter?"

I raised my hand. Lila poked me in the arm and said, "She goes by Charlie."

Mr. Drummond looked at me. I smiled, because it was the only thing I could think of doing. "You look more like a Chuck," he said.

The class laughed, and I felt my face heat up. Why had he singled me out? Was he making fun of me?

When he was finished taking attendance, he reached into his bag and pulled out a thick old book, bloated with age. The spine was so creased it was almost entirely white.

"I'll pass around a syllabus in a second," he said, "but first I want to find out what your favorite books are and tell you about mine."

Lila smirked. Mr. Drummond turned to her and said, "Lila? Did you want to say something?"

Lila looked straight at him and said, "I was just wondering what your pick was."

"We'll get to mine," he said. He leaned back on the desk so his arms were propping him up. "So what's your favorite book?"

"Um, probably *The Cat in the Hat*."

A few people laughed and my heart started kicking in

my chest. It was happening again: Lila was goading him and in a minute everyone would turn. I silently begged her to stop talking.

"All right," said Mr. Drummond. "I can't dispute a classic, especially one written in anapestic tetrameter."

"Coincidence!" Lila said. "That's why I picked it."

"I suspected as much. Any other reasons, besides your appreciation for poetic meter?"

"Um, probably because it's the last book I actually read for fun."

"Really? You never read Judy Blume or J. K. Rowling or *From the Mixed-Up Files of Mrs. Basil E. Frankweiler*?"

"Okay, I read some of those," Lila said, putting her hands up in surrender. "But the general point is that mostly what I read now is for school, not for fun. I can't remember the last time I read a book because I wanted to." I understood suddenly that she was flirting with him. I looked at him: was he handsome? Not really, though he was young for a teacher. Was she just bored?

He wasn't flirting back, but he didn't look put off either. "Luckily for you, Lila, that's what I wanted to talk about today. But let's ascertain what everyone else's choices are first." He turned to me. "Chuck?"

The class laughed again, and again I wasn't sure whether they were laughing at me or with him. The knot on my head throbbed. "Um . . . can you skip me?" I said. "I need a minute to think."

He nodded and turned to Asha.

Lila passed me a note. *Asshole but I kind of like him,* she'd scrawled in large looping letters.

I scowled at her, but she didn't seem to notice. More

kids gave him their favorites: *Harry Potter, 1984, Superfudge, The Shining, A Scanner Darkly, The Da Vinci Code,* and three votes for *The Catcher in the Rye.* I hated *The Catcher in the Rye.*

Finally it was back to me. Mr. Drummond nodded again.

I still couldn't think of anything. "Um . . . *The Brothers Karamazov*?" I blurted it out. I'd never read it. I knew it was famous, and I'd always had a hazy idea it was about acrobats in turn-of-the-century Russia. I'd only ever seen it on my parents' bookshelf, its spine cracked like the bark of an old tree, looking foreign and imposing.

"Really?" Mr. Drummond said. He looked unconvinced. "That's a tough one."

"Mm," I said vaguely.

"Did you read it for class or for . . . pleasure?"

"Uh, over the summer. I thought we might cover it in class, so I wanted to be prepared."

"I admire your initiative." He paused and I prayed he would move on. Instead he crossed his arms and tilted his head at me. "Which part was your favorite?"

I cleared my throat. "The part in . . . Russia."

He tried not to laugh; he brought his fist to his mouth and pretended to cough, but he was smiling underneath his fingers. I'd embarrassed myself already. If he hadn't thought I was dumb before, he certainly did now. I looked down at my notebook.

"I can't argue with that," he said finally. "Okay, guys, I guess at this point I have to reveal my favorite book. It's the one we're going to be reading first this year. I realize that's not very democratic of me, but it's one of the only benefits of being a teacher besides the incredible pay: I can force you to read stuff I like."

He held up the book—*Catch-22*. The class was quiet. "No takers?" he said. "Silence. All right. Well, let me tell you why this is my favorite book and why I've forced you to admit that you've never read anything better than *The Cat in the Hat*—or maybe just that your reading skills haven't improved since you did."

Lila's mouth dropped open and she slapped her hands on the table in indignation. I winced; this was exactly the kind of attention she wanted. Mr. Drummond glanced at her sideways as the class started to vibrate with shocked laughter, but fortunately he continued before she could say anything.

"I first read this book when I was a senior in high school like you guys, back when people marked time by pointing at the sun and grunting. Before that I'd enjoyed books, but I'd never felt understood the way I did when I read this one. It was like someone I'd never met knew me and was saying something about the world I thought only I had noticed. I hope you connect with it too, but if you don't, don't worry, because I also want you each to choose one of the books that someone else mentioned as a favorite. Yes, including *Superfudge*"—he frowned at Frank—"and *The Brothers Karamazov*"—he shook his head at me—"and even, God help me, *The Da Vinci Code*." He looked at Sean, who shrugged.

"Two books at once?" Katie said incredulously.

"You can read someone else's favorite book at any

point during the semester. I hope that'll encourage you to read some of the longer books, but if you all want to read *The Cat in the Hat* and write an excellent ten-page paper on it"—he waited a beat as we groaned—"then I won't stop you."

He put the book down on his desk and folded his arms. "Every book is an argument. What I'm asking you guys to do is to respond to that argument. Liking a book or disliking it is a good starting point, but it's not enough. I want you to learn how to make your own arguments. I want to hear your voice. I want you to tell your own stories." He looked at me. "So good luck with Dostoyevsky, everyone."

chapter 4

"His name's Tom," Lila said when I answered my phone that night.

I paused. "Who is this?"

"Charlie! That joke does not get funnier on the thirtieth outing."

I scratched the spot between Frida's eyes that she loved the most. "You do know comedy," I said. "Is it just Weird Al's greatest hits that you've paid actual money for, or his complete works?"

" 'Eat It' is a classic—you know what, I'm not even going into this with you again. So I found out. Drummond's first name is Tom. Or Thomas, I guess, but the secretary called him *Tom*." She said this in a way that implied the secretary had a crush on him.

"Oh," I said. "Okay. Well, it's good his name isn't Marvin or something, I guess."

"Marv," Lila said. "Or Ralph."

"So why were you so interested in this information that you sought it from the administrative staff?"

"You're *not* interested?" she said.

I waited to see if she'd elaborate, but she didn't. "Not particularly. I mean, I wasn't wondering."

"Even though he was flirting with you in class?"

"He was not! He was making fun of me."

"No, he wasn't, *Chuck.* He liked you."

"That's what I'm talking about. What was he implying with that nickname?"

"He was implying that he thought you were funny, you dork."

"He thought *you* were funny. If he likes anyone, it's you."

"Whatever," she said. "I don't know why but I do kind of like him. It's not like he's hot, plus he clearly thinks he's the cool teacher. And he's kind of a jerk. I couldn't believe he called me out like that."

"You wanted him to! You were asking for it."

"I was not! I just wanted to see what he was going to be like as a teacher."

I sighed; arguing with her was pointless. "Okay, so you have a disgusting and shameful crush on a teacher. Why do you think *I* do?"

"When have you *not* crushed on a teacher? I thought he'd be right up your alley. He talked for like twenty minutes about how much he loves *Catch-22*. I thought you'd have a book boner for him, at least."

She was right, as much as I hated to admit it. I'd had crushes on teachers since the sixth grade. And English teachers were the worst—they liked books as much as I did, and I always got As in their classes. But the crushes were fleeting things, moments of gratefulness for the kindness and attention they showed me.

"Well, I don't," I said. "He was mean to me from the minute we walked in."

"Will you listen to me? He was teasing you because he liked you!"

"Great, so he's a perv." I knew my joke was more about

the idea of a grown man lusting after a teenager. I didn't have to worry about teachers getting ideas; it wouldn't cross their minds to consider me.

"I'm not saying he's a perv. But he did nearly crack up when you lied about reading *The Brothers Karamazov*. Bold choice, by the way."

"God, I don't know why I did that. I panicked. It was the only book I could remember. Like literally out of all books."

Lila snorted. "I picked *The Cat in the Hat*. At least yours had chapters."

"I wouldn't call it your proudest moment," I said.

"The worst part is that I can't read it, since I picked it. Maybe I'll go for *Superfudge*." She sighed. "Oh, I forgot to tell you about PE. You didn't have it today, did you?"

"Nope." We only had it three days a week, and I'd gotten a study hall on the other two days.

"Well," she said, "bring a pillow."

chapter 5

If there was a class I hated more than math, it was gym. It baffled me that people actually chased after the ball as if they wanted to catch it instead of nonchalantly stepping back when play got too close, or, if pressed, loping after it halfheartedly until someone else got to it first.

Our gym teacher, Mrs. Deloit, surveyed us with the tired, watery eyes of a woman who had supervised far too many sessions of listless square dancing. "We've got a new activity this year, girls," she said. "This semester you'll be able to take yoga. There are only twenty places, but the boys won't be joining us."

The other activities were basketball and soccer. I knew yoga was probably what Lila had been warning me about, but I couldn't pass up an activity that didn't involve either boys or sweating. Once we'd all chosen, Mrs. Deloit said, "All right, lap first, and then the girls who are taking yoga can come with me."

We headed outside, where the boys were already trudging around the far end of the track. I started jogging with the others, moving somewhat faster than usual so the guys who finished first wouldn't be standing there watching my breasts parabola as I ran. As I neared the end of the track, I noticed with a jolt that Mike from the pool was standing near the back of the group of boys. He saw me looking at him. He hesitated for a minute, and then he started to move toward me. I froze, but a boy clapped his shoulder and he turned away, distracted.

I looked around to see whether I could find anyone to talk to who would make me look a little less desperate. I didn't want Mike reporting to Austin how vulnerable I was without Lila. I noticed Dev and Asha from my English class talking to each other, but once everyone finished their lap and the boys left, Asha was alone too. I'd only ever said hi to her, though, and the thought of starting a conversation just for it to stall out was enough to keep me away. Why would she want to talk to me anyway?

Once we were back inside, Mrs. Deloit said, "All right, ladies. Everyone go get a mat and then we'll begin." She sat down in a plastic chair and started the music. She already looked exhausted.

I could see why Lila had warned me. The recording was some old relaxation guide, probably something Mrs. Deloit had found at a garage sale. There were wobbly panpipes on the sound track, and the instructor was vaguely British. A few girls exchanged smiles, and by the time we were doing a downward dog to the echoes of whale song, some had broken into cautious giggles. When it came time to relax our bodies and the instructor urged us to loosen our groins, a gale of laughter shot out. By that point Mrs. Deloit was half asleep.

I glanced at Asha, who was on the mat next to mine. She gestured at Mrs. Deloit's drooping eyelids. That small invitation was enough. I nodded and whispered, "She must have really relaxed her groin."

Asha's eyes widened. "I hope not too much or this room's going to smell even worse than it already does."

I laughed, surprised that she'd made a joke. She hadn't spoken much in class the day before, and I had assumed she was shy.

The music finished and there was silence for a moment. I realized a couple of girls were breathing heavily. It took another minute for Mrs. Deloit's head to bob up. Asha and I snickered.

"Okay, girls," she said, blinking slowly. "That was very relaxing, wasn't it? I see a few of you were as relaxed as I was. Let's head back."

I deliberately avoided walking to the changing rooms with Asha. The sudden pressure of having to talk to her stopped up my thoughts, and it was easier to avoid conversation entirely. But when I started toward Mr. Drummond's classroom, she appeared out of nowhere in the hallway.

"My mom would not have called that yoga," she said.

"I don't think most people would have," I said. I smiled at her tentatively.

She was silent for a few steps, and then she said, "Mr. Drummond is interesting."

I laughed. "Yeah, that seems to be the general opinion."

"You don't think so?"

"Don't really know him well enough yet," I said. "But hopefully he's a step up from Mr. Mickler." Mr. Mickler had been known as the English department's tenure jockey until he'd retired the year before.

"Oh, him," she said. "Dev heard that last year he made them watch movies while he napped."

"And you're sure he won't come out of retirement?"

Asha laughed. "Not likely."

Lila gave me a smug look when we walked into our classroom. I quickly waved goodbye to Asha as she headed to her seat. Lila glanced at her suspiciously.

"What now?" I said.

She looked back at me. "I've solved your dilemma. I accept Weird Al merchandise."

I sat down next to her. "What's your brilliant solution?"

"Drummond's taking over the newspaper," she said. "So you've got your extracurricular."

I glanced at him. This time he really was ignoring us, scribbling something in a notebook. "That involves a substantial amount of interaction with people. You know how I feel about people. All that talking."

"You can be a columnist. Have strong opinions on things you know nothing about." She pointed at me. "Don't say it. I am not a writer."

"So I have to do it alone?"

"Sorry. I actually would like to, but field hockey is every afternoon."

I considered it as the class started discussing *Catch-22*. I'd been too overwhelmed on the first day of school to think about spending a minute longer than I had to in the building, so I hadn't come up with any alternative ideas. Our school paper came out maybe twice a year. I'd never joined because it was mostly a stoner occupation—it was called *Truth Bomb* and it mainly contained rants about how overpriced the vending machines in our school were—but it did sound like the most painless option. I'd always liked writing, and it probably wouldn't be too much work.

Mr. Drummond confirmed my suspicion at the end of class.

"Before we wrap up, guys," he said, clapping his hands together as he stood up, "I just want to let you know that I'm reviving the school paper this year."

"*Truth Bomb*?" Katie said.

"Indeed," Mr. Drummond said. *"Truth . . . Bomb."* He said it slowly, waiting for the laugh that he must have known he would get. "I heard it was defunct, so I found an old issue, which contained an article on whether we should allow cigarette smoking in school bathrooms. It will probably not come as a surprise to any of you that the author of the article was pro."

"Was there a con article?" Frank asked.

"No," Mr. Drummond said. "I guess they assumed the smell coming out of the bathrooms was argument enough."

"So how do you feel about smoking in the toilets?" Dev asked.

"As an educator, I am of course against. As a fellow human being, at least open a window." He lowered his head almost shyly as we laughed. "So I'm looking for volunteers. Three days a week after school for an hour. This will count toward a college credit, but of course the main benefit will be the fantastic education you will get at the feet of this communications minor." He pointed at himself. "Who graduated from a school that did not offer a journalism degree. I assure you, though, that I am very pro crossword puzzle. So if you're interested, let me know, and please also tell your literate or semi-literate friends about it. And if you know anything about newspaper layout software, I will pay you cash money to join."

I lingered after the bell rang, and Lila nudged me as she left.

"Just get it over with," she said. "Like a Band-Aid. *Right off.*"

Soon everyone was gone. I'd be late to lunch, but Lila would save me a seat.

Mr. Drummond noticed me after a moment. He put down the papers he'd been looking through. "What can I do for you, Charlie?" he asked.

"I thought I was Chuck now," I said, and then felt my neck heat up.

"Sorry," he said, "I just started calling you that without asking you first, didn't I? Would you rather I called you Charlie? Or Charlotte?"

"No, no, Chuck is fine. Or Charlie. Or whatever." I realized I did like it. It was the first nickname I'd had in a long time.

"Okay." He leaned back in his chair slightly, making it creak. "So are you interested in journalism?"

"I'm interested in an extracurricular," I said, and he smiled. "I mean, yes, I am interested in writing."

"Great," he said. "I was hoping you'd sign up, actually. Even if it's only because you need an extracurricular. We could use bright kids like you on the paper."

All I could hear was him saying I was bright. Any compliment from a teacher snagged in my head and looped there for hours. But how did he know? Had he looked at my report cards? It certainly wasn't because of my performance in class. "I'm not actually— I am actually interested in writing. I don't know why I said that about needing an extracurricular."

He spread his hands. "Doesn't matter to me why you sign up as long as you sign up. I'm hoping it'll be fun, though. I'd like to put out an issue every month, which I know sounds like a ridiculously low bar to clear, but when you're starting from nothing it's a lot of work just getting everything together."

"I can imagine. So you have experience running a paper?"

"Yeah, some," he said. "I was the editor of my college paper for two years. We're not talking about the *Crimson* or anything, but we did a few good stories. Exposed a financial aid scandal. Traced the origins of the dining hall's Tater Tots. The Tater Tots thing was actually much more disturbing."

"If they were anything like the Tater Tots here, I can't imagine the depths of malfeasance you exposed."

He laughed. He had a nice laugh—low, almost private, as if he were laughing to himself. "Malfeasance. See? You're a natural. I'll put you on word search detail."

"I'm just good at studying my vocab words," I said. "So you're keeping the name?"

"Are you suggesting that *Truth Bomb* is not a worthy name for a school paper?"

I laughed. "I don't, uh . . . no?"

The bell rang.

"I should go," I said. "Lila gives me shit—uh, crap, sorry—if I make her save me a seat at lunch."

He waved at my apology dismissively. “Swearing is the last thing you have to apologize for in front of me. We’ll start meeting in a week or two, I think, but I’ll let you know more in class when I’ve gotten things organized.”

“Well, I can’t fucking wait,” I said, thinking for a moment that it would be funny. Then I lost my nerve and skittered out of the room, but all the way down the hall I could hear him laughing.

chapter 6

I found my dad in the basement later that afternoon. He was hitting his computer monitor and cursing softly.

"Sounds like it's going well," I said.

"Hey," he said. "Can you get me that hammer over there, sweetheart? I need to fix something."

"Let me look before you break it," I said.

"Thanks," he said. He got up and went to his worktable, which bristled with scraps of unfinished projects. "How was school?"

"Fine, I guess," I said. "How do you manage to screw the website up so much in so little time?"

"Practice," he said. "Tell me about your classes."

"Not much to say. Boring as ever."

"I'm here with Frida all day and no one else to talk to. Give me something."

"You're not missing much. We did yoga for gym class and learned how to relax our groins. Oh, and we have a new teacher."

"A new teacher who's instructing you to relax your groins? Do I need to get in touch with someone about this?"

I laughed. The basement door creaked open and Frida came bounding down. My mother was home.

I turned toward my dad. "Mrs. Deloit was teaching her first yoga class. Well, I say teaching. She fell asleep."

"Yoga?" my mother said as she came down the stairs, flushed from the sun. She must have come back from a workout. She flicked on the overhead light, and my dad and I both winced. "I don't know how you can work down here when it's so dark," she said. She'd scraped her hair back into a clean glossy knot, but she was wearing a baggy T-shirt, thin and corroded with age, that had been my dad's. "That must have been fun. Remember when we took that class together, sweetheart?" Her voice was high and constricted. She knew I was still mad at her.

My dad and I both watched her for a second; she looked bright and out of place. Then I said, "Yeah, vaguely, I think," and returned to the computer screen.

My dad went to give her a kiss. I knew he would; he always did.

"So what are you guys doing down here?" my mother asked. "I didn't realize you still needed help, Paul."

"Charlie's just saving me from myself," he said.

"This whole operation is going to fall apart without me," I said.

I could hear them talking to each other behind my back, but I didn't move. I didn't want to know what they were saying.

"So what else happened today, Charlie?" my mother said eventually.

"Got an extracurricular, like you wanted."

"Did you? That's wonderful."

I turned around again. "It doesn't involve marching in lockstep, so that's something."

"I'm glad to hear it. So what will you be doing?"

"Our new teacher's restarting the newspaper."

"The newspaper!" she said. "You've always wanted to work on the paper."

She sounded so pleased that for a moment my resolve crumbled. I looked down shyly. "Yeah, it seems like it might be fun."

"I'm really happy for you, honey," she said. "That will be a great fit."

"Thanks," I said, still looking down. I tried to hide my smile.

She paused. I saw her grab my dad's hand. "I know I shouldn't say I told you so, but do you think you would have joined if I hadn't made you?"

My mouth tightened. "Maybe not," I said. "Um, I should do some homework before dinner. Dad, you want to take over here?"

"Sure," he said, and let go of my mother.

She watched me as I passed her, but she still let me go upstairs.

Half an hour later my dad knocked on my door. "I brought a peace offering," he said, and let Frida inside. She was carrying a package of Oreos in her teeth. "I wanted to talk to you right after you came upstairs, but it took this long to get her not to chew it."

"So this is how you spend your time while we're gone all day," I said. Frida offered me the Oreos with a faint wag of her tail.

"Have to occupy the hours somehow." He sat down on my desk chair. "Your mom is just looking out for you, kid."

"And she had to brag about it?"

"You know she didn't mean it like that."

I snorted. "How *did* she mean it? And why did she get you in here instead of coming to talk to me herself?"

"You're so upbeat and charming, I can't imagine why she wouldn't."

I ignored him. "And how did she mean it when she stopped me working for you?"

"That wasn't a punishment, you doofus. We—as in *both* of us—just realized it wasn't fair to keep you locked in the basement, and you are so ridiculously stubborn that the only way to do that was to kick you out."

I looked at him. "I like helping you."

"I like it too," he said. "But if I were a real employer, I'd be prosecuted for breaking about three hundred child labor laws."

I hefted the Oreos. "This is enough payment for me."

"Go talk to her," he said. "Please. For me."

I sighed. "Okay."

"Tonight," he said. "Not when you get around to it."

"All right, all right, I promise."

He paused. "The other thing I wanted to tell you, which I must stress is contingent on you being less of a pain in the ass in the future, is that I'm going to let you start using my car to get to school. I know it'll be difficult to stay late if you can't get the bus."

"Really?" I said. I sat up. "Are you sure? I'll pay for gas with the pathetic wages you've given me."

"I know you will. And half the insurance. And any required maintenance."

"Yes, all of that, and I'll even leave you some music so you can see what uncool teenagers are listening to."

"That's very generous, but you know how I feel about post-Beatles music."

"You're old," I said.

"I just learned many—"

"Many."

"—many years ago that anything not available on LP wasn't worth bothering with," he said. "Just talk to your mom for me, okay? You don't realize how much of an effect you have on her."

"Okay," I said. I offered him a cookie and he crunched it loudly in the silence. Frida looked at him with wet, pleading eyes. "How's it going with work now that I've averted disaster?"

"Not bad, actually. I just got commissioned to make a sculpture for Holmesdale Park."

"The one on the other side of town?"

"Yep."

"Wow, good job. Can I offer some input?"

"No."

chapter 7

About fifteen students showed up to the first meeting of *Truth Bomb:* a mix of kids I recognized and some people I'd never seen before. The only ones I really knew were a few students from my literature class: Asha, Dev, and Frank. I exchanged smiles with them but sat at the other edge of Mr. Drummond's classroom, since an underclassman was sitting in my regular chair.

Mr. Drummond sat in his usual spot on the front of his desk. "Thanks for showing up, everyone, even if you were bribed to do so," he said. "I hope at least one of you understands newspaper layouts. First of all I want to find out if you have any thoughts about what the newspaper should be, or if you've got any ideas for features or editorials. Keeping in mind, of course, that we cannot endorse anarchy or libertarianism. Or mayonnaise, which is the devil's condiment."

There was a silence. Eventually Mr. Drummond said, "Frank? I know you have some ideas."

"Word search," said Frank, and a few people chuckled.

"Well, obviously. We need to keep people like you occupied somehow," Mr. Drummond said in a way that I realized was deliberate. He'd used Frank to warm us up. "Anyone else?"

"How about a profile of new teachers?" said a guy with

a cloud of curly red hair that crackled out like it was full of static.

"Fine, Scott, before you ask again, I wear boxers. Happy now?" The kid laughed and held up his hands as if he couldn't help his curiosity. Mr. Drummond turned and wrote on the board: *Find out Drummond's favorite baked good; use for bribes.* "Let's also think of less obvious ideas. What have you wanted to see in a school newspaper but haven't?"

"Why so many bad teachers have tenure," said a short girl with glasses.

"Generally I'd like to stay away from topics that will get me blackballed from the teachers' lounge, but it's a good subject," said Mr. Drummond. "We'll see what we can do with it." He wrote *Tenure jockeys—the only thing they ride out is the clock.* "No one tweet that."

Dev said, "What about the statistics for who gets into advanced placement classes? Like the number of non-white students in them versus white students."

"Yes, good," Mr. Drummond said. "You might want to look into socioeconomic class as well. I have an article about it somewhere around here."

"Gender too," Asha said.

Mr. Drummond inclined his head toward Dev. "Gender too," he said.

Dev sighed as if he and Asha had argued about this before. "Feminists," he said.

Asha hit him. When she saw me watching them, she rolled her eyes toward Dev. Dev grinned at me.

Suddenly I felt out of my depth. They knew about things like that? *What* did they know? Who had taught them?

"That'll be interesting," Mr. Drummond said. He wrote *Advanced placement elaborate scam to fuel sales of graphing calculators?* "Anyone else?"

"What about government subsidies for school lunches? Pizza sauce being classed as a vegetable because of agricultural lobbies," said a guy in a Weyland-Yutani T-shirt. I stared at him. Where had these people come from?

"Excellent," Mr. Drummond said. On the board he wrote *Tomato sauce a vegetable, high-fructose corn syrup a fruit?*

I was ashamed of staying silent, but fear made my tongue thick. I listened while a few other people made suggestions and Mr. Drummond wrote them out on the board.

"Okay," he said finally. "I think we've got enough for a respectable issue. Now, who wants which story?"

There was a murmur, and the curly-haired kid said, "I thought we'd get to do our own ideas."

"That would make sense and be fair," Mr. Drummond said. "But I want you to stretch yourselves. So let's go around and choose. Chuck?"

I started as if he'd shocked me. "Sorry, what?"

He smiled patiently. "Which story would you like? First choice."

"Uh." I frowned feverishly at the board. The letters all looked like runes. "The first one, I guess."

"It's éclairs," he said as he wrote my name next to the story idea. "For future reference."

"I'll make a note of it," I muttered.

chapter 8

"So what did you guys think of the end?" Mr. Drummond held up his battered copy of *Catch-22*.

There was a pause. "I didn't like it," Sean said.

A couple of kids laughed nervously, but Mr. Drummond held a hand up for silence. "Why not, Sean?"

"Okay, I liked Doc Daneeka. He just, like, owns being a dick. But Yossarian's supposed to be a hero and he's actually a complete loser." The class laughed again. "And like I needed to know that war is bad. It's funny at first, I guess, but toward the end it's just, like, well, life sucks and then you die."

"Isn't that kind of the point?" Lila said.

"How is that a point?" Sean asked.

"You don't think that's the entire point of the book?" Asha said. "That war is futile?"

"If it is, that's a really dumb book."

I looked to Mr. Drummond, feeling panicked. He was watching them with a placid expression. He glanced at me and I looked away again.

"Okay, Sean," he said. "Do you have to agree with all of a book's ideas to like it?"

"Uh," Sean said. "Yes?"

"No?" Lila said. "Unless you're a dumbass like Sean?"

That got another laugh. Sean stuck his middle finger up at Lila and she blew a kiss at him. Ugh.

"All right," Mr. Drummond said. "Let's keep the level of discourse above obscene gestures at least until we get to Jane Austen." He paused. "So. Sean thinks the book is arguing that life is pointless, and that argument doesn't convince him. Let's take a step back. Why would a book make an argument like that?"

Sean shrugged. "Dunno."

"Do you think it could encompass a larger argument? Like, say, one for atheism?"

I looked up sharply.

"Explain," Lila said.

"Think," Mr. Drummond said.

Lila grinned. I felt something turn in my stomach.

"What do we find out about the catch-22?" he said.

"It doesn't actually exist?" Lila ventured. "But the powers that be tell them it does exist, so it kind of does."

Mr. Drummond leaned forward and Lila did too. I suddenly noticed how low-cut her top was.

"And who does it benefit?" he said.

"The people in power."

"How?"

"It . . . keeps them in power?"

"The idea does?"

"Yeah."

"So it's an idea that benefits the status quo, keeps people afraid and complacent, and is almost impossible to disprove once it's been established," Mr. Drummond said. "That remind you of anything?"

I'd been distracted by Lila's cleavage, but when he said that, I looked up at him in surprise. I could feel something inside my mind twist open. When he noticed me watching him, he raised his eyebrows at me. Again I looked away.

"So you're implying that the book's talking about . . ." Lila trailed off as if she would get in trouble if she continued. Her eyes looked luminous.

"You can say it," Mr. Drummond said. "But keep in mind that I have a duty to report any seditious thoughts to Dr. Crowley."

Lila was delighted. "Is it talking about God?"

"Let me get this straight," Mr. Drummond said. "You think it's saying God might not exist but we've been led by people in power to believe he does, for their own benefit."

"Yeah, I guess," Lila said.

Mr. Drummond leaned back and pointed to the door. "Get the fuck out," he said with mock ferocity.

The class exploded into laughter with the sudden force of a balloon popping. Lila and Mr. Drummond grinned at each other. I stared at him. I felt unmoored, as if I were out at sea for the first time and everything was slightly off-kilter, shifting unsteadily when I tried to get a fix on it.

"This is just one interpretation," Mr. Drummond said, "but I don't want you to be afraid to make intellectual leaps like that. If you feel like a text is leading you somewhere, don't be afraid to go with it, no matter how odd your idea might seem."

I looked at Mr. Drummond, and he looked back. I smiled.

* * *

He caught up to me as I was leaving after school. He was wearing a battered leather jacket and carrying an equally weather-beaten messenger bag the same dark brown as his hair. A hot shiver ran through me, as if dozens of needles were pricking me from the inside.

"You wanted to speak up today, didn't you?" he asked. When I didn't answer immediately, he said, "Sorry, that was a really presumptuous thing to say."

I laughed; it came out sounding like a car trying to start. I wasn't used to talking to him, especially alone. I wished Lila were there for backup. "Why was it presumptuous?"

"Maybe more condescending than presumptuous. I suspect you don't need another teacher telling you that you should speak up more in class."

"I do get that a lot," I said.

"Well, in that case I will tell you to feel free to stay silent," he said. "It just struck me that you might have had something you wanted to say."

We had slowed down to an amble. Our steps fell into sync until I deliberately took a few short strides so he wouldn't think I had done it on purpose.

"I did, I guess," I said. "It wouldn't have been anything helpful, though. It would have just been, how the hell did you think of that?"

"I doubt that," he said. "But I know that not everyone gets comfortable at the same speed. Back when I was in school, whenever anyone told me to speak up, it just made me shyer."

"You were shy?" I said. "I find that hard to believe

somehow." I was nervous about teasing him; I felt a blush spread on my face like a sunburn.

"You mean because I'm such an annoying loudmouth now?"

I looked at him; he smiled, inviting me to complete the joke. I noticed suddenly how blue his eyes were. "Yes," I said.

He laughed. "Would you believe I'm actually less annoying than I used to be?"

"No."

"Fair enough," he said. "But I mean it when I say we get plenty of noise from the usual bloviaters. It's good to hear from people with fresh insights."

"So you're telling me to find a way to shut Lila up."

"I wouldn't ask you to do what I can see is clearly impossible."

I laughed out of surprise. Was he just teasing about Lila? Or was he confiding in me? Even teachers I liked had never talked to me like that.

We stepped outside, into the newly chilly air. I was relieved that the seasons were finally changing. Autumn had always felt like the hinge of the year to me. Summer was stagnant—it was too hot to move or to think—but fall swept in with fresh air. There was always a chance that things would start over, better than they had been.

We walked a little way in silence. I wasn't comfortable with pauses in conversation; I assumed they were my fault.

"It's pretty out today," I said, to say something.

"If you like sunshine and vivid colors and that sort of nonsense," he said.

"You'd do well in England."

"I do like being damp." He stopped in front of a beat-up Volvo station wagon.

"Is this your car?" I asked.

"Afraid so." He fished his keys out of his coat pocket. "I'd offer you a ride, but it has this funny quirk where none of the doors except the driver's open."

"Oh," I said. "Oh, no, I—I have my dad's— I'm fine."

"Ah, good," he said. He smiled again. He had dimples when he smiled.

"All the doors work, at least."

"You've already got me beat." He jiggled his keys in his hand. "See you tomorrow, then?"

I realized that he was trying to cue me to leave. "Oh," I said. "Yes."

"Okay."

I didn't move.

His forehead creased. "Did you need something else, Charlie?"

"Um," I said. "Just—thank you for the compliment. I'm going to try harder."

"I look forward to it," he said.

"All right," I said to Lila that night. "I get it."

"Drummond?"

"Yeah."

"Ha!" she said. "Knew it."

"Congratulations."

"So what was it? Nice outfit today."

He'd been wearing a V-neck sweater and jeans—

admittedly some of his nicer clothes. "Since when do you get hot for sweaters?" I said.

"When he's wearing them."

I snorted. "Next it'll be cardigans with elbow patches."

"He would look good with a pipe. Come on, tell me."

"It was the . . ." I felt stupid saying it had been sparked by the conversation in class and then fueled by our chat after school. I couldn't tell her he'd sought me out privately. "He's really smart."

"You'd hope," she said.

"You know what I mean," I said. "You looked awfully interested when you were talking to him about atheism."

"That was kind of hot, wasn't it? He kept looking over at you, though."

"No, he didn't," I said automatically.

"Charlie," she said in a way that allowed no argument. "I told you, he likes you."

"I thought you said he wasn't a perv."

"No, but he likes you."

"I think he likes *you*."

Lila laughed. "I *was* giving him some serious eye sex."

"Ew. I really don't need to know where your eyes have been."

"I'm just planting a seed."

"Ugh, that's even worse."

"Speaking of seeds—I'm just going to tell you now that homecoming is in a few weeks. No pressure or anything, but I want to go."

"You'll go even if I don't?"

"Yeah, of course, but I want you to be my date. I'm just

telling you now because I know you need time to freak out about it first."

"You're a good friend."

"I wouldn't go that far," she said. "I've just been burned a few too many times. Oh, and no excuses that you need to help your dad. I know he does not need help on a freaking Friday night."

I had a habit of agreeing to things and then backing out at the last minute. I said yes partly because it made Lila happy, and mostly because I didn't want to make her angry by saying no. When I flaked, she was usually much angrier than she would have been otherwise.

"All right," I said. "I'll think about it. How was last period?"

"Fine. Papakostas is as riveting as ever. You know that girl Asha, the one from our English class?"

"Yeah, she's in my gym class too. She's okay. Why?"

"She just creeps me out a little. Why is she talking to me?"

"Because she's trying to be friendly?"

"No, I don't buy it. I think she wants to be friends with you and she knows *I'm* friends with you, so she's trying to be nice to me."

"You jealous?"

"Obviously." She said it sarcastically, but I wondered. Lila had had me to herself for as long as we'd known each other.

"And why is she trying to be friends with me?"

"Far be it from me to guess at anyone's reasons for being fascinated by the enigma of you. Is it your sparkling, bubbly personality? Your enthusiastic approach to sports? Your disdain for printed material?"

"I'm hanging up now."

"For all I know, she's just trying to get to Frida. And who could blame her?"

"Good night."

"Or your dad. Who is, may I point out, still hot."

"I hate you."

"Love you too."

chapter 9

I'd had crushes before, but this was worse than anything I'd ever felt. It started in my stomach and soon it was everywhere, spreading outward like an infection; it swallowed my concentration, blotted out my other interests, consumed whole days I would have normally spent reading. I felt like a tuning fork perpetually vibrating at his frequency. It happened suddenly: one day I barely noticed it and the next it felt like it had always been there and I would never be able to shake it.

Some mornings I'd see him in the hallway before class and quickly look away before it took hold; other days he'd notice me and smile and for the next hour I'd ache inside. After a few weeks I knew his schedule, and some days I would take detours just so I had the chance to glimpse the back of his head.

In class I was still mostly quiet, but Lila talked enough for both of us, and now and then I'd roll my eyes at him while she was rambling. Lila said smart things, which I hoped cast a reflected glow on me, but she also just *talked,* like ordinary people did, whereas I, in my silence, contained mysteries. He looked at me often, gauging my reactions to things—more often, I was sure, than he looked at the others. He teased me like he teased everyone, but now I looked forward to it; I could usually get a laugh from the class with a well-timed expression.

No one seemed to notice except Lila; my mother was happy that I was working on the newspaper, and my dad was happy that I was happy. I hadn't been happy at school in a long time.

I made up excuses to talk to him or seek him out. It wasn't hard; we had lunch after English, and *Truth Bomb* got quiet if I hung around long enough after school. He usually left as late as the last student did, and I had been working up the nerve to stay last. I still preferred to talk to him with Lila buffering our conversations, but I was getting braver.

"Mr. Drummond?" I'd thought of something to ask him after English. It felt odd using his title; no one ever called him that. It was usually "Drummond" or, more often, "dude."

He looked amused. "Yes, Chuck?"

"Sorry to bug you if you're busy—"

"I'm never that busy," he said, shoving his papers aside with a flourish. "What's up?"

I hovered by his desk. "I just wanted to ask about the paper . . ."

"Sit down," he said. "Make yourself comfortable."

"Oh, okay." I pulled a chair over and sat on the edge of it. "I wanted to ask about the favorite books thing."

"Sure." He picked up a tennis ball on his desk and tossed it into the air. "What about it?"

I cleared my throat. "You remember how I read *The Brothers Karamazov.*"

"Oh yes," he said. "I may even remember it better than you do."

I looked at him and he grinned and said, "Sorry," but he didn't look sorry at all.

"Right," I said. "The thing is, I loved it so much that reading it once really wasn't enough."

"You didn't get enough of the parts in Russia, you mean."

"Yeah, exactly."

"*More Russia,* you said as you finished a nine-hundred-page novel about Russia. *There just wasn't enough Russia in that for me.*"

"Uh-huh. So I wondered if you would make an exception and allow me to, uh, reread it for my paper."

"Well, what aspect of it were you hoping to get more insight into? Besides Russia."

"The, uh . . ." I felt myself cracking. "The acrobats."

"The acrobats."

"Yes. Their . . . plight."

"So what you took away from reading *The Brothers Karamazov* was that it in some way involved a circus."

"At the turn of the century. Is that wrong?"

"Oh no," he said. "Just like *Madame Bovary* is about a cow who wants to be human."

I laughed; I couldn't help it. That made him laugh too.

"I'm sorry," I said. "I was nervous. I didn't mean to lie."

"You know, I'd expect this behavior from Lila, but not from you."

"Lila doesn't have the class to pretend to have read *The Brothers Karamazov.*"

He laughed at that, a low chuckle that made a shiver of

pleasure run down my arms. "Fine, 'reread' it if you want, you glutton for punishment."

"Thanks?" I said; it came out like a question.

"You're welcome? But I hope, Charlie, that someday you write a novel about Russian carnies."

"I'll make a note," I said.

"Do." He leaned back and his chair screamed on its hinges. "Good Lord," he said, and I started laughing helplessly, partly at his reaction and partly to let out what felt like helium in my lungs.

He smiled, looking baffled. "I'm glad my bumbling has given you such amusement."

"You're funny," I said. "I like you." As soon as I said it, I wished I could take it back, but his expression lightened and I realized I'd caught him off guard.

"I like you too, Charlie," he said. "Even when you lie to me."

october

chapter 10

Attendance at our school's first pep rally of the year was mandatory for underclassmen. As a senior I could have escaped early, since I could drive, but Lila was a field hockey player, and she'd instructed me to show up and at least pretend to be enthusiastic.

Normally I would have sat with her, but she was in another room with the field hockey team, waiting to be cheered as they strutted into the gym. I wandered around the half-full bleachers, trying to act like I was looking for a friend. I knew Drummond wouldn't be there—he'd left early—but I half hoped he'd turn up anyway. Finally I spotted Katie from our English class. She was popular but she'd always been nice to me.

"Mind if I sit here?" I asked. She was alone, texting someone.

"Course not," she said, smiling at me. "How's it going?"

"Okay," I said. "Hate these things."

"Oh, really?" she said. She peered at her vibrating phone again. "Sorry, just a sec," she said, and resumed texting.

As her thumbs tapped the screen, I looked around the gym, trying to seem like I was coolly observing the action and not just being socially outmatched by a phone. The bleachers were filling up as groups of kids barreled in, already giving off a dangerous hum of electricity.

"Sorry," said Katie, looking up. "Insecure boyfriend."

I knew I was supposed to offer my own boyfriend anecdote here. "Oh," I said. "Isn't he coming to this?"

"He doesn't go here," she said. "He's in college."

"Which college?"

She ducked her head a little. "Chatham Valley." The local community college.

"Ah, right," I said.

"K-Dawg!" someone shouted. It was a girl I didn't recognize; she sat down next to Katie and they started whispering frantically, their foreheads practically touching.

I pulled out my own phone and fiddled with it, wishing I had a text to respond to, even from my parents. The last text from my dad had been a picture of Frida with a sombrero on her head. The last one from my mother had been a reminder that she was going to be late and I needed to pick up some eggs for her. Cage-free.

"You meeting that loser later?" the girl said.

Katie hit her but laughed. "You're one to talk."

"Sean may be a loser but at least he's got a gigantic . . ." The other girl spread her hands (Jesus, that was way too far, wasn't it?), and Katie laughed. That must have been Sean Varniska from my class. I was embarrassed that I suddenly knew this about Sean, that anyone in our school knew such a private thing about him.

"Hey."

I turned to see Asha and Dev standing on the bleacher below mine. I'd never been so glad to see them, or anyone.

"Hi!" I said, and Asha laughed, clearly taken aback by my enthusiasm.

"Want to sit here?" Dev said, pointing at their bleacher.

"Please," I said. I moved to their row.

"Guess you're not a fan of these," Asha said, sitting down with me.

"How could you tell?"

She laughed. "Just a hunch."

Dev sat down on my other side. "So why are you guys here?" I asked.

Dev pointed at a camera Asha was pulling out of her bag. It looked professional. "They let her take photos for the yearbook because no one else is interested."

Asha glared at him. "Dev is here because he can't drive."

Dev laughed and said, "Fair point." I didn't usually trust guys my own age, but there was something about his laugh I liked: it was quick and friendly, like he was always ready to be amused by your jokes, no matter how terrible.

"And our brother is on the lacrosse team," Asha said.

I turned to Dev. "Not you."

"What an assumption! Look at these muscles," he said. I started to blush, but then he rolled up one sleeve and poked at his flaccid bicep. He was joking. I relaxed.

"You're wasted on the paper," I said. "They probably need a water boy."

He laughed again; his whole body shook with it. "I'll look into it," he said.

"It's our little brother, Jai," Asha said. "I doubt he cares whether we're here, but our mom would kill us if we didn't show up. What about you?"

"Lila's on the field hockey team," I said. "She said I have to whistle when she comes out."

"Doubt she'll be able to hear yours above all the others," Asha said.

I glanced at her to see her expression, but she was looking down at her camera, adjusting the settings. "Sorry," she said when she saw me looking at her. "It's hard to get the white balance right with these artificial lights."

"Ah," I said. "Of course. But that camera's . . . good?"

"It's her Christmas and birthday presents for the next five years," Dev said. "You know what I got for Christmas last year? A pair of hiking boots. I don't even hike."

"I think they were trying to give you a hint," Asha said as I laughed. "Like, go outside more than once a month."

"I play plenty of sports," Dev said.

"I don't think playing them on your Xbox counts."

"It's okay," I said. "The outdoors is overrated anyway."

"*Thank* you, Charlie," Dev said. "I'm glad someone here makes sense." We smiled at each other.

The gym had mostly filled up. There was an expectant thrum in the air like the murmur of a band tuning up.

"Here we go," Asha said.

Dr. Crowley crossed the gym with long fluid steps, looking crisp and cool despite the damp heat. "Welcome, everyone," she said when she got to the microphone. The crowd whooped; kids drummed their feet on the bleachers.

"This is our inaugural rally, so let's make the most of it." She smiled indulgently at the crowd. "First up is Coach Rick Perona."

"Thanks, Dr. C.," Coach Perona said as he took the microphone. "All right, children, settle down." His eyes gleamed as the crowd cheered. "As you all know, we haven't had the best couple of seasons. We've had setbacks; we've had disappointments." He paused to survey the crowd. "But this year, that's all gonna change." The noise swelled. "Introducing your new quarterback, Ethan Salvato!"

Ethan burst through the gym doors as if the sound itself were propelling him out. He whooped as he jogged through the gym.

"Sean Varniska, running back!"

Katie stood up and screamed. As Sean ran past, I imagined his penis flopping around in his shorts like an uncooked hot dog hanging out of a split-open pack. I wondered how he could run with it if it was really as big as that girl had said. Wouldn't it be uncomfortable, slapping him on the leg or something? I tried thinking of him with an erection, but I couldn't picture Sean's goofy face contorted in . . . effort.

Dev pointed out their brother when they sent out the lacrosse team's players. As Jai stood in line he searched the bleachers, and when he spotted Asha and Dev, he waved like a little kid, looking excited and proud to see them.

"Good thing you came," I said as Asha waved back.

"Ah, I wouldn't have missed it," she said.

Finally there was the field hockey team. Lila came out third, to a good level of applause. A few boys wolf-whistled at her, and a couple more groaned "Lila!" like it was a dirty word. She bowed and lifted her skirt at the hip, just enough to show some thigh. A few more guys shouted "Yeah!" in guttural moans.

Asha rolled her eyes. "Boys," she said. "They do it to everyone."

Lila looked up into the bleachers; I waved at her and she spotted me and waved back. Then she noticed Asha and frowned. Great.

"You want to get out of here?" Asha asked. "We can beat the crowd if we leave now. I think Dev's more than ready to go." He had already shuffled into the aisle and was motioning for us to hurry up.

"Oh, I think I might need to wait for Lila," I said. I knew she'd be busy celebrating with her team afterward, but I wasn't ready to be real, outside-school friends with Asha yet. It wasn't that I didn't like her; I did, despite Lila's disapproval. It just made me clammy, how guileless and straightforward she was. She didn't seem to care that I could reject her. I was much more comfortable with people who made me work for their affection.

Asha considered me. I tried not to flush. "Okay," she said finally. "See you Monday?"

"See you," I said. I watched them walk out. Dev turned back to wave and I waved too, feeling even guiltier now that Asha had caught me lying. I told myself I'd make it up to her somehow.

I waited a few minutes after they'd left to get up. When the doors closed behind me, it was like I'd plugged a hole; the noise and confusion was safely encapsulated on the other side.

"Ugh," I said aloud.

"I know what you mean," someone said, and I jumped. It was Ms. Anders, my trigonometry teacher. "Sorry, Charlotte," she said. "I didn't think anyone would be out here."

"Oh, I—I didn't think I needed to stay—"

"Oh, no, no, no," she said, waving her hand dismissively. "Do what you want. I couldn't stand these things when I was your age either."

"Thanks. Um, have a good weekend, then."

"I'll walk out with you," she said. "I need a cigarette anyway." She fell in line beside me and we walked the few steps to the outer doors. When we got outside, she rummaged in her bag and dug out a crumpled pack of cigarettes. I was about to escape to my dad's car when she said, "Are you liking trigonometry?"

"Yes," I said automatically.

She looked up over the cigarette she was lighting. "It's okay; you don't have to lie."

"Well, math's not my best subject, I guess, but I'm enjoying it so far." I hated every second of thinking about math, and Ms. Anders still didn't have control of the class; she was lucky if she made it through a day without someone throwing something or trying to derail her.

She blew out a gray exhaust cloud of smoke. "I'm glad if that's the case," she said, clearly not believing me.

There was a silence as she inhaled deeply. I wondered how much longer I had to stand there.

"I don't think I'm getting through to them," she said.

"Oh, you are," I said. "They just act like jerks sometimes."

"You think?"

"Yeah, of course," I lied. "It just, like . . . it just takes a while for some people to settle down."

"Yeah," she said. "So you like Tom, huh? Sorry—Mr. Drummond. I've seen you two talking."

"Oh," I said. I hadn't realized they knew each other. "Yeah. He's, uh . . . yeah."

She laughed; smoke puffed out of her mouth. "Yeah, I know what you mean." She gazed up at the building. "You couldn't pay me to do all this again," she said after a minute. "I know it must be rough for you. And I guess you can see that not much changes."

I knew she was trying to be nice, but somehow the fact that she included herself made it worse. I pitied her; I consoled myself sometimes that at least I *wasn't* her.

"So you're . . . you're here for the whole year?" I asked.

"Oh," she said. "Yes. Mrs. Morgan isn't coming back."

"Okay," I said. "Good luck, then."

She gave me a smile; her eyes looked glazed. She stubbed out her cigarette. "I'll need it," she said.

chapter 11

"So any initial thoughts on *Pride and Prejudice*?" It was a Friday and Drummond knew we were flagging. The homecoming dance was that night and we'd just come back from a dress-code assembly. No shorts for guys; no skin for girls.

When no one answered, he said, "I'm not going to get *Dangerous Minds* on you and try to link Jane Austen to your homecoming dance, but they're not entirely unrelated." Silence again. "Lila, any brilliant theories?"

Lila looked up from doodling. "Paul Rudd was really hot in *Clueless*."

He sighed. "That's not even based on the same . . . You know, I don't even know why I'm bothering today." He put the book down so its pages splayed out on the table. "All right, Frank, you're obviously dying to tell us, so—what color is your dress?"

Frank tapped his pen against his bottom lip. "If I tell you, then someone else might steal my idea."

"Mine's purple," Dev said. "The color of royalty."

"An excellent choice," Drummond said. "Frank could learn something from you."

"What's yours, then?" Frank asked.

"My dress?" Drummond said. "Red, obviously. Slinky, to show off my curves. Short, because I've got great legs."

Everyone was laughing now. "You are way too old to pull off a dress like that," Katie said.

An "ooh" went up from the class and Drummond said, "That's ageist."

"So you're coming to the dance, then?" Lila asked.

"If Frank doesn't upstage me," Drummond said.

"But are you really?"

"If Dev promises he will wear purple. I don't want to clash."

"Cross my heart," Dev said.

"But are you *actually* going?" Lila said, exasperated.

Drummond finally looked at her with mock annoyance. "*Yes,* Lila, I am actually going. As a chaperone. Apparently it's illegal for Frank to take me as his date."

Drummond turned back to the class, and Lila whispered, "Coming now?"

I rolled my eyes. "You think I'm that predictable? But, yes."

Lila came over to my house to get ready that night. She brought three outfits: all, she said, in increasing factors of sluttiness.

"This one's a three," she said, holding a glittery top and a long skirt against her body. She curled her lip. "Senior bingo?"

"A little," I said.

She tossed it onto my bed. "How about this?" She held up a red dress with a shiny bodice and ruffles on the flared skirt. "Too nineties?"

I nodded. When she threw it onto the bed, I picked

it up and stretched it experimentally. "Is the top of this spandex?"

"Yep. My aunt bought it for me," she said. She held up a short black dress. "This will have to be it."

"Just slutty enough," I said.

She wriggled into it while I averted my gaze. "So?" she said after a minute.

She looked fantastic—older and sexy and confident. It made my throat constrict with fear.

"You look great," I said.

She turned to the mirror and smoothed the fabric over her flat stomach. "I look fucking hot, actually." She turned back to me. "Now you."

"Me?" I said. "I'm just wearing what I have on."

She squinted at me like she was scrutinizing a poorly drawn map: I had on a pair of loose jeans and a button-down shirt.

"It's not a T-shirt," I said. "It has buttons."

"It's plaid," she said.

"It's festive."

"At least try on the dress."

"No way."

She looked at me seriously. "Please?"

"It's not going to fit."

"Don't," she said. "Anyway, it's stretchy."

"Oh good," I said. I considered her, looking hot in her dress. "I'll try it on. But no promises." I grabbed it and went into the bathroom. I didn't have any strapless bras, so I pulled it on over my bare skin. My boobs sagged a little, but not too badly. It fit, at least, and the ruffles didn't look that stupid. There were no horrible bulges or gobs of fat leaking out the sides. But it looked all wrong on me; I didn't recognize myself in it. I was about to take it off when Lila burst in.

"You look good!" she said. I couldn't tell whether she was just trying to make me feel better.

"No, I don't," I said. "I feel safe in plaid."

"No plaid!" she said. "Wear this. You look hot."

"I won't feel comfortable."

"You will. Just give it a few minutes."

I sighed. "All right."

"Now what about your face?"

I looked at it in the mirror. "What about it?"

"Makeup? I brought a whole bag full of crap. I think I've had some of it since before puberty." She rummaged briefly and extracted a tube of glittery purple lip gloss. "See?"

"You think I need it?" I was afraid of makeup. It felt like using a toothpick to try to dam a waterfall. I knew that without it I didn't have a chance with guys, but I was also afraid that if I did wear it and still no one noticed me, it would confirm all my worst fears about myself.

"Just put on some mascara," Lila said. She never made me feel bad that I wasn't interested in girly things like she was. I wondered how awful she must think I looked if she was suggesting it.

"Okay," I said. "Just don't make it look like I have spiders crawling out of my eyes."

There was a soft knock on the door. Lila and I glanced at each other.

"Yeah?" I said.

My mother's blond head came into view. "I just wondered if— Oh my God! Lila, did you get my daughter into an actual dress?"

Lila grinned. "I did. High five, right?" She held her hand up.

"Absolutely," my mother said. She stuck her palm out but nearly missed Lila's hand. She let the door slide open. "Can I come in, girls?"

"It's a little crowded," I said, but she was in already.

"Are you putting on makeup too?" my mother asked. "You should have told me! I thought I'd never get you wearing mascara, Charlie. Good work, Lil."

"Mom, we need to go soon," I said.

"Sure, I know, honey," she said. "But you've got that mascara on a little thick, and if I could just . . ."

She always did that. *You look fine, but if I could just . . .* Like I was some deteriorating project of hers that needed constant shoring up.

"Okay, but fast," I said.

"One second," she said. She jabbed at my eyes with some kind of pencil. "Okay. That's . . . well, it'll do. Do you want to borrow a pair of my shoes? They might be a little small for you, but I think I have a pump that ran wide—"

"I have shoes," I said. "We really need to go."

She lifted her hands up. "Okay, okay, your interfering mother is leaving you alone now." She paused for a second to survey her work. "Oh, honey," she said. "You look beautiful."

My throat closed. I grabbed her into a hug suddenly; I could hear her breath puff out with surprise.

"Thanks," I said into her hair. "I love you."

When I pulled back, her eyes were shiny. "Okay," she said. "Go have fun. Take pictures, all right?"

I was already out the door. "No chance!" I called from the hallway.

"Do you actually have shoes?" Lila asked.

"Technically," I said.

"Your gross old sneakers?"

"Yes."

We passed my dad on our way to the door. His head shot up when he saw me.

"Charlie," he said. "What are you wearing?"

"I don't know," I said. "Lila made me. Is it horrible?"

"Don't answer that," Lila said. "She looks great."

"I look like an idiot," I said.

"No, you don't," he said. "You look wonderful."

Lila moved toward the door, as fluid as water. "Let's go, okay? It'll be in full swing by now."

"Get home safe," Dad said. "If you need a ride, just call me, all right? I don't care how late it is."

"You're awesome, Mr. Porter," Lila said.

"I haven't even gotten to what you're wearing, Lila," he said, frowning.

"Bye, Mr. Porter!" Lila rushed through the door.

"Bye, Dad," I said.

"You do look lovely, Charlie," he said.

"See you in half an hour," I said.

The gym was heaving when we arrived. Noise spilled out in waves and hung in the air like smoke. I lingered behind

Lila, watching as people's eyes swiveled to her and then to me.

"We'll find Drummond," Lila said, "if that'll make you feel better." I knew, though, that she wanted to show off for him too.

He wasn't with the other chaperones, who were laughing with one another in a loose circle, their clothes and hair drooping. And he wasn't anywhere else either; it was just purple-hued teenagers grinding as far as the eye could see.

"Sorry," Lila said. "Let's dance until he gets here, okay?"

"I'm fine," I said, gesturing at the buffet table. "I need to get a drink. Fortify myself."

Lila looked me over. "All right. I'm making you dance in a few minutes, though." She wandered off into the crowd, her hips swaying in a way that made me feel uncomfortable.

I watched the dancers for a while—the way the rhythm of the songs guided their movements, and how groups spontaneously formed and then fell apart. Some people didn't get a partner when a slow song came on, and they'd wander to the buffet table as if they'd just remembered they needed a snack. I exchanged resigned smiles with a few of them.

I kept my arms crossed over my chest and tried to stay as inconspicuous as possible. I felt like people were staring at me but I couldn't tell for sure. Whenever they laughed and looked in my direction, I thought about retreating to the bathroom. I filled a cup with punch and held it like it was a piece of armor. I didn't know how to carry myself in a dress. I couldn't figure out where to put my hands or how to stand. The sneakers had seemed like a good idea at home, but all the other girls were in heels and suddenly I wished I'd borrowed some from my mom.

Then I spotted Drummond—he'd finally arrived. A gaggle of kids surrounded him already. One of the girls touched him flirtatiously. He withdrew a little but she didn't seem to notice; she clung to his arm even as it moved.

As a song wound down, Lila returned, looking sweaty and flushed and terrifyingly sexy. "What's going on?" she said, knocking into me as if she were a wave and I were a concrete barrier. She grabbed the cup from my hand and took a long swig, draining it. "Thanks, babe."

I took the cup back and fiddled with it. "Drummond's here," I said, pointing.

She looked around. "Polo shirt and Dockers. Hot. He seems to be getting attention, though."

"Freshmen."

"Ew. How about we distract him a little? Come out and dance with me."

"You think my dancing is going to *attract* him? You've seen me dance, right?"

Lila tried to pull me away from the buffet table. "Come on, I'll teach you how to look hot. It's all in the calves."

I glanced at Drummond. He was still talking to the kids, laughing now, enjoying himself.

"All right," I said, but I didn't move.

"Really?" Lila stopped pulling. "You've never actually danced at a dance."

"I guess I should do it once in my life."

"You really do like him, don't you?" she said. She gave me a look I couldn't read. "Okay, come on, then."

The music pulsed and I shuffled as much as I could without feeling ridiculous. I could just about sway my hips to the beat, but anything more complicated made me feel awkward and gangly. Lila tried to guide my movements, but she had an internal rhythm I found impossible to mimic.

"Just listen to the music!" Lila shouted into my ear. "Don't try to move; just let it move you."

"Oh please," I said. But a song I liked came on, and Lila started dancing so shamelessly that I laughed and started dancing too. After a minute, I felt my joints loosening and my muscles going slack. The music was loud—so loud that normally it would have overwhelmed me, but instead I felt like I was inside it and it was pounding into me as I danced. Lila sang at me, bouncing and laughing, and I found myself laughing and singing back.

I glanced at Drummond. He was finally looking at us, but he didn't see me watching him. As much as I hated dancing in public, I had imagined this scene many times at home: pretending to sing to him into my TV remote as I listened to a love song. But now the thought of him seeing me was humiliating. At home I was a siren and he was enraptured by my performance, but here I was just another awkward teenager and he was a bored teacher, wondering when he could get home.

I settled down to slow swaying. Lila was still dancing with a kind of liquid ease I knew I couldn't match. I felt like a shadow of her. I watched Drummond, who was alone now, to see how often he looked at her. He never watched her very long, but his eyes flicked back a couple times. Every time he glanced in her direction, a clot of fear stuck in my throat. Eventually he noticed that I was watching him, and he smiled at me and waved.

I left Lila to a group of dancers she'd found. She didn't seem to notice that I'd left.

"You made it," I said, standing close to him so he could hear me over the music.

He leaned in closer, shaking his head. He smelled warm, like clothes fresh from the dryer. "Sorry, you might have to shout at me—the loudest thing I listen to these days is NPR."

"It wasn't important! Are you having fun yet?"

"In a Jane Goodall kind of way, yes. Why aren't you out dancing with your very, uh, dexterous peers?"

I turned back to Lila, who was now being humped by Jason Tierney.

"Not my speed," I said.

He nodded. "I was never much for dancing either. I looked sort of like a monkey being electrified."

"Seemed like you were about to be dragged out to dance earlier."

He rolled his eyes. "Kids."

I didn't know whether to laugh with him, as if I weren't a kid myself, or feel chastised.

"You're wearing my dress," he said.

I looked down at it and then up at him. "What?"

"The dress I said I was going to—"

"Wear in class. Right." I looked down again. "You'd probably pull it off better than me."

He laughed. "I doubt that very much."

I blushed, not sure how to take that.

He looked over at Lila's group. "Why don't you go

back?" he said. "I'm just going to stand here and be boring and drink disgusting spiked—what is this? Punch?" He took a sip and grimaced. "RC Cola? Mr. Pibb?"

"Tang, I think," I said.

"That explains the metallic note," he said, "but not the burning."

I wanted to tell him I felt more comfortable standing there with him, but I wasn't sure whether he wanted to get rid of me so he could talk to the other chaperones.

"Or stay," he said. "I could use the company. You can make sure I don't start slurring in case I've been drugged with off-brand cola."

I smiled at him, hoping I didn't seem too relieved. I watched Lila for a few minutes as she flirted with Jason, grinding against him in her tight black dress, which was so short that it seemed to dare you to look up under it. He pretended to slap her ass and she laughed and moved closer. I glanced at Drummond, but he wasn't watching her anymore. Then I noticed Jason's friends—the ones who'd been at the pool. The tanned one—Austin—had been hovering behind him, but now he moved forward, not dancing, just looking at Lila and Jason.

I watched him out of the corner of my eye as Drummond said something I couldn't hear. I knew as soon as Austin saw me he'd come over: me with my ruffled dress and old shoes like a flag at full mast. It wasn't even that I knew he would say something cruel. It was that he'd do it in front of Drummond, and then there would be no way to pretend that he could ever feel anything but pity for me.

"It's you!" Austin said as he came close. He leaned

down next to me, his breath hot in my ear. "He's never going to fuck you, sweetie," he said. "You can stop trying." Then he straightened, turned away, and shouted, "Jason! We're going, asshole!" Jason kept grinding on Lila. When Austin got no response, he stomped toward the emergency exit and pushed the doors open. Mike hesitated, turned to me, said, "Good dress," and then followed him out.

"He seems nice," Drummond said as he watched Austin leave. When I didn't say anything, he looked at me and frowned. "You okay, Charlie?"

"Um," I said. Had he heard? Talking to him—pretending I was someone worth talking to—suddenly seemed impossible. The music clogged my head. "I need to—I just need a minute."

"Did he say something to you?" He looked worried and stepped backward as if he was going to follow Austin. "I'll take care of this."

"No!" I said, loud enough to stop him. "No, it's not—it's not that. I just—I just need to go." The noise and the crowd and the darkness were pulsing in on me, pushing me down, binding me in. I hurried to the doors and opened them onto the cool, silent hallway, then headed for the bathroom.

I wriggled into a stall and slammed the door, then twisted the lock. There was no toilet seat cover, so I sat fully clothed on the seat itself and waited for my breathing to slow down. I should never have come in the first place.

I stared at the cubicle door and listened to other girls coming in and going out. Every time the door opened, there was a whoosh of music, like water gushing out of a leak, and then it gradually became a distant thumping again. The rhythm of it was soothing: it was out there, and I was in here. As long as I stayed in here I'd be fine.

The door opened again. "Charlie?"

I considered not answering, but I knew Lila would find me.

"I'm here," I said.

"Are you going to let me in?"

"Sure," I said, but I didn't move.

"Are you okay? Drummond sent me in here to check on you."

"Drummond?" I unlocked the door. Lila squeezed into the cubicle with me. Her knees pressed against mine. Her lip gloss was smeared and her mascara had collected in little black globs around her eyelashes, but she still looked sexy.

"Why are you in here?" she asked. "I've been looking for you for, like, ten minutes."

"I just needed to go somewhere quiet. Why did he want you to check on me?"

She shrugged. "He didn't say."

"What *did* he say?" I knew I was pushing it.

"I don't remember *exactly*. He was worried enough that it made me jealous, okay? He cares about you." She smoothed my hair and I tried not to shy away. "So what happened?"

"I'm— Nothing. I've just had enough and I want to go home."

"We only just got here!"

"Fine, I'll call my dad. He'll pick me up."

Lila sighed. "Don't be a baby about this. You did this to me when we went to the pool too. Suddenly wanting to leave, no explanation."

"Lila, all you need to know is that I need to go home," I said. "If you want to stay here, fine."

"Well, I do. You seem to take some kind of perverse delight in thinking everyone hates you. Don't flatter yourself that you're that unpopular. Plenty of people like you, and the rest of them don't even think about you at all."

"I really don't want to get into this, okay? Just go back to the dance. I'm sorry I came and ruined your night."

"You should be," she said as she left the stall. I heard her heels clicking as she ran to the gym.

In the bathroom mirror I looked pale where I wasn't bright red and blotchy. The top of Lila's dress sagged and my mascara had smeared and I looked idiotic. I went outside, passing the gym, and stood in the cool air. I called my dad but he didn't pick up.

"Dammit," I muttered, and tried him again.

"You need a ride?"

I turned, and it was Asha, of course.

"How do you always show up at the right time?" I asked.

"I keep very close tabs on you," she said.

"Creepy," I said.

She laughed. "Or I get bored of social things at the same time." She looked elegant in a short navy dress, much too posh for a sad gym full of strobe lights.

"Why'd you come?"

She held up her camera, which was hanging from a strap on her shoulder. "And I wanted to see what it was like."

"You're odd," I said before I could stop myself.

She laughed again. "Why'd *you* come?"

"Lila dragged me here," I said. I decided not to go into the Drummond thing.

"I think my reason was better than yours," she said. "Come on, I'll take you home."

I followed her to a dark sedan. It smelled new and the inside was trimmed with wood and leather.

"It's my mom's," she said when she saw me admiring it. "Mine's at the mechanic's."

I nodded. "I use my dad's car. This one looks like Lila's."

Asha turned on the ignition, and the engine vibrated gently, like water simmering in a pan. "Her parents bought it for her?"

"Yeah," I said.

"Not surprising, I guess."

Even though I was mad at Lila, I tensed. "She contributed."

"She has a job?" The headlights swerved across the trees next to the parking lot as we pulled out, illuminating the branches so they looked like veins. "Which way are we going?"

"Left and then straight for a few miles," I said. "She babysits."

"Okay," Asha said. We sat in silence until I directed her to take another left at the first stoplight. "I saw you talking to Mr. Drummond at the dance."

"Briefly," I said.

"I talked to him too."

"A lot of people talked to him. He was the most popular guy there, apparently."

"He was," Asha said. "It's because he flirts with everyone."

I glanced at her, glad it was dark. "You think so?"

"He flirts with our whole class. You haven't noticed?"

"I guess," I said. I knew he did, but I thought the way everyone loved him so much was charming.

"He does," she said. "I don't like it."

"I thought you did like him," I said. "At least, you did a few weeks ago."

"He is charismatic, I'll give him that," she said. "But he's too . . . I don't know. He's immature. Glib. He makes fun of people more than I'd like."

"He's just teasing them," I said.

She glanced at me. "I thought you *didn't* like him."

"I never said that," I replied, feeling my face heat up. "He's grown on me."

"Hmm," she said. She pushed a button to turn the radio on; it was a classical station and she didn't change it.

I looked out the window. What would Lila think of my getting a ride home with Asha? I knew Lila didn't consider her worthy of friendship, but I didn't know whether that was because Asha wasn't popular enough or because Lila was trying to be. I was sure she kept me around only because I'd been grandfathered in; we were friends long before she got cool. And I knew about her Weird Al obsession.

"Did you dance with anyone?" I asked finally.

"No," she said. "I don't dance."

"I don't either," I said. "That didn't stop me."

"I think Dev operates on the same principle. I made sure to get lots of photographic evidence."

I laughed. "Wish I had a brother."

"You don't wish you had a Dev," she said.

"Well," I said. Then I blushed fiercely and looked out the window again.

We were silent until she pulled up in front of my house. I lingered before I opened the door.

"You okay?" she said.

I hesitated. "I just . . . You ever feel like this is the absolute worst time in your life and it has to go up from here?"

"Always," she said. "I feel like I'm watching other kids in better movies."

"Right?" I said. "Like you're the sidekick and someone else is the star."

"With a better sound track," she said.

"Definitely better," I said, widening my eyes at her stereo.

She glared at me. "Get out," she said. "You've been reduced to obnoxious extra."

I laughed. "Thanks for the ride. See you Monday?"

She smiled back. "I'll bring a new yoga mat."

I found my dad in the basement. "Hey," he said. "You're home early."

"It was stupid," I said. I sat down at his worktable. "What is the point of dubstep, do you know?"

"Is that a dance?"

"I'm not even sure," I said. "I don't think I'm very good at being a teenager."

He turned around from his computer. "You're better than I was," he said. "You've seen pictures, right?"

I laughed. "That's true. That mullet was definitely ill-advised." I reached for a piece of clay and squashed it flat onto the table.

He considered me. "Everything okay, kiddo?"

"It's fine," I said. I looked at his desk, which was stacked high with papers. "You need any help with those invoices?"

"Nah, it's okay," he said. "I've decided I don't need to get paid anyway."

"Come on," I said. "Mom will never know."

He looked at them and then back at me. "Just half an hour. Then you need to go eat some junk food and watch bad TV."

"Deal," I said.

chapter 12

Lila called me while I was still in bed the next morning. "Sorry I stormed off last night."

"I'm used to it," I said. "Are we okay?"

"Of course," Lila said. "I was being a dick."

"You were. You were a real asshole, actually."

"All right, we've established that. Let's move on, okay? Did you get home all right? Did your dad pick you up?"

"Uh," I said, "no. Asha actually took me."

"Asha?" she said. "Are you friends with her now or something?"

"No," I said. "She was just there and she had a car." I felt a coil of guilt in my stomach as I said it.

"Hmm," she said. "As long as you were just using her."

"I told you you were jealous. You'd like her if you got to know her."

"I am *not* jealous, you loser!" she said indignantly.

"And yet somehow I don't believe you," I said. She laughed. "So how about you? How'd you get home?"

"Um, I'm not home yet."

I sat up. "Explain, please?"

"Vodka," she said. "Vodka is the only explanation."

"Who was it?" Every time Lila hooked up with someone, I felt worse; another guy and her tally of conquests pulled further and further away from mine. It was particularly depressing because mine was zero. I knew I wasn't supposed to mind. I didn't *want* to mind. I pretended not to mind. I hoped someday I actually wouldn't.

She sighed and mumbled a name I couldn't make out.

"Sorry?" I said. "Did you say James Joyce?"

"Jason," she hissed. "It was Jason. I can't say it again or I'll have to desecrate this cemetery with a loogie."

"You're . . . on foot?"

"Charlie, don't make my walk of shame even worse. I'm wearing one shoe and I look like a raccoon with pinkeye."

I tried to laugh, but panic rose like bile in my throat. The previous night I had been pretending to read *The Brothers Karamazov* but actually watching *Sex and the City* reruns and feeding Frida cheese. Lila had been fumbling down Jason Tierney's pants. "Well," I said, "how was it?"

"Awful," she said. "Like kissing a badger."

"What's that like?"

"Horrible pointy teeth and a weird musky smell. I'm not sure if it was coming from his bedroom or his body." She paused. "Hang on, I just found a bag of Ruffles by the side of the road."

"How many times have we gone over this? Do not eat garbage."

"Fine, I'll starve." She huffed and I heard the bag crinkle as she dropped it. "I'm taking a shortcut through the gravestones."

"Don't eat out of any vases you find," I said. "That's not Pixy Stix dust."

"Ha-ha," Lila said. "I do need something to wash my mouth out."

"So how far did it get?"

"Oh, that. I don't know. I touched his penis. Not impressed."

"Small?" I said. I made up for my lack of experience by reading extensively about sex. I knew the average erect penis was six inches long. I'd studied pictures on the Internet to determine what they looked like so I wouldn't be surprised when I saw one for the first time, and for other, less scientific reasons.

"Medium, I guess? I don't know, I'm not *that* much of an expert. It was kind of . . . purplish. It looked angry."

I laughed. "Also like a badger?"

Lila laughed too. "Yeah, exactly. He wanted me to suck him off. He just, like, *presented* it to me. Like I'm going to be like, 'Oh my God, your dick! What a thrilling surprise!' "

I thought of making out with Drummond, seeing that he had an erection, that he wanted me to touch him. I shivered. "So you needing to wash your mouth out . . ."

"Oh, no, I couldn't go through with it. As soon as he showed it off, I pretended I had to throw up. By the time I got back from the bathroom, he'd passed out on his desk chair, so I took his bed. I left before he woke up this morning. Thank God he has a separate entrance. That was convenient, huh? Can you imagine if I'd run into his mom?"

"So I guess you don't like him anymore," I said.

"I don't know. I might give him another chance. Maybe I can teach him how to pull his lips over his teeth."

Panic fluttered in me again. She could keep him if she

wanted him; it was her choice. He wanted her either way. I would never have that.

"You're lucky," I said.

"Lucky like a badger."

"That doesn't mean anything."

"Shut up."

november

chapter 13

"You want to do it now?" I asked.

"Sure," he said. "Let's get it over with."

"That's a promising start."

I was finally interviewing Drummond for the newspaper. Our first issue still hadn't come out, a combination of hardly anyone having written articles and our inability to crack the layout software, although Dev was trying. Drummond was the only new permanent teacher, and I'd put off interviewing him because whenever I tried to, we ended up chatting instead. Besides, I'd already written a column, about why tennis was a metaphor for college admissions.

"It'll be fine," he said. "I'm just warning you now that I'm not going into those years at the smelting plant. Some memories are too painful."

"All right. So where did you go to school?"

"Well, it was mostly on-the-job smelting experience."

I cocked my head. "That's your answer?"

"Yes," he said.

"You want me to write, 'Tom Drummond, newly hired AP literature teacher, says of his education, "It was mostly based on smelting."'"

"Are you implying I don't know anything about, uh"—he turned around in his chair and typed something on the computer—"extracting base metals from their ore?"

I was partly happy that he was trying to make me laugh and partly dismayed that he wouldn't give me a straight answer. Sometimes it felt like he pummeled me with jokes until I gave in and laughed. But I always did eventually. "So just to be clear, in your capacity as my newspaper adviser, you're encouraging me to lie."

He rocked back in his chair. "You don't win Pulitzers without some truth stretching. You think Woodward and Bernstein didn't embellish a few details? How plausible is it to you that Nixon added a tape recorder to his office just before he began committing crimes?"

"Are you saying this to annoy me or because you think the word *smelting* is funny?"

"Yes."

I paused. "Okay, next question. Where did you work before this?"

"I told you I wasn't going into the smelting years."

I sighed.

"Tom?"

We both looked up. Ms. Anders stood in the doorway, looking at us quizzically.

"Is there something about your past you haven't told me?" she asked.

"Secret's out now," he said. He let his chair drop to the floor and slapped his hands on the table. "What can I do for you, Tracey?" It was strange—and weirdly hot—seeing him turn professional and solicitous in an instant.

She stepped into the room and perched on the edge of a table. "It's Olivia," she said. I knew she must mean our principal, Dr. Crowley. "Did you hear about that bullshit directive?"

Drummond glanced at me, and she said, "Oh, sorry, Charlotte. I forgot you were there. Apologies for the swearing."

She forgot I was there? I was sitting right in front of her. "No worries," I said. "It does sound like a bullshit directive." I stood up. "I'll come back and you can tell me about your smelting days another time."

I could see Ms. Anders was about to nod me away.

"Don't be silly," Drummond said. "I have so many stories. We'll only be a minute." He raised his eyebrows at Ms. Anders.

I moved to the other end of the room, desperate to overhear their conversation but worried they'd notice if I did.

I hadn't seen Drummond interacting with other teachers very often, and I wasn't sure how I felt about it. What did they talk about? Students, I assumed, and apparently Dr. Crowley. They were talking in low voices, conspiratorially, and occasionally Ms. Anders threw her head back and yelped with laughter. Drummond laughed with that low, private chuckle I thought he reserved just for me. I wondered why I had stayed. I felt sure that they were talking about something so hopelessly adult that I wouldn't be able to follow it even if I could hear them. It probably involved political humor.

Tracey, I thought, *how perfect a name.*

I watched them from the corner of my eye. She touched him on the shoulder and he smiled. Then she got up—at last!—and said, "Have a good one, Tom."

"Yep, you too," he said. He waited until her footsteps had faded, then turned to me and said, "Sorry about that."

"Everything okay?" I asked as I sat down.

He rolled his eyes. "Yes. Just the usual gossip."

I smirked as if I had the faintest idea what he was referring to. "What about?"

"The same things bored people at work always complain about."

"I haven't been lucky enough to experience that yet."

"Enjoy it," he said. "You'll have plenty of time to experience it when you get older."

"I'm sure it's more interesting than the things high schoolers talk about," I said.

He shook his head. "It's the same stuff, I'm afraid. It's just polished to a higher sheen."

"I doubt that," I said, "but thanks for trying to make me feel better."

"It was more of a warning." He nodded at my notebook. "All right, what's the next question, Woodward?"

"You never answered where you worked before this," I said.

"Ah, right," he said. "It was Bloomfield High over in Peterborough. Three hellish years teaching freshmen how to parse sentences."

I looked up and he raised his eyebrows at me. "What?" he said.

I shook my head and tried not to smile. "Nothing."

chapter 14

"We are actually going to discuss *Pride and Prejudice* today, kids," Drummond said. "If I hear any groans, I'll probably just put up with it."

There was a knock on the door.

"What did you do this time, Drummond?" Frank asked.

"You're still here, so it couldn't have been that bad," Drummond said as he got up.

Dr. Crowley was at the door. They talked quietly for a minute, and then she smiled at us in a perfunctory way and moved inside, toward the windows at the end of the room.

Drummond sat down again. "Dr. Crowley's going to observe, guys, so let's not embarrass ourselves quite as much as usual."

I was immediately anxious on his behalf: what if he got a bad evaluation? They couldn't fire him, could they? I didn't want to imagine the rest of the year without him.

"So, any thoughts?" he said.

Everyone was silent.

"Really?" Drummond said. "Not even about Paul Rudd?"

I nudged Lila, who was a reliable breaker of silences, but she shook her head and whispered, "Didn't do the reading. Jason."

I wrinkled my nose. "At least you're getting an education."

"All right, what about Elizabeth?" he said. "Did you like her? Dislike her?"

Another silence. This never happened; Crowley's presence had shut everyone up.

Katie had her phone in her lap and was clearly texting someone.

"Katie?" Drummond said. "I bet you identify with Elizabeth."

Katie looked up guiltily, then scowled when she realized what he'd said. "Identify with her? She's completely dependent on her parents."

Drummond raised his eyebrows, and Katie scoffed.

"Are you saying Katie is helpless?" Sean said.

"No, Sean," Drummond said, but he caught my eye for a moment and I could see he wasn't as calm as he sounded. Embarrassment for him abraded my stomach, and then a fleeting moment of disgust did too. I hated seeing him not in control. "What makes you say that?"

"Elizabeth is lame," he said. "She sits around waiting for a guy to marry her."

"What other options does she have?"

"I don't know," Sean said. "She could go out and get a job."

Drummond laughed, and Sean frowned at him. "Is that really an option for her?"

Sean shrugged. "Some women had jobs. What about their servants?"

"Okay, true," Drummond said. "But do you think Austen's condoning this kind of society?"

Sean paused. "What's condoning?"

I couldn't stand it. "Elizabeth isn't helpless," I said.

All the heads in the room snapped toward me and I had to stop myself from shrinking back. I looked at Drummond for help and he smiled at me pleasantly but didn't say anything.

"She has some power," I said.

"What power?" Sean asked.

I tried not to freeze up at Sean's question. "She uses her intelligence," I said. "It's the only real power she has."

"Yeah, but for what? To get a husband?"

"A husband is power," I said. "At least for her."

"What about *love*?" Sean said. Drummond frowned at him and then looked at me, his forehead still creased into worry lines.

"That's power too," I said. "Darcy gives her that when he marries her."

"You mean social capital?" Dev said.

"Yes," I said, relieved that he'd stepped in.

"That's true," he said. "Darcy is her way of getting ahead in the world."

"But I think she actually loves him too," Katie said.

"Yeah, she does, but that's just a bonus," Asha said.

Then people were talking over each other and I couldn't keep track of it anymore. I glanced at Drummond. He mouthed, "Told you so."

When I went in after school, Drummond's classroom was deserted. It wasn't a *Truth Bomb* day, but I was meeting Lila so we could go shopping—or rather, so Lila could shop and I could trail behind her, halfheartedly picking up shirts and then putting them down again. I headed for my usual seat, then stopped. I looked at his desk, which was a drab military beige. It was covered in curling stacks of paper and the occasional thumbed-through book. His chair was an old, squeaky metal thing lined with cracked vinyl padding. I sat down in it. It shrieked when I reclined—I smiled, remembering that day we'd talked alone in the classroom—but it was surprisingly comfortable.

"You taking over after my performance today?" Drummond was standing in the doorway. He looked as if someone had popped him and he'd half deflated.

"Crowley hasn't told you?" I said. "This is awkward." I gestured at the empty space in front of the desk. "Pull up a chair. I'll give you some suggestions for improvement."

"I'm looking forward to this," he said. He dragged over a chair and sat down.

I settled my feet on his desk. "First of all, always sit like this when you're addressing the class. It tells us you're in charge, but you're also a maverick who doesn't play by the rules."

"How many times have you watched *Dead Poets Society*?" he asked.

"Not important," I said. "You can jump up here"—I rapped on the desktop—"when you really want to inspire us."

"I guess I'll have to memorize all of 'If' by Kipling," he said. "I've always hated that poem." He leaned back and looked at the ceiling.

"You were flustered," I said.

He sighed. "Those were my incredible coping skills under pressure. It's too bad I didn't become a pilot." He held out his hands and shook them as if he were having a seizure. "Steady as a rock."

"You'd be excellent at bumper cars."

"I am renowned at a local track for several reasons."

I picked up a couple of books and pretended to read the blurbs, then tossed them down again. There was something thrilling about looking through his things while he watched. "You really find Dr. Crowley intimidating? I've seen her drinking Go-Gurts."

"I find anyone who's spent that long in academia suspicious."

"Why do I find that odd?" I said, and ruffled a stack of marked papers.

"All right, smart-ass," he said, grabbing them from me. "There's a reason I teach high school. It's so I know I'm definitely smarter than most of you." He looked at me. "Thank you, by the way."

"For what?"

"Don't play dumb when I'm complimenting your intelligence."

I smiled. "I had to step in when it became clear you were going to give the game away."

"The game?" he said. "You're referring to the one in which I appear competent to the outside world?"

"That's it."

"Oh, is that where this conversation is headed? You're uncomfortable with me complimenting you, so you're insulting me?"

I paused. "Yes."

He picked up the tennis ball from his desk and tossed it at me. "Typical."

We were laughing as Lila walked up.

"Hey, nerds," she said. "What's so funny?"

"Besides your face?" I said.

"Oh ho," Lila said. "Good one." She turned to Drummond. "You have any bon mots for me, dude?"

"Not after today," he said.

"Oh yeah," Lila said. "Pathetic performance, really."

"Lila!" I said.

"It's fine," he said. "I was only trying to put in as much effort today as Lila did."

"I resent that," she said. "I watched the entire BBC adaptation, which is really long."

"In between 'dates' with Jason?" I asked.

"No. We watch them *on* dates. Or I do. He usually falls asleep."

"Who's this Jason character?" Drummond asked.

"He's Lila's boyfriend," I replied, enjoying her face when I said it.

"Not my boyfriend," she said. "I just spend time with him occasionally on a recreational basis."

"'Recreational,'" I muttered.

"Enough with the air quotes, Captain Sarcasm," Lila said.

Drummond looked at us as we laughed. "This relationship seems fulfilling."

"He's very muscular," she said.

"Why don't I know this guy?" Drummond asked. "He sounds like an intellectual titan." He grinned at Lila.

Lila gave him her warm, slow smile back. "He's not in any advanced lit classes. I'm not entirely sure he can read, come to think of it."

"He's on the lacrosse team," I said. "He's one of their stars."

"Lacrosse is a rube's game," Drummond said. "I prefer curling. Tactical sweeping."

"I heard you liked swimming, actually," Lila said. She had that tilt to her head and cock of her hip that always made me nervous.

Drummond considered her. "Where'd you hear that?"

"I have sources," she said.

They both laughed. My pulse began to hammer.

"I bet you wear a Speedo, don't you?" she said. "One of those bright red ones."

I stood up and tugged on her arm.

"We're late," I said.

"We're talking," she said.

"Go," Drummond said. "You kids already spend way too much time in my company."

Once we were in the hall, Lila whispered, "What was that?"

"What were you doing?" I said. "You were embarrassing yourself."

Lila stopped. "What the hell, Charlie? *Embarrassing* myself?"

"He looked really uncomfortable."

"We were just talking. Jesus." She started down the hall and I followed.

I let a moment pass, then said, "I had to pull you

away. He was clearly getting a dangerously large erection."

She glanced at me. "Bet it'd look better in a Speedo."

"True," I said. "Let's hope someday we find out for sure."

chapter 15

The newspaper had become my favorite part of the week. Our lit classes weren't long enough, and Drummond was more relaxed after school; most days *Truth Bomb* became an excuse to chat rather than a legitimate enterprise. Even Asha seemed more tolerant of him now, though she was usually at a computer working while the rest of us talked.

That day she was taking pictures. I mostly kept my head down so she wouldn't notice me, but eventually she came over and stood in front of me as I read one of my most recent library selections.

"You know I still exist even if you keep your head down?" she said. "I think they call that object permanence."

I laughed despite myself. "What's up?"

She slid onto the edge of the table. "I don't want to interrupt when you're clearly busy, but can I get a picture with you and Dev?"

"No pictures."

"Come on, you have to. Otherwise how will they know who to complain to?"

I looked at Dev, who was working at a computer with Drummond.

"With Dev?" I said.

"You guys are the two opinion columnists. In theory, anyway."

"Oh, right," I said. I could tell she wasn't going to leave

until I agreed. Asha didn't brook argument when she'd made up her mind. "Okay, if I have to."

She turned around. "Dev!" she said. "Get over here."

He looked up and so did Drummond. He said something to Drummond, and Drummond nodded. He watched as Dev came over to us.

"I need you to pose with Charlie," Asha said.

Dev looked at me. "I take it she's bossing you around too?"

"I'd call it decisiveness," I said.

He huffed. "You know, I'm older by ten minutes."

Asha ignored him. "Come on, kids," she said. "The quicker you do this, the quicker it's over."

Dev sat across from me so we were on either side of the table, and we posed a few times with pencils askew in our teeth. I saw Drummond glance at us occasionally and it thrilled me, knowing he was watching. Everything I did in his presence had become a performance I hoped he would notice.

"All right," Asha said finally. "You can get back to your little golf column."

"What's the golf column?" I asked.

Dev looked at me without turning from Asha. "I'm writing a column on whether golf is a sport or an activity."

"It's more like pin the tail on the donkey for adults, isn't it?" I said, and Asha laughed.

"It takes skill!" he said, but he laughed too and turned toward me.

"I didn't say it didn't," I said. "But you could definitely improve it with blindfolds and alcohol."

"Since when do you like golf, anyway?" Asha said. "I thought it was Xbox sports only."

"Dad took me a few weeks ago."

"What, when he was home?"

"Yeah, and when he's on leave for Christmas, he's taking me and Frank again."

"Hang on," she said. "I thought the two of us were—" She glanced at me. "Never mind. I have to upload these pictures." She passed Drummond as she left. I looked at Dev and he shrugged and rolled his eyes in a long-suffering sort of way.

"What's this ruckus about?" Drummond said, and rapped his knuckles on the table.

Dev looked up. "Ah, good. We need you to arbitrate something for us."

Drummond sat down on the table, between me and Dev. He'd never gotten this close to me.

"What's up?" he said. He leaned back and put his hands out behind him so that he was nearly touching my hands, which I'd let rest on the table. He always sat like this in class, his shirt dissolving into wrinkles where he slumped, his shoulders low, as if he were chatting with a group of friends at a party. I liked that he was so comfortable with us, because I so often felt uneasy inside my skin, like I was wearing an ill-fitting coat and the seams were all irregular.

I had to angle myself to see Dev; Drummond was practically blocking him. "Dev thinks golf is a sport, because he was dropped on his head as a child," I said.

"My dad plays," Dev said.

"See, dad sport," I said. "Does that not prove my point entirely?"

Dev looked so hurt that I laughed. "I'm sorry," I said. "I do like a sport you can play in khakis."

"All right," Drummond said, "I'll settle this if I have to."

I looked up at him. His eyes were glittering.

"You have a lot of experience arbitrating this kind of thing?" I asked.

"It was basically my major in college," he said. His dimples puckered as he smiled at me.

"Yeah, but you think curling is a sport. You can't be trusted."

He bumped me on the arm with his elbow. This was new. He'd never touched me before. He was casually affectionate with a lot of people in our class—he'd chuck them on the shoulder or shove them playfully—but never me. Giddiness filled my head like helium.

"Dev," Asha called. "I need you over here for a second."

"Sorry, guys," Dev said. "We'll finish this later."

"Yep," Drummond said. "Just remember your grade depends on whether you answer correctly." He had moved closer to me now; I could feel the heat from his torso, he was so close. I looked down at his hands—big hands. Nice fingers as well.

Once Dev was on the other side of the room, Drummond looked down at me and said, "You guys going to do anything about that flirting?"

I pulled away from him. "Dev?" I said. "No, afraid not." I was relieved he'd said it out of Dev's earshot, but embarrassed that he'd considered the idea at all. I hated it when adults assumed that just because you were younger than they were, you wouldn't mind pairing off with anyone of a similar age. I'd thought he understood us better than that.

"Sorry," he said. He bounced his arm slightly; he was still so close that his elbow touched my shoulder. "I didn't mean to embarrass you. I just thought you guys . . ." He shrugged. "It seems like Dev likes you."

I tried not to blush. Had he really thought of me that way? I looked around. No one was paying attention to us, at least. I was torn between wanting someone to overhear and being mortified by the thought that they might. He wasn't supposed to say things like that, was he? Did he like me enough to say them anyway?

"I think he and Frank are a better fit," I said finally.

"True," he said. "And they both look better in formal wear."

"Unlike you," I said.

He shoved me with his elbow again, and this time I shoved him back. It was the most I'd ever touched him.

After a minute he said, "So you don't like any of the guys here? Or girls?"

I looked at him. Did he really think I had a shot with anyone? "Nope," I said.

"Well, Sean might be available if Katie could possibly relinquish him," he said. He knocked me on the head and then he finally sat up. "Think about it."

I thought about him instead, the entire drive home. We'd touched for less than five minutes, but I managed to replay it for twenty. I felt as if all the charge from his skin was in my body and I had to release it somehow or I'd burn up.

When I got home, I found a note on the kitchen table: my dad had taken the train into the city to meet a client and my mother was working late. I looked at Frida.

"We're alone, huh?" I said.

She unfolded her ears into triangles, but her head stayed on her paws.

"You need to stay downstairs. Your owner has something sinful to do." I shivered as I climbed the stairs to my bedroom. Lila and I had talked about it before, but I'd never tried it. Neither of us really understood what to do. She said she'd tried using an electric toothbrush once but it didn't work. She couldn't look at it after that. "My dentist is going to be so angry," she'd said. "But what can I tell him?"

I locked the door and lay down on my bed. Then I got up, pulled the covers down, lay down again, and pulled them over me. Then I lay still, waiting for inspiration.

I closed my eyes and thought about watching him in class, looking at the inch-long vertical space between the waist of his pants and the part of his shirt that puffed outward—where it was obvious how flat his stomach was, how it didn't slop over his belt. Sometimes when he stretched, I watched his shirt pull taut against his torso; there was something erotic about seeing the fabric straining upward, threatening to pull out of his jeans and expose his belly.

His belly, his hands, his mouth, his legs, his eyes. His eyes.

I thought about being alone with him, working on the newspaper at night, resting my head on his shoulder in frustration. He'd wrap his arm around me and rub my shoulder. I'd look down and notice he had a giant—

I laughed, thinking of Lila and Jason. Start again.

He'd put his arm around me. I'd lean into him. He'd kiss me on the forehead. "Mr. Darcy wasn't the only one with social capital," he'd say. "Something of mine has capitalized too."

Oh God. Start again.

We were lying in my bed together. My mind started trying to fill in how he'd gotten there, but I made myself accept that he had and it didn't matter how. It was a sunny afternoon and he was backlit next to me, fringed with sunlight. His hand was warm and solid on my rib cage and he was laughing at something I'd said. He lifted himself up and lowered himself onto me. His loosened tie pooled on my stomach. He was pleasantly heavy. He started kissing my shoulder, then my collarbone, then my throat. His hands slowly pulled up my shirt.

My heart was pounding hard enough to make me shudder now. Parts of me were pulsing that I'd never realized could have a pulse. My hand moved lower and lower to relieve the welcome ache, and after a few minutes of fumbling, I realized what to do.

Afterward, everything I had thought about seemed ridiculous, but that didn't stop me from doing it again.

chapter 16

After she got home that night, my mother knocked on my bedroom door. By then I was reading and trying not to think about what I'd done.

"You're home," I said.

"We had a big project today," she said. She sounded annoyed. "I only work this late when it's really important."

"I wasn't judging you," I said. "Calm yourself."

She stepped inside. "Sorry," she said. "I was just—I just came to say that dinner will be done in a minute. Your dad's boiling the pasta."

"Okay," I said. "I'll be down in a sec. I just want to finish this chapter."

"Oh?" she said. "What book?"

I held it up.

"Pride and Prejudice," she said. "I loved that book when I was your age."

"That's a surprise," I said. It wasn't that I didn't like the book. It was that I didn't think she liked Austen the same way Drummond did—that is, the way I did—or for the same reasons. The right reasons.

She didn't seem to know whether to laugh. "What does that mean?"

"I mean, you just—did you like Darcy or something?"

"Does anyone *not* like Darcy?" she said.

"I don't," I said.

"So you're just reading it for the intellectual satisfaction?" she asked. She smiled like she had me.

"For class!" I said, laughing despite myself. Although I'd read enough to contribute (I always skimmed endings first; I couldn't stand the suspense of not knowing how a story turned out), I had never finished it. It was better than I'd expected. "Darcy's okay, I guess."

She sat down on my desk chair. "Is this for Mr. Drummond?"

I hated how my heart kicked up a gear when she mentioned his name. "Yeah," I said.

"You're enjoying it, right? His class?"

"Sure," I said. I could only skirt the subject when I talked about him.

"He's a good teacher, then? You like him?"

"He's okay. Better than Mr. Mickler, at least."

"There were stories about him, weren't there?"

"Yeah. One of my friends told me he took naps during class."

"Oh, really? What friend?"

"You don't know her."

"Invite her over," she said. "Then I will."

I started to say something and then stopped. "Okay," I said. "Maybe."

She looked pleased. She sat up straighter and recrossed her legs.

"So I missed Parents' Night," she said, "and I know your dad went, but I thought maybe the two of us could go see Mr. Drummond together."

"Oh," I said. "Why?"

"So I can brag about you," she said.

I rolled my eyes, but I laughed.

"And he might have some advice about internships. Get you out of working in the basement next summer."

"I like the basement," I said.

"I know," she said. "But internships are important if you want to get into a writing program."

"It's a bit early, isn't it?" I said.

"The earlier the better," she said. "Any more objections?" She pursed her lips ironically.

I glanced at her and then out the window. I loved the thought of showing Drummond off, but I wasn't sure I wanted him to meet her. What if she embarrassed me? What if I embarrassed myself? "Is Dad coming?"

"I was thinking it could just be the two of us," she said. "We could go get something to eat afterward."

"I do like free food," I said.

She stood up. "I won't make you, but think about it, okay?"

"Dinner!" my dad called from downstairs.

"Saved by the bell," she said. "Let's go." I watched her leave, and then I looked down at the book again. I still didn't like Mr. Darcy.

chapter 17

"So I have an idea," Lila said.

"It's great when you have an idea, because it's usually something I really want to do."

Lila reached over and pulled the magazine out of my hand. "I was talking to this girl from the field hockey team," she said. "She swims at the community center three times a week."

"Gross."

"I know. So guess what she said? If you make a joke, I am going to slice your neck open with this copy of *Cosmo*. Why are you reading this filth, anyway? You don't wear makeup, and I give you all the blow job tips you'll ever need."

"I think blow jobs are probably a little more complicated than 'get out of the way when he starts to look constipated.' "

"Well, it's true," she said, flicking the pages noisily. "I don't see that advice in here anywhere. Listen to this one. 'Cook your man a spaghetti dinner naked, then dip your breasts in a little tomato sauce and ask him to lick it off.' Is this satire?"

I pried it away from her. *"Anyway,"* I said.

"Yes, back to Drummond," she said. "So he swims there. And he does wear a Speedo. Apparently it's black."

I wasn't sure what expression to make. I thought of how Lila had been flirting with him that day in the classroom, and how he would look in a Speedo—good? or humiliatingly saggy?—and what he would think if he saw me watching him.

"So you can probably guess my idea," Lila said.

I turned to face her. She was lying on her back, her hair cascading over the side of the bed.

"What are we, thirteen?" I said.

"It's a social outing and it's perfectly legal."

"I'm not stalking him."

"Oh come on, it'll be fun. Apparently he doesn't look bad."

"Does 'not bad' mean six-pack or does it mean not entirely covered in moles?"

Lila snorted. I suddenly wished he were there to see me making her laugh. "I'm going to assume 'not entirely covered in moles' is the baseline," she said. "Think about it, at least."

"You know I'm going to say yes."

"I did." She grabbed the magazine back. "I'm burning this."

The next day, I found Asha on my way to Drummond's class. The thought of stalking Drummond alone with Lila made me anxious (what if she approached him and started flirting while he stood there half naked and dripping wet? what if she decided to get in the pool herself?). Maybe she and Lila would even be friends by the end of it. There was no better bonding experience than a semilegal stakeout.

"Hey, Ash," I said, sidling up next to her. "How's it going?"

She glanced at me suspiciously. "Fine, I guess. Do I want to know how you are?"

"I'm good, thanks for asking," I said. "Listen, I know this is kind of . . . uh, do you want to hang out this weekend?"

Her forehead creased. "Um, I'm not sure. What were you thinking of doing?"

"Ah," I said. "That's the thing. I don't think you'll be interested, but I want you to come."

"Okay," she said slowly.

"We're—Lila and I—we're going to go to the community center."

"For . . . Why?"

"Because we heard that . . ." It seemed so stupid suddenly that I stopped. "Never mind, it's really dumb. I'm sure you have better things to do."

"You'd be surprised," she said. "Come on, what is it?"

"Well, you said you don't even like Drummond, so . . ."

"This has to do with Drummond?" she said. "Him being at the . . . Oh, disgusting." But she laughed as she said it.

"I know, it's idiotic," I said. "He swims, apparently. It was Lila's idea. I guess I thought if you were there, I'd feel better about the whole thing."

"You know I don't really like him. And I definitely do not like him like *that*."

"I know. You can mock us the whole time if you want. Bring your camera."

She was silent for a minute as we jogged up a stairway.

"And Lila wants me to come?" she asked.

"Yes! She wants to actually get to know you."

Asha looked down at the book she was carrying. "I'll think about it."

"I invited Asha," I whispered before class started.

"What?" Lila said. "Why? Why would you do that to me, Charlie?"

"I want you to get to know her. You'll like her."

"You know I think she's weird."

"This is coming from someone who's about to stalk her half-naked teacher at a public pool."

"Can the peanut gallery settle down so we can get started?" Drummond raised his eyebrows at us.

Lila smirked, and I hit her. That made her start laughing helplessly.

Drummond walked up to us, smiling as if he were in on the joke. "You guys found *Othello* that hilarious, huh?"

"'The fault is not in our stars, but in ourselves,'" I said.

"That one's from *Julius Caesar,* Cassius," Drummond said, "but nice try." He rapped his knuckles on the table in front of us and turned back to the class. "All right, guys, let's get started. What did you make of Desdemona?"

"She was kind of pathetic," Frank said. "She whimpered a lot."

"She whimpered," Drummond said. "So do you think she deserved what came to her?"

"Of course not," Lila said. "She didn't deserve to be smothered."

"Ah," Drummond said. "Would she have deserved it if she *had* cheated on Othello?" He turned to Sean, who was slumped back in his chair, looking out the window. "Sean? What do you think?"

"Hell yeah," Sean said.

"Why's that?"

"She would've been a slut."

A few people protested, and Drummond held his hand up. "A slut," he repeated. He pronounced it in such a way that it sounded obscene: something about the slide of the *s* and the clip of the *t*. "Does a woman who has sex outside of marriage deserve to be killed?"

You could see Sean was pleased he'd had an effect on us. "She wouldn't just have been having sex," he said. "She would've been cheating on him. Good for him if he took it into his own hands."

"And would it have been okay if Othello had cheated on her and she'd killed him?"

Sean looked at him sharply. "That's not the . . ." He looked back out the window, his fingers curling.

Drummond let Sean trail off into silence. I could tell from the faint lines on his forehead that he was annoyed. "So, guys," he said, "even if Desdemona cheated on Othello, would it have been okay?"

"No," I said. "It wouldn't."

He turned to me. "Why not?"

"Uh, because it's not okay to kill someone even if she cheats on you?"

His eyes lit up, like they always did when we hit on something he wanted to pursue. "An excellent point. And yet our empathy for Othello rests on us believing he would be justified if she had cheated."

"Yeah, but he is hot-blooded," Lila said. "Iago uses that against him."

"He's also an outsider," I said. "Actually, so is Desdemona. He's a Moor and she's a woman."

"And how does that affect them?"

"Desdemona sort of helps him fit in."

"So you're saying Desdemona has a kind of limited agency."

"I guess so," I said. "She's his voice in legitimate society. But then he smothers her voice. He actually takes her voice away."

"She's in a double bind," Asha said. "They both are."

Drummond raised his eyebrows. "What was that, Asha?"

"He thinks the only thing that makes him worthwhile is the fact that he's defending white society, but it's white society that brings him down. And Desdemona choosing Othello is the thing that dooms her—the fact that she's strong enough to have her own will is the thing that makes him so paranoid and ultimately kills her."

"Excellent," Drummond said. "And a double bind is . . . ?"

Asha sat up a little. "It's like . . . it's like a catch-22. Like how women are told not to care about male attention but also that they're not worthwhile if they don't get it. Or how they're expected to wear makeup, but they have to look like they aren't. Or how they're allowed to have power as long as it's sexual, but then if they use it, they get called sluts." She glanced at Sean. "And if they don't have sexual power, then they're worthless. It creates a situation where the person in the double bind can't win."

Drummond frowned. "Why would society do that?"

Asha gave him a small smile. He smiled back. "To keep us policing each other and trying to live up to an impossible standard instead of turning our anger on the society that's telling us to act that way."

Drummond turned to the class. "Welcome to feminist criticism, everyone." He pointed at Sean. "You too, Sean, if I have to drag you there."

Sean looked at Drummond. "You're a feminist?"

"Yes, I am," he said.

Sean paused for a moment, and then his fingers uncurled. "I'm not saying I wouldn't do her," he said.

Drummond allowed our class the laugh. "A terrifying glimpse into the mind of the teenage male."

"You were one too," Lila said.

"Never," he said. "I came out of the womb covered in prematurely gray stubble."

I looked at Asha. I knew he had her. She pretended for a minute that she didn't see me watching her, and then finally she glanced at me and said, "Fine, I'll go."

chapter 18

"It's been two hours," I said. "I don't think he's coming."

Lila looked into the rearview mirror. "What do you think we should do?"

"I was ready to go an hour and forty-five minutes ago," Asha said.

Lila sucked in her cheeks. "What about you, sunshine?"

"I'm having a great time," I said. "I can't feel my hands."

"You're not helping," Lila said as she started the car.

"I'm freezing," I said. "Maybe because you're too cheap to turn on the heat."

Lila looked at Asha again. "I promised to be nice today, so you're going to have to take this one."

"I'm wearing a scarf," Asha said.

"Let's get some lunch," I said. "I need hot chocolate."

"Horsemeat?" Lila said.

I nodded. The Horseshoe was our favorite diner. The menus were fraying at the edges and we were always brushing crumbs off the vinyl seats and wiping the crust from the lid of the ketchup bottles, but we could usually get a table in the corner and the waitresses always let us linger there for hours.

Asha studied the menu for a long time. "This is extensive," she said. "Ten pages? What's good?"

"The chicken parm is . . . well, I'm not going to say it's

definitely chicken, but it probably lived on a farm at one point," I said.

She laughed. "Maybe I'll stick with the burger."

Lila glanced at her. "Really?"

Asha looked up. "Is that surprising?" she said mildly.

"Of course not!" Lila said, but her voice went up too high. "I just thought since you're . . . you might not eat . . ."

Asha flipped her menu over. "Actually, maybe I'll have the veal."

I could sense Lila trying to catch my eye but I didn't look at her. Let her be unsure of herself for once.

"So what are you up to later?" I asked Asha after we'd ordered.

"Movie night with the family," she said.

I was sure Lila would think this was stupid, and I braced myself for what she would do, but she said, "Do you know that Charlie has seen a total of two movies her whole life?"

"It's more than two," I said.

"But she is on a first-name basis with the entire staff of the town library."

"At least my favorite movie isn't *UHF*."

Asha raised her eyebrows. "What's *UHF*?"

"It stars Lila's favorite musician, Weird Al," I said. "A forgotten classic, really."

"Don't even," Lila said, but she was laughing.

I relaxed a little as we ate. Asha grimaced at her burger, but she finished it. After we'd pushed our plates away, Lila said, "Sorry that was a bust. The girl on my team said he's there every Saturday without fail. Maybe she was just punking me."

"I bet he knew," I said. "He knew, and we're going to see it in his eyes on Monday."

"Silently accusing us of perving over him?" Lila said. "He'd be flattered."

"Of course he would," Asha said. "He'd love it."

"You don't like him?" Lila said. She arched her eyebrow at me.

Asha folded her arms on the table. "He's fine," she said. "But I think he likes the fact that everyone loves him a little too much."

Lila waved away her words as if they were an unpleasant smoke. "I'd be flattered too if half my students had a crush on me."

"He encourages it," Asha said. "Can you imagine the ego boost he'd get if he knew we tried to spy on him?"

"That's assuming he looks good enough to get an ego boost," I said.

Asha laughed and wrinkled her nose. "I can't say I was all that curious."

Lila looked at me. Then she sat back and slung an arm across the empty booth next to her. "So you're on the yearbook staff?"

"Kind of," Asha said. "I take pictures for them."

"So you're not quite on staff."

"You've met them, right? I'm as much on staff as I want to be."

Lila smiled tightly. "Not a fan of the people here, then?"

Asha shrugged. "Didn't say that. People are kind of the same everywhere."

"So people are equally unlikable wherever you go?"

Asha looked like she was amused by Lila's rudeness. "Yeah, if you want to put it that way."

"You're not exactly helping your case, Lila," I said.

Lila ignored me. "So why didn't you bring your camera today?"

"Ugh," Asha said. "I don't want this immortalized."

Lila's forehead began to crease, and to cut her off I said, "That's true. We're going to cringe when we think about this in ten years. We're not going to want photographic proof."

"Oh please, Charlie," Lila said. "You came along. Don't act like you're better than this."

I frowned. "Don't act like it wasn't your idea in the first place."

"Yeah, okay. You may have pretended to protest but you were desperate to see him."

"I was not!" I said. "You didn't even—"

Asha moved to stand up. "I think I might leave you guys to it. I've got to get home—my mom was expecting me an hour ago."

"It's the middle of the afternoon," Lila said. "Your curfew couldn't be that early."

"I need to get back," Asha said in a voice that didn't allow argument. "But thanks for the adventure, and for lunch."

"You didn't drive here," I said.

"It's not far. I'll see you Monday." She left some money on the table and walked away.

"Thanks," I said when she was out of earshot. I stabbed at a fry.

"What?" Lila said, her eyes wide and guileless. "What could I have possibly done wrong?"

"You've been rude to her since we picked her up this morning," I said. "And to me." I couldn't look at her, so I watched the fry collecting ketchup as I swirled it around the plate. "And she lives about five miles from here, so you must have really pissed her off."

"She was rude to *us,* Charlie," Lila said. "Why did she even come if she was just going to dump on what we were doing?"

"Because I asked her to?"

"No one told you to do that. I wanted to do this with just you. I thought it would be fun and instead she just disapproved of us the whole time. And then you joined in on it."

"You weren't exactly welcoming to her."

"She's not exactly friendly."

"She takes a while to warm up to people," I said. "They only moved here a few months ago."

"She's a snob."

"She's not."

"She *is.*"

"I was like that with you at first."

"No, you weren't."

"You probably didn't notice because you were being so loud and obnoxious."

Lila picked up one of my fries and threw it at me. "At least she seemed interested in Weird Al."

I snorted a laugh. "So he has two fans now."

She crossed her arms in front of her chest, but the corner of her mouth turned up.

"She was trying to be friendly to you, you know," I said.

"I know," she said. "I was being friendly with her too."

"Is asking her whether she likes people a friendly thing to say?"

"Oh come on," Lila said. "She can grow up and take it."

I sighed. "So much for that."

Lila stood. *"Fine,"* she said. "I will try. Now get up. I need to give my library card a spin."

chapter 19

I caught up with Asha on my way to lunch on Monday. "I'm sorry about Saturday," I said once I was next to her.

Asha looked at me. "I'll live," she said. "Don't worry about it."

"Don't worry about making you walk five miles home?"

"Ah, I called my mom and she picked me up."

"Bet that was a fun conversation in the car," I said.

"You mean when I told her I was trying to see my English teacher shirtless? Luckily she didn't ask. I think she was glad I was out with other people."

We stopped inside the cafeteria. "I just—I'm just really sorry about Lila," I said. "She's not usually like that. Well, she is, but . . ." I stopped when I felt a hand on my shoulder. I turned; it was Drummond. Fear shut me up.

"Uh, bye," Asha said. She moved off before I could say anything.

"Can I talk to you for a minute?" he said.

Oh great. "Um, yeah, I guess."

He motioned me back into the hallway. He hadn't acted different in class, but he hadn't been especially friendly either. Now I was sure he knew. I imagined the various ways he could humiliate me and was only about halfway through when we got to his empty classroom.

"Make yourself comfortable," he said as he closed the door.

I sat on the edge of a table and let my legs swing. At least I'd be higher up than he was.

"So your mom contacted me," he said. He sat down in front of me.

"About—wait, what about?"

"She said she wanted to know if the three of us could meet up to talk about internships."

My breath gushed out. "Oh my God. I forgot about that." Annoyance shot through me along with the relief: she'd called him already? Summer was so far away. I hated thinking about it.

He laughed. "Sorry, did I scare you?"

"Uh, a little bit."

"Don't worry, you're not in trouble. I just wanted to make sure it was okay with you before I called her."

I was still reeling from the scare. "If what was okay with me?"

He looked at me quizzically. "You all right?"

"Sorry," I said. "I was ready for you to yell at me."

"Never," he said. "If I were trying to let you know that you'd disappointed me, I'd ignore you for a couple of weeks and hope you'd get the hint."

"That works?"

"No, not at all," he said. "People just assume you're busy." He crossed his arms loosely. I tried not to stare at his chest, but I couldn't help wondering what it would be like now if I'd seen him shirtless. I was suddenly glad I still had to imagine it. I didn't want to know if he didn't look good.

"If you don't want me to meet your mom," he said, "I certainly understand. I know it'll only be a letdown for her, meeting me in the flesh after months of your incessant praise."

I fought back a blush. "She wouldn't be swayed by anything I said. I'm sorry she's bothering you about this already."

"She's just trying to help," he said. "I probably should have asked you this before, but have you thought about what you want to major in?"

I wanted to tell him I hadn't thought much about the future since I'd met him. Deciding on a major seemed trivial now. "A little," I said. "I like writing."

"Have you applied anywhere yet?"

"Yeah," I said. "But they don't have a journalism program. I was thinking maybe creative writing, but I don't—I don't know, really."

He reared his chair up so it was balanced on two legs. "Let's pretend. It's forty years from now. You're looking back on your career. What were you doing?"

I thought about it for a second. "Writing a bestseller about Russian circus folk."

He laughed. "You called it *The Plums of Europe.*"

"It sold ten thousand copies."

"A hundred thousand. Mostly to English teachers."

"The critics called it a rollicking journey full of luminous prose."

"I bought it," he said. "I read it seething with envy. How did you make those circus folk come alive like that? Especially One-Legged Vlad."

"Ah, you were okay. You became an eminent visiting professor at NYU."

"Well, I had insight into you that no one else did. I wrote an analysis of it called *Strange Fruit: Digesting* The Plums of Europe."

We started laughing before he'd finished. He liked the story too, I could tell. It made me feel like we were intertwined, like he too imagined a future in which we still knew each other.

"Did that help at all?" he asked.

"What?" I said. "Lying to ourselves about how great our future's going to be?"

"We weren't lying," he said. "We're just imagining a possibility. Something to believe in. That's all writing is: making sense out of chaos; giving random events narrative and purpose and meaning. That's what you'll be doing, right? So it's good practice."

"Sure, I guess," I said. "I would like to write someday, if any publishers still exist by then."

"They say dying industries are the most thrilling."

"Do they?"

He shook his head. "No. No one says that."

"At least having to live in a garret will give me material." I sighed. "I think my mom's just worried I'll never leave home and get a job."

"She has nothing to worry about on that front, I'm sure," he said.

"Thanks, I think," I said, looking down. "I won't object if you want to talk to her. Just . . . be prepared."

"I like a challenge," he said. "I'll get in touch with her and set it up."

There was a silence, and I knew the conversation was

over, but I didn't want to leave yet. "It'll be weird," I said. "You meeting my mom."

He looked amused. "Why's that? Am I the embarrassment or is she?"

"A little of both," I said.

"I'll try not to break wind or visibly bleed for an hour," he said. "That's the best I can promise you."

I laughed a little too hard, giddy that he was trying to entertain me. "I can't say the same for her."

"I've known you long enough that I'm prepared for anything," he said, and laughed when I scowled at him. "I'm sure she's lovely and most likely not a huge, unrepentant racist," he added.

"So you'll call her? And actually speak to her on the phone?"

"Is she mute?"

"No, it's just . . ."

"Weird, I know."

"Yeah." I got up. "All right, I'm really leaving this time."

"I'll believe you when you're gone," he said.

chapter 20

The afternoon of our meeting, I paced Drummond's classroom while we waited for my mother to arrive.

"You look like you need a cigarette," he said.

"I don't smoke," I said. "Though this seems like an excellent time to start. You have any?"

"Not anymore." He looked annoyingly relaxed. He was wearing jeans and a plaid shirt that was open at the top, and he had his hands in his pockets like he was chatting with someone at a barbecue.

"You used to smoke?"

"Why does everyone laugh when I say that? It was just for a year in college."

"I don't know, maybe because of your impeccable fashion sense?"

For a moment he looked genuinely hurt. "I like this shirt."

I stopped pacing and laughed. "Sorry. I didn't mean it." I liked it too. It was one of my favorites, in fact. He looked outdoorsy in it, as if he spent his weekends chopping wood. And he always rolled the sleeves up in a way that seemed to invite me to slip my hands inside them.

"You get mean when you're nervous," he said.

Even though it was perfectly obvious I was nervous, I was still pleased that he'd noticed. "Does it help if I say you look like an off-duty Brawny paper towel man?"

He frowned. "No."

"Sorry I'm late," my mother said from the doorway. I knew she'd hurried because she always hurried, but she looked immaculate. She held her bag in one arm as if it were a carefully wrapped present she was afraid of damaging.

Drummond sat up when he saw her, as if she were the teacher and he were the anxious parent. "Hi, Mrs. Porter," he said as he shook her hand. "It's good to meet you."

"Oh, please, call me Julia," she said.

"Tom," he said, glancing briefly at me.

They both found seats in a way that was so awkward and polite that I nearly had to turn away in embarrassment. I slouched next to my mother and tried to catch Drummond's eye, but he didn't look at me.

"As you know," my mother said, "I wanted to have this meeting to see if you had any ideas about internships for Charlotte." So she'd be taking control. I stared at the ceiling so I wouldn't roll my eyes. There was a water stain up there that I'd never noticed. I couldn't find any shape in it other than a blob. *Blob,* I thought, and nearly started laughing.

"Well," he said, "I know Charlie had a few ideas already, and I'm happy to help you look for some more places. I know a couple of journalists, and I can get in touch with them and see if they have any openings this summer. I also know a few creative writing programs if she'd rather go in that direction."

"That would be perfect, thank you," my mother said. "I just want her to get some experience and see if writing is something she really wants to do. The creative writing is maybe a bit . . . Journalism's a little safer, isn't it?"

"Not necessarily," he said. "But it's good to get experience in both."

"I work on the paper here," I said, to remind them I was still in the room. I was careful not to let the petulance I felt creep into my tone.

"I know you do, honey," she said. She patted my leg. "But it's different working at a professional paper." She looked at Drummond for backup.

"It is," he said. "They actually put out issues, for one thing."

Her mouth sagged open. "Oh, I didn't realize you hadn't finished any issues yet. I was wondering when I could read one of Charlie's articles."

"Technical problems," he said. "By which I mean none of us understand computer software. But it'll be worth the wait."

"I'm sure of that," she said.

They both looked at me. "What?" I said.

They laughed like they were sharing a private joke. Drummond turned back to my mother and said, "I'll get on that soon. Summer internships fill up fast."

"So I've heard."

"It was bad enough in my day, but it's gotten ridiculous now. You should've had Charlie studying Latin in kindergarten."

"You couldn't have gone to college that long ago," she said as if there was no way he could be telling the truth.

"Ah, it was longer than I care to remember," he said.

She chuckled throatily. "I doubt that," she said. I hit her leg and she shot me a look like grim death. Then she straightened her jacket and ran her hand through her hair. "So the other thing I wanted to ask about was scholarships. Charlie applied early to Oberlin, but—"

"You applied to Oberlin?" he said. "Why didn't you say anything?"

"Yeah," I said, pleased I had his attention. "I thought I'd told you."

"No," he said. "I would've remembered a hippie college like that."

"Where'd you go, then?"

"Will you believe me if I say Oberlin?"

"No you didn't."

"I've got the Phish ticket stubs and the enormous student loans to prove it."

"Well," I said. "Did you like it? Do you think I'll like it?"

"You'll love it," he said. "You couldn't be a better fit."

"That's good to hear," my mother said. She was watching us with an expression I couldn't read.

"Sorry, Julia," Drummond said. I tried not to smirk when he used her first name. "I interrupted you."

"Oh," she said as she looked at me. "I was just going to say that even though Charlie applied early to Oberlin—and we hope she'll get in—"

I rolled my eyes this time.

"—we'll most likely need to rely on some scholarship money. And while her humanities grades are great, her math scores are . . ." She trailed off as if to mention them would be like telling him an embarrassing family secret. "Let's just say that in math, she takes after her dad."

"Math is overrated," he said to me. "Where has it ever gotten us? What's your dad do?"

"He's an artist," I said.

"We don't know where the writing came from," she said. "Neither of us is any good with words."

"Maybe the milkman," I said cheerfully.

She looked at me out of the corner of her eye. "The sense of humor comes from her father. I don't take any responsibility for that."

Drummond laughed. "Nor should you. Anyway, that shouldn't be a problem. There are plenty of scholarships that reward ability in a particular subject."

"Oh, that's a relief," my mother said.

"Thanks," I said.

"You know I think you're a great writer," she said. "And Mr. Drummond clearly thinks so too." She looked at him conspiratorially, like it was their accomplishment, not mine.

"Clearly," he said. "I'd be happy to go over applications with you, Charlie, but I don't think you need it." He turned to my mother. "She'll be fine on her own."

"I hope she will," she said.

I shot her a glance.

"Thank you for this," she said finally. "Charlie's our only child and we tend to be a little overprotective."

"It's a pleasure," he said.

"So she's doing all right?"

"Mom!" I said.

Drummond laughed. "She scrapes by."

"I'm glad to hear it," she said.

"That was weird," I said, clutching the handle above the passenger-side window.

"I thought it went well," my mother said. Her voice went up like I'd hurt her feelings.

"No, it was fine," I said as she started the car. "Just strange having you guys in the same room."

She looked straight ahead. "Did I embarrass you?"

I paused and then said, "You were both acting different."

"How so?"

"I don't know," I said. "Just different."

She was quiet as we approached a red light. After we'd been idling for a moment, she said, "I had a lot of crushes on teachers when I was your age."

My heart knocked and I tried to laugh. "You?"

"Mm-hm," she said. "I preferred them to high school boys. They always seemed so young and immature."

"I guess," I said. Was I that easy to figure out?

"And it was safe," she said after a silence. "I was afraid of boys and I knew nothing would ever happen with a teacher. I knew I wouldn't have to deal with having a real relationship."

I wasn't sure whether to take the bait. "Mom, are you possibly trying to imply something?"

She glanced at me and gripped the steering wheel tighter. "I'm just saying I understand."

"What's to understand?"

"All right, pretend you don't know what I'm talking about if you want."

"I'm not pretending!" I said. "You seem to think I have a crush on my teacher, which is both illegal and gross."

"It's not *illegal,*" she said. "Well, for him it would be, but that's not really . . ."

"He's not—this is not—"

"Charlie, calm down, please. Look, I can see why. He's funny, he's young, he's cute—"

"*Mom!* Please stop talking."

"It's normal! I was trying to . . ." She trailed off. "Never mind."

She thwacked on the blinker and took the turn too fast. I braced myself against the door. I looked out the window toward the park, where two girls were chasing each other and screaming with laughter.

"Thank you for trying to . . . understand," I said finally, "but I honestly don't have a crush on him. He's nice and I like him, but I don't have, I don't know, *feelings* for him."

"Okay," she said. "I won't bring it up again."

Then I felt guilty. But how dare she intrude on me and pretend to know how I felt? She knew I was lying, but there was no way I could admit that I did have a crush on him, no matter how obvious it was to both of us.

"Sorry I snapped," I said.

"I'm sorry too," she said.

We rode in silence for a few minutes.

"Can we get some ice cream?" I asked.

She laughed. "I suppose."

chapter 21

I spent most of that evening reading over my paper on *The Brothers Karamazov,* which Drummond had returned to me at the end of our meeting. At the top was a large *A*, and at the end, in cramped red lettering, he'd written, *Excellent examination of the intersection of free will and morality as experienced through Ivan—but I still felt it was lacking in circus folk.*

"Hey," my dad said. He stood in my bedroom doorway next to my mother. "You need a break?"

"Sure. What's the occasion?"

"No occasion," he said. He sat down on the bed. My mother sat next to him. "We just thought we'd come sit on your bed and watch you for a while."

"Come on," I said. "Am I in trouble? Did I win a raffle? Did *Frida* win a raffle?"

Frida's tail thumped like a heartbeat.

"You didn't check the mail today," my mother said.

"No . . ."

"You got a letter," my dad said.

I knew what it was. From the way they were smiling, I could tell it wasn't bad news. "Can I see it?"

"We didn't look," my mother said as she pulled a thick envelope from behind her back.

"This could turn gloomy in a minute," my dad said, but he was grinning.

"Probably," I said. I took it and opened it, and there was a letter welcoming me to Oberlin College.

I laughed. "I got in."

My mother squealed—I'd never heard her squeal before—and they both grabbed me into a hug. Frida stood up and nosed her way in, wagging her tail as if she'd had something to do with it. For a moment I let myself think about it: a new start where no one would know me, in a place where he had been. But also a place where he wasn't anymore.

My dad pulled away first. "You look less excited than I expected," he said.

"I'm just in shock," I said. My gaze fell on the letter again. I picked it up and rolled it into a tube and squeezed it. "Let's celebrate."

december

chapter 22

I spent a lot of time watching him. He was tall, and his shoulders were broad. He wasn't stocky, exactly, but he wasn't thin either; he was as solid and sturdy as a cart horse. His body always seemed on the verge of overspilling its boundaries, but he swam often enough that it was roped in by muscle. I spent a lot of nights imagining what it would be like to hug him and decided he was big enough to enclose me completely, until we were so close that I could dig myself inside him and curl up in the hollow spaces. I loved watching him move around the room, juggling a tennis ball or sweeping his arms as if he were conducting our conversations. He could get our attention just by drumming his fingers on a table.

He was casually graceful—quiet and steady in class, never quick or impatient, but if pressed, he could move with surprising speed. He'd effortlessly take the stairs three at a time or leap over the low wall in the courtyard if he was running late; boys would wolf whistle at him and he'd give them the finger without turning around. When he ran, it was with the easy springing rhythm of an athlete; one day after school, a group of kids tossed a Frisbee too far and he raced after it with long loping strides and leapt up to catch it with a nimble curl. He moved not as if he were weightless but as if the weight didn't matter.

He didn't wear nice clothes—usually combinations of jeans or khakis and polos or sweaters—but one day he had a meeting with Dr. Crowley and he came in wearing a dress shirt and tie, and I wanted him so badly my vision blurred. For a moment it was so overpowering that my muscles went slack and my skull felt full of concrete. I had to put my head in my hands and close my eyes to ride it out. Halfway through class he'd loosened the tie and unbuttoned the top two buttons of his shirt as he listened to Frank ramble about *Wuthering Heights,* and I spent the next twenty minutes thinking about slowly unhooking the rest of them. He glanced at me while I was imagining freeing the lip of his shirt from his belt, and I blushed shamelessly and looked away. By the time I came back after school, he'd rolled up his sleeves: he'd started neatly, folding the sections of fabric over each other, but eventually he'd shoved them the rest of the way up his forearms until they bunched around his elbows like bloomers. "Nice," I'd said, and he'd replied, "I know; I just can't stand suits. I feel too restricted." I'd said I felt that way about skirts and he'd nodded solemnly and said, "Me too."

His hands were big, his fingers notched evenly at every joint, not thick or tapering but square at the tip. They looked capable of both strength and precision. The bones in the back of his hand showed through sometimes like the ribs of a piano. I stared at them during class, watching as he restlessly clicked a pen or tapped a finger against his thigh. His arms were contoured with muscle, but the soft undersides were as pale as the white of an eye. Blue veins traced a meandering path down his forearms like rivers in a topographical map. When he squeezed his fists, the veins would bulge slightly, and when we cracked him up, the one that crossed his forehead popped out like an extra laugh line.

His chest was solid but not particularly muscular. When he wore button-down shirts, he'd leave them open so that small tufts of his chest hair were visible, not dark and masculine but blond and sparse. He had a tag of skin on his throat, like a leftover bit of paper from a hole punch, that I was forever tempted to pull off.

His ass was round, curved both in profile and straight on, and where it met his thighs they were almost chubby, swollen with slightly too much flesh. They were powerful legs, thick as tree trunks. I tried not to stare at his groin, out of fear he'd catch me doing it more than anything, but every once in a while I couldn't help looking at the bulge where sometimes the seam of his jeans would push against his balls, and I'd think about what he'd look like with an erection. I'd never seen one in real life, clothed or otherwise, but I liked thinking of him being startled by it, embarrassed and apologetic but unable to stop it. The daydream usually involved us being pressed together and me feeling it on my hip, at which point I was often interrupted by Asha coughing or the scratch of pens on paper as everyone finished their quizzes, or even his rapping the table in front of me with his knuckles. I'd look up at him and blink, my vision briefly doubling as I tried to reconcile the fantasy image with the one of him looking stern as he patrolled us, his groin decidedly flaccid.

He never wore shorts, but sometimes I'd catch him idly scratching his leg, his pant leg rucked up and a crumpled sock exposed. His calf was milky white, knitted with dark hair, and it startled me how much I recoiled when I saw it. I think it was the sock, dark against his pale skin. It made him look ordinary, vulnerable, the way it sagged, the way it made his calf look like any man's calf, like a sixty-year-old's, like my father's. I thought of him in sandals with socks and winced.

He wasn't handsome, not unless you squinted. He had thick, dark brown hair, but cowlicks always threatened at the back, and it looked like the most thorough combing he gave it was when he dragged his hand through it in class. His mouth was too wide; his lips were too thin; his chin lacked a confident jut. His nose was straight but his profile made him look too young, like a college kid playing at being a teacher. He usually had traces of stubble sweeping his jaw like pencil shavings, but there were always angry red dots along his throat where he'd shaved too quickly.

But I loved his eyes. They were a striking shade of blue—the kind that made you look at them twice to ensure you'd gotten the color right—and they were big and warm and always ready to laugh. They caught mine every day in class, whether I was whispering to Lila or laughing at something he'd said or listening to someone ramble and grinning at him when he shook his head at me.

His crow's-feet fanned out into sunbursts when he laughed, and the crisp lines that bracketed his mouth pooled into fat dimples. I often imagined tracing those lines with my fingers, mapping his face until I could draw it from memory. His voice was soft in conversation but deeper in class, especially when he was joking with us, as if our whole course were an elaborate parody of teaching. I liked his laugh best when it was low and guttural, but I also loved it when we made him crack up; he'd bury his face in his arms as if he was ashamed to be so defenseless in front of us.

Even the books we read were different to me now, and took on his cast: every one felt like something our class shared, some secret we had together. We joked about them like they were a language only we understood. He made us feel like we had conquered them, understood them, unlocked them in a way other people hadn't, or couldn't, or would never be able to. Once I'd read a book for his class, it felt like it was mine, like it said something about me, and we were the only ones who would ever know what it was.

Everyone was infatuated with him to some degree; he pulled us in like a magnet. It started that way for me too, but after a few months I was absolutely helpless in front of him. It was exhausting, feeling as much for him as I did; it was big and violent and felt like it would never end. Some days I felt like a branch trying to hold up under an enormous weight; the pressure got worse and worse until I was sure I would snap. I was so giddy sometimes that I felt manic. I knew it would be wrong for him to feel anything toward me—and in a way I wanted him to feel something but not to allow himself to act on it, to be tortured and desperate but too noble to hurt me—but there was something even more appealing about the thought of him giving in: he'd have to want me so much he'd break the rules to act on it.

I would have done anything he'd asked me, formed any opinion he'd told me to, laid myself bare in front of him and let him do anything he wanted. I often pretended he was on my bed with me, overlit by the afternoon sun, running his hand down my leg. Then I'd try to picture what he was actually doing at that moment—swimming at the community center, laughing with a group of friends, talking to his parents, having sex with a girlfriend—and I'd think about how small I must be in his life, while he was everything in mine.

I knew nothing would ever happen. He liked me, of course, and sometimes I let myself think I was his favorite. But I told myself I didn't even cross his mind outside school. I was an ugly girl with a crush. I didn't have to worry that it would be wrong of him to be interested in me; he wouldn't ever be interested. I cringed to think of how he described me to his friends. I'd make myself imagine it: *You wouldn't believe how some of the girls throw themselves at me. Yes, really! And not even the good-looking ones. I get the ones the boys won't touch. There's this one . . . Jesus, it's painful. I want to put her out of her misery and tell her, Listen, I wouldn't be interested if you* weren't *my student.*

But there were other times I could have sworn I saw something else in his eyes, or we shared a grin as if it were a private joke, or he'd pass me kneeling at my locker and gently kick the soles of my shoes, and when I'd turn, he'd feign ignorance, whistling loudly and looking around for the perpetrator. Maybe it was just pity. I'd seen him do similar things with other kids in our class, and maybe it was the only way he knew how to relate to us. Why should I be any different?

chapter 23

When I went downstairs for breakfast on Christmas, my parents were kissing.

"Ahem," I said. "Good morning."

They pulled apart reluctantly. "Merry Christmas, kid," my dad said.

"Merry Christmas," I said. "I'll thank you not to give me a Christmas kiss like that."

"How about a Christmas noogie?" He squeezed my mother, and then he came over and ruffled my hair until I squealed and ducked away from him.

My mother watched us from the kitchen, smiling vaguely. "You in the mood for pancakes, Charlie?" she asked.

"When am I not in the mood for pancakes is a better question," I said. "And the answer is never."

"Well," she said, "your dad's making them, so he should probably get that griddle fired up."

My dad raised his eyebrows at me and I raised mine back.

"Sounds like you've got your orders," I said. "I take pure maple syrup. None of that Mrs. Butterworth's shit."

"I'll allow you that profanity because it's Christmas," he said. "But don't you dare insult Mrs. Butterworth like that again."

My mother slapped him on the butt as he walked past

her into the kitchen; then she grinned at me like she'd done something delightfully outrageous. I rolled my eyes, but I laughed.

"You know," she said, "agave's good on pancakes. You can barely taste the difference."

I squinted at her. "Just this once."

We sat by the tree in our pajamas to open presents. My mother had put Christmas music on and my dad had made a fire, something he attempted only once a year. My favorite Christmas memories involved watching him swear at great length and with increasingly florid creativity as he tried to get the logs to stay lit for long, squatting minutes.

"Last presents," my dad said. "Charlie, I believe yours is at the back there."

I splayed out under the tree to grab it; it had slid down near the wall, amid a carpet of browning needles. It was a large, heavy package in silver paper and the contents shifted slightly when I shook it.

"It's from your mom," he said. She looked at him and smiled and then said to me, "It's not something from your list. I just thought . . . well, you'll see."

She looked nervous. I readied my face so I could smile when I opened it, whatever it was. I ripped open the paper and saw the humped backs of a line of hardcover books. "Books!" I said in surprise.

"If you don't like them, we can exchange them," she said.

"Okay . . . ," I said. I ripped the paper off the rest of the way. It was a boxed set of all Jane Austen's books. The box itself had embossed lettering and a leather cover that gave a little when you pressed it. I slid the books out; they seemed to sigh a little as I released them, like their seal had popped. They were heavy, their covers smooth, the pages stiff, the paper heavy and creamy and expensive-looking. I turned them around to see the flat lips of their covers; the pages sandwiched between them were ragged at the edges.

"Wow," I said. "These are beautiful."

"I thought, you know, since you were enjoying *Pride and Prejudice,*" she said. "And I know your teacher liked Jane Austen, right? Mr. Drummond?"

"Yeah," I said. "I didn't think you remembered."

"I did," she said. She allowed herself a small smile. "So you like them?"

"I do," I said. I ran my hands down their spines. "Thank you." I glanced up and smiled back. "These are really—thank you. They're perfect."

Her smile grew wider. She put her hand on my dad's thigh, and he fastened his hand on hers. "So there's something else that goes with them. . . . It's in the bottom there."

I reached down into the slipcase and pulled out a thick white envelope. "What's this?"

"It's a—it's a certificate for a salon I like. I want to treat you to a spa day. We can both get dolled up and have a girly day out."

"Oh," I said. "Is that . . . What does that have to do with the books?"

"You know," she said, "like the way the girls do, getting ready for their suitors before a ball."

"That's not really the . . . the point of them."

"I know that, Charlotte," she said. "I just thought it might make you more enthusiastic."

I pushed my tongue against my teeth and sucked in air. "And you . . . that's why you gave me the books? They were a bribe?"

"No!" she said. "No. But I thought it couldn't hurt. One present for you and one for me. Right?"

"Right," I said.

"I know it's not your favorite thing," she said, "but I think it would be fun for both of us. Maybe you can see it as a gift to me?"

"Sure," I said. "Okay. No, that's great. Thank you, it's really . . . really generous." I glanced at my dad. I needed to exchange looks with him, to reassure myself that he still knew me, but he kept watching her. I should have known the books were just a stealth gift. She couldn't let it go, even on Christmas. I suddenly felt like I was going to cry, and I swallowed hard and said, "So is that it? Anything else?"

"Yes, now that you mention it," my dad said. "This last one is from Santa." He slid an envelope from a pocket in his frayed robe and handed it to my mother.

"What's this?" she said. She didn't take the envelope from him, and it hung in the air between them, trembling slightly.

"It's from Santa, like I said." He wiggled it in front of her as if it were bait. "Come on, you'll ruin his Christmas if you don't open it."

She raised her eyebrows at him and took it tentatively. She looked at me. "Were you in on this?" she asked.

I shook my head.

She slid her lacquered nail under the flap and gently freed it. She watched my dad the whole time. Then she pulled out what was inside—two neatly folded sheets of paper. She unfolded them and read, then looked up at my dad.

"Paul, you can't afford this," she said. She didn't sound angry, just surprised.

"Santa paid for it," he said.

Her eyebrows sloped together like poised knitting needles.

"Don't worry about it," he said. "My last commission went better than I'd hoped."

"It didn't go *that* well."

"You haven't had a vacation in years," he said. "Don't protest."

"So, uh, what's going on?" I asked.

My dad smiled at me, looking pleased with himself. "Your mom and I are flying to Hawaii the week after you go to Oberlin."

"Oh," I said.

He turned back to my mother. "I thought we could both use the break. And there's no better occasion."

"To celebrate getting rid of me?" I said.

"Charlie," he said sharply.

"What?" I said. I felt stung; he never spoke to me harshly.

He frowned at me. "It's quite the opposite," he said.

"This is wonderful," my mother said. "Thank you, honey."

"It sounds great," I said. "I wish I could be there but I'm just so busy."

"Jesus, Charlie," my dad said. "Could you not make this about you for once?"

I stared at him, too shocked to say anything. Then I picked up the books and stomped upstairs.

That night I stood outside in the snow and called Lila.

"How was it?" she asked.

"I don't know," I said. My eyes started to burn with tears.

"My day was fantastic," she said. "My dad got me sweatpants with 'Juicy' written across the butt for Hanukkah. For Hanukkah, Charlie."

I laughed and swiped at my eyes. "I didn't even know they still made those."

"I know, right?" she said. "He couldn't find some Ed Hardy or something? So was it bad?"

I kicked at a snowbank. "It was just . . . She tried, I guess. I know I was a brat about it. She just thinks I'm . . ." My throat felt thick and I tried to clear it. I couldn't say it, even to Lila. "I had to leave. It's freezing outside, by the way."

"I ask this without judgment: are you in your pajamas?"

"I have a coat on too." I sighed. "I miss school."

"I'm not even going to tell you how weird that is."

"Thank you," I said, "for not saying that."

"You miss Drummond."

"Not just that."

"No, it's that."

I shrugged farther into my coat. "What do you think he's doing?"

"Like right now? Sitting in front of a fire with a pipe, rereading one of your essays and shaking his head in wonder at your brilliance."

I laughed. "I bet he's trying to get a call through to the *New Yorker* about it."

"Definitely," she said. "'Publish this young woman's essay about how *The Cat in the Hat* is a metaphor for communism or risk complete cultural irrelevance.'"

"He probably has a lot of sway with them," I said.

"Well, he does teach advanced placement classes, so . . ."

I looked at the sky. "What do you really think he's doing?"

"Dunno," she said. "Wanking?"

"Good night," I said.

"Love you," she said.

By the time I hung up, it had started to snow again. The chill had gone out of the air and everything was silent. It was the kind of silence that made it seem like the snow had stuffed itself into every crevice and gap, buried the landscape under layers of padding, and now there was just this neighborhood, just this street, just me, and no matter how far I tried to run, nothing would ever look different.

Talking about it with Lila had made it worse. The loneliness felt like an infection I couldn't shake, something hollowing me out from the inside. It wasn't the longing for him that hurt the most; it was the gnawing feeling that no one wanted me and I had no idea when, or if, that would ever change. I stood and watched the snowflakes come down, more and more of them, until the plows cut swaths through the streets, peeling the snow back like a rind, and I had to go back inside.

chapter 24

In the disappointed sigh of a week between Christmas and New Year's, Asha came over to watch movies. I'd been worried that she wouldn't accept after our aborted stakeout, but she said Dev had been busy golfing with their dad and she'd had enough of the rest of her family by the time I texted. Meanwhile, I had finished all my library books and was staring warily at the Austen boxed set.

"This is Frida," I said as she stepped through the door one dark afternoon, brushing snow from her shoulders. Frida sat down and wagged her tail hopefully.

"She's gorgeous!" Asha said. "A malamute?" She leaned down to pet her, and Frida stood up and pressed herself in an arc against Asha's knees.

"She likes you," I said. "I trust anyone Frida likes."

Asha looked up at me, her dark hair falling into her eyes. Frida's tail kept time like a metronome. "Has she ever disliked someone?"

"Not yet." I moved toward the stairs. "My room's up this way. We can bring her with us."

When we got to my room, I said, "So did you bring anything to watch, or—"

"I've been there!" Asha interrupted. She was pointing at a poster I had up on my wall—a photograph of a German castle on a cliff, surrounded by a forest, that I'd found back in middle school. I'd hung it up because it was the farthest place I could imagine from where I was then.

"You have?" I said. "I wasn't sure it actually existed. It looks like something out of a fairy tale."

She nodded. "It's beautiful. Musty, but beautiful."

"I always thought I'd get married there," I said.

Asha kept looking at it as if she hadn't heard me.

"So when were you in Germany?" I asked. "Family trip or something?"

She sat down on my bed. "Kind of. My dad used to be stationed in Berlin. We went to visit him a couple of times."

"Wow," I said. "Did you ever live over there?"

"Nah, never out of the country," she said, "but we moved around a lot before we came here. Ohio before this."

"Did you mind?"

"You kind of get used to it," she said. "Which is not the same as liking it, I guess."

"Would be hard to make friends," I said.

"Yeah," she said. She paused. "Especially if you and your brothers are the only brown people in the whole school."

"Oh," I said. "Yeah, I guess . . . I guess so."

She smiled, not unkindly. "So then you get disgustingly close to your family. Especially if you aren't the biggest fan of other people to start with." She looked back at the poster. "I'm just saying that theoretically. One would. If they were like that."

"I've lived here my whole life and all I have to show for it is Lila, so you're doing better than I am."

She laughed. "I'm sure you have your reasons."

I laughed too and then felt guilty for laughing. "I'm sorry she's been such a bitch to you," I said, and immediately felt worse. You probably weren't supposed to say *bitch* to a feminist.

"You don't need to keep apologizing for her," she said. "Not everyone needs to be friends."

"You're right," I said. "I'm sorry."

She widened her eyes at me playfully. "Stop apologizing! It's really patronizing!"

"So . . . ," I said. "I'm— Okay, I will. I just feel like I'm responsible for her somehow. We grew up together and she's . . ." I shrugged. "She's like my embarrassing racist uncle. She's family."

"I don't think she's a bad person," Asha said. "She just seems to think that the more you talk, the more interesting you are."

"God, I know," I said. "I don't think she even does it intentionally. And she's threatened by you, but she'd never admit it."

Asha frowned. "Threatened by me?"

I blushed. "Just, you know, we're, um, hanging out, so . . ."

"Oh, right," she said. It had gotten darker and it was hard to see her expression. "She's with that guy Jason, isn't she?"

"The one who looks like a giant sentient slab of meat?" She laughed, and I relaxed a little. "Yeah, but she refuses to acknowledge that they're together. Which, fair enough. He'd be my secret shame too."

She made a face. "She could do better."

"Seriously," I said. "I don't know if she doesn't know how pretty she is or she just has low standards."

"You think she's pretty?" she said as she gazed out the window.

I turned to see what she was looking at. It was just houses swaddled in snow, the lights in their windows like golden eyes in the dark. "You don't think so?"

"No, she is, I guess." She sighed. "Ugh."

"Yeah, I hate it when you can tell people are attractive," I said.

Asha laughed and bowed her head. "I'm just being catty."

"Oh," I said. "No, I didn't mean— I mean, I feel that way too."

"It's not really about her, anyway," she said. "I just feel like . . . why do girls like her get all the attention?"

Asha had never brought up her love life, so I'd assumed she was indifferent about it. Some kids I knew—academically minded ones, mostly—walled off romance as a topic of conversation, as if it were a distraction from their real future. "Are you interested in someone?" I said.

"No, there's no one in particular. I just . . ." She trailed off. "I just feel completely invisible sometimes."

"Yeah," I said. It was easier to admit in the gloom, when I didn't have to look at her. We were silent for a few minutes as the room got darker and darker.

"I got catcalled this one time," Asha said quietly. "I thought he was insulting me at first."

I took a moment to think about how to respond: with

shock or laughter or commiseration? "Was he?" I said finally.

"He was complimenting me, I think—or what he thought I should take as a compliment, anyway," she said. "He told me I had a nice ass. And then he tried to grab it."

"Hot."

"Yeah," she said. "But even though I hated it, I felt sort of . . . relieved that he'd noticed. Which just made me feel worse."

I wanted to tell her I knew what that felt like, but it was too humiliating to admit it out loud. I sat back on the bed so I couldn't see her face. "You know those friends Jason has? Mike and Austin?"

"I think so," Asha said. "Mike's in our gym class, isn't he?"

"Yeah. He . . . well, I don't know what his deal is. But Austin has—he's said some things. I don't think he was flirting. I couldn't tell Lila because she wouldn't . . ." I swallowed, tried to say something else, and then stopped when I realized I was perilously close to crying.

Asha didn't say anything. We were so still that I could see my shirt tremble every time my heart beat.

"I've had that happen," she said finally.

The heat clicked on with a sigh. I thought about how pathetic I was, for not being able to resist telling her and for letting it happen to me at all.

"I wonder sometimes," Asha said at last. "Why does it matter whether you're beautiful at all? What does it even get you?"

I stared at her silhouette. I didn't know how to answer.

"I mean that," she said. "The way people talk about women's beauty like it's a personality trait. It's just . . . it's depressing. Why should we bother?" She glanced at me quickly. "I mean, not that you're— Sorry, I didn't—"

"It's okay," I said. Suddenly I desperately wanted to hug her, but instead I grabbed a pillow and pulled it to my chest. "Is the feminism what Dev is always teasing you about?"

She laughed. "Among other things."

"I don't think he's serious."

"No, he's not. He just likes being a pain in my ass."

"And his girlfriend's, probably," I said.

She raised her eyebrows. "What girlfriend?"

"Oh," I said. "I thought he had one."

"Dev with a girlfriend?" She laughed. "No, he is, uh, definitely single."

"Oh," I said. "Right." I paused. "So there's no one you're interested in? Not even Frank?"

Asha glared at me. "No."

I smiled. "I guess as a feminist you're a secret man-hating lesbian, right?"

She looked at me quickly to check whether I was joking. "Funny," she said.

"Yes." I paused. "But it'd be totally cool if you were. I didn't mean—"

"I knew what you meant."

I put my chin on my hands and batted my eyelashes. "So tell me more about feminism."

She looked at me again thoughtfully. "If you're sure."

"I am. It's mostly about not shaving, right?"

"Mostly."

"Excellent," I said. "Reduces the need to shower. And I like when I can feel the wind through the hair on my legs."

"Are you interested in feminism or an excuse for questionable personal hygiene?"

I laughed. "Both. So tell me."

"You're really interested in this?"

"I really am." I got up and turned on the light. "By the way, do you want to stay for dinner? My dad cooks. He's very good."

"Yeah," she said. "I'd like that."

january

chapter 25

"Go home, Charlie, really," Drummond said. He and I were working late on the newspaper layout—or rather, he had stayed after everyone left and I'd stayed with him.

"It's okay," I said, trying not to turn hot with embarrassment. "I don't mind."

"And I appreciate it," he said, "but both of us banging our heads against the wall is just going to make a bigger hole." He made a sound between a sigh and a whimper that made my stomach curl. I hesitated, not sure whether he was just trying to be nice or he really wanted me to leave.

"Why are you two still here?" Asha had appeared at the door.

"The first issue is almost finished," I said.

Drummond shook his head. "Charlie has an interesting take on the word *finished*."

"Why are *you* here?" I asked her. "I thought you left with everyone else."

"Watching Jai practice," she said. "I was walking past and I heard shouts."

"He's mad at the software," I said, jerking my thumb at Drummond.

"It's fine," he said. "I'm going to find the people who made it and force them to create pie charts for the rest of time."

"What's wrong with it?" Asha asked.

"No, no, don't worry about it," he said. "I'm sure both of you need to get home."

Asha moved toward us. "Let me see if I can help," she said. Drummond got up with a *please, go ahead* gesture and Asha took his seat next to me. He stood behind my chair, his hand on the backrest. I moved deliberately to see what would happen; my shoulder brushed his hand and he pulled it away.

Asha shifted things around on the page for a few minutes. "What about this?" she said. "If we moved the editorial over two columns and then pushed the response to the right, that would make sense and still fit on the page."

"Asha, you're a genius," Drummond said, and chucked her on the shoulder. "That's perfect. We should have you doing layout. We're terrible at it." A gust of jealousy swept through me: he'd never chucked me on the shoulder and called me a genius.

Asha brushed her shoulder off. "I'm sorry to run, but I really need to get home for dinner. Will you guys be okay?" She raised her eyebrows at me.

"Sure, sure, go home," he said, waving her out. "Charlie, seriously, you go too. There's no reason you should be here this late on a Friday. I'll finish up and then we can tackle it again next week."

"Oh, I'm fine," I said. "My parents are out for the night, so I don't have to be home." My parents were definitely not out for the night, but I decided I could apologize to them later.

Asha glanced at me again. "You sure you don't want a ride?"

"No, it's okay. I've got my dad's car," I said, not quite meeting her eyes.

"Okay. Well, have fun, guys." She waved at me and then she was gone. Her footsteps faded quickly.

"You sure you want to be here? I'm just going to be a grumpy jerk," Drummond said, sliding down into his chair. His leg bumped against my knees as he settled himself.

When I didn't answer right away, he said, "What?"

I swallowed. "How's that any different than usual?"

"Good point," he said. He paused. "I didn't mean to imply that I wanted you to leave earlier."

"Oh," I said, "good. I wasn't going to." I looked into the hallway. The building was completely silent. Usually by then there was the narcotic drone of a vacuum in the distance. "This is the only time of day I like this place."

He grabbed his tennis ball from the desk and threw it into the air. "With the notable exception of my class," he said.

"Uh, yes, sure," I said. He threw the ball at me, and I laughed and caught it. "It has a different feel at night, though, you know? It feels—I don't know—warmer. Safe."

"Mm," he said. "Back when I was in high school, lo those many—"

"Many."

"—many years ago, I always came in early or stayed late so I could do my homework in peace."

"Ugh," I said. "You came in just to do homework?"

"I had a big family. I shared a room with my brother

and there was always noise coming from somewhere. Sometimes school was the only quiet place I could find." He held his hands out and I tossed the ball back to him.

"That sounds hellish," I said. "On both counts."

"You're an only child, right?" he said.

He remembered. "Yep."

He tipped his chair onto two legs and looked at the ceiling. He threw the ball up and caught it, up and caught it. "I often wished I were an only child."

"How many brothers and sisters do you have?"

"One brother, two sisters. Two parents, which was more than enough."

It was strange to think he had parents, people who had known him when he was young. Whenever we asked him personal questions in class, he'd deflect them with a joke. I knew I had to be careful.

"Do you get along with them?"

"Sure," he said. "Mostly. How about you?"

"I liked my imaginary brother a lot, but they told me I couldn't bring him to kindergarten."

He smiled at me, still balanced on two legs. His hair had gotten shaggy and it curled like a wave cresting when he moved. "And your parents?"

"Well, you've met my mom."

"Yes. Oh, I still need to find out about internships for you, actually."

"Don't worry about that," I said, waving the words away. "Anyway, you can imagine how well that goes." He had put the ball down on the table and I picked it up and squeezed it. "I do love them."

"But . . . ," he said.

"You know how when your best friend gets obsessed with somebody and you feel like a fifth wheel when you're with them?"

"That bad?" he asked.

"I don't know," I said. "Sometimes I think I'm imagining it."

He rocked forward so the front legs of his chair hit the floor. "My parents got divorced when I was thirteen. Hated them for a good few years."

"I think you have to hate your parents at least a bit when you're a teenager."

"Very wise. I went a little crazy at your age."

"You?"

"Yes, *me,* Charlie. Got suspended once, even."

I stared at him in surprise. Every time I felt like I knew him—had quantified him, made him containable—he would say something like this and a vast space would open behind the words, hinting at oceans, deserts, planets full of things I didn't know. "Really? I always thought you were . . ."

He laughed. "I was a loser, don't get me wrong. I just had a night of drunken stupidity."

"What did you do?"

He grimaced as if even the memory was painful. "Vandalized a science lab."

"Why? And how?"

"There was this girl," he said. "Rachel."

"Ah," I said.

"Yes," he said as if we were old friends, which made me flush with pleasure. "Anyway, she was an atheist—a very vocal atheist, as seventeen-year-old atheists tend to be. She was the one who introduced me to the idea that *Catch-22* might be about atheism, actually. She used to tell me how she suspected our biology teacher was a creationist, so one night I snuck in and—you know those bumper stickers they make, the ones where the Jesus fish have legs? I stuck those up all over the walls, into the books, onto the Bunsen burners. Stuck one right onto his reading glasses."

"That is a pathetic prank," I said.

"It was," he said. "I thought I was Yossarian. Turns out I was Doc Daneeka."

"So did you impress her?"

"What do you think?"

"What happened?"

"Never got up the nerve to tell her I'd done it."

I slapped my hands on the table. "No!"

"Yes. But I did turn myself in, because the guilt was eating me up inside. Have I mentioned how I wasn't popular in high school?"

I enjoyed the thought of him in high school. "What were you like?"

"Picture me now but thirty pounds heavier, with what can only be described as a visual assault of hair, and a hundred times more obnoxious and determined to get people to laugh at my jokes. I say this with a very loose definition of the word *jokes*."

"You were Frank?" I said.

He laughed. "Now you understand our fraught relationship."

"So was Rachel your great lost love?" I said. I tried to keep my voice light.

He cleared his throat. "Not exactly."

I knew I had hit on something personal, but I wasn't sure what. Maybe he still liked her. "Do you keep in touch with anyone from high school?" I asked, to change the subject.

"Some people," he said. "I still talk to a couple of my friends, and a few people I became close to after we got older."

"Are they different now?"

"Yeah, to varying degrees," he said. "Some people change a lot."

"I won't," I said. I rolled the ball to him.

He picked it up. "Maybe not," he said. "You never know." I didn't know what to say to that, so I didn't say anything. "I, however, am not someone you would have liked in high school." He was silent for a long time, bouncing the ball against the table. "We really should do some work," he said eventually. But he didn't move.

I wanted to draw him out before he snapped shut again. "I guess you probably have someone to get home to."

He snorted. "The only thing I have to get home to is your classmates' papers."

"Oh," I said. "Not even like a goldfish?"

He shook his head. "You're fishing, though."

I laughed. "You do tend to be stingy with the personal details."

He leaned back in his chair and looked at the ceiling again. "You seem to be pretty adept at getting them out of me tonight."

I swallowed. "I guess I should ask for your credit card number while I'm on a roll."

"Aim a little higher than that, Charlie. Fuck knows I don't have any savings for you to plunder." I felt a jolt of delight every time he swore in front of me—like he was including me as an adult, an equal.

"You really want me to ask you something personal?" My heart was pounding so hard now I was surprised my voice wasn't shaking.

He was still looking at the ceiling, watching the ball as it arced up and down. "Sure. Why not? Three questions."

"Three," I said. I looked at my hands; they'd left damp palm prints on the table.

"Think of me as the shittiest genie ever. Instead of endless riches and immortality, you get the meaningless personal details of some schlub of a high school teacher."

"You're not—" I said, and stopped myself.

He looked at me. "I am, kiddo. But go ahead."

"All right. Just give me a minute." What could I possibly ask him? I knew what I wanted to ask—*Do you ever think about me when I'm not here? Do you think about me at all? Do you think about Lila?*—but I couldn't think of anything appropriate.

"Oh," he said, "and no questions about when I lost my virginity. There is a limit to how much I'm willing to humiliate myself in front of you."

"All right," I said, though it threw me to hear him mention himself in a sexual context. Finally I said, "How much do you make a year?"

He laughed. "What did I just say about my lack of savings? What's the next question?"

"You didn't answer!"

"I didn't say I would answer them. Just that you could ask."

"Ugh," I said. I got up and started pacing the room, trying to think of another question. The windows were black, and I watched my reflection follow me, looking sick and sweaty. Were my eyes really that hollow? "Some game."

"It's the only one I've got, Chuck."

"Why do you call me Chuck?"

"Is that one of your questions?"

"Yeah," I said, sitting down on the window ledge, "sure."

"It's just a nickname."

I pressed my finger onto my nose and made a noise like a buzzer. "Sorry, you'll have to do better than that."

He stared at the ball as if it would provide an answer. "Honestly, I'm not sure. It just fit you somehow." He smiled up at me. The lines around his eyes crinkled.

"I looked like a man?" I said, trying to put some power behind my voice so it didn't come out in a whisper.

"No, of course not. But you didn't feel like a Charlotte to me."

I made a face. "I don't feel like a Charlotte either."

"Maybe you'll grow into it," he said. He squeezed the ball so that his fingertips turned white. "I overheard you talking to Lila as you guys walked in and you struck me right away as really sharp. I meet a lot of new people every year, but it's not—" He paused and started again. "I guess I wanted to give you a stamp."

I could barely get the words out. "A stamp?"

"Something that made you stand out. Marked you out. Even if I didn't really know I was doing that at the time."

I was silent. Had he really just said that? I hadn't imagined it?

"Oh," I said finally.

He turned to look at me. "I hope that didn't sound creepy and patriarchal. I just want you to know I think you're . . ." *Wonderful. Beautiful. Incandescent. Really, really amusing.* ". . . going to go on to better things than this."

"Thanks," I said, giving him half a smile. "That only sounds a little creepy."

He laughed softly. "Minorly creepy is sometimes the best I can hope for. So what's the next question?"

"Oh," I said. I couldn't think. "God, I don't know. Um, so you're not married?"

He laughed. "No," he said. "But I was."

"I mean like to a person."

"Yes," he said.

"Come on," I said. "I thought you weren't going to bullshit me."

"I'm not bullshitting you," he said.

"I know you think I'm gullible, but—"

He laughed again, a nervous sound like a cough. "It was not . . . Anyway, it didn't last, so . . ."

"Wait. You're serious? When was this?"

He smiled and looked down. "Just after my senior year of high school. She was . . . You know that girl Rachel I just mentioned?"

"I'm familiar, yes."

"I didn't tell her about the prank, but word that I'd done it got out. She thought it was idiotic, but we started talking more often, and then we became good friends, and then eventually we ended up together. She was funny and smart and—you would have liked her—and she was the first girl who ever showed interest in me and, well . . ." He shrugged like that filled in all the rest. "And, uh . . . we were young and stupid and after a little while I got scared and left her." There was silence. He looked down at the ball, which he was running back and forth under his palm. "Sorry," he said. "I don't know why I told you all that."

"It's okay," I said automatically so he wouldn't feel uncomfortable, though I had no idea how I felt about it. Were we still bantering? How did he want me to react? How was I *supposed* to react?

After a minute he stretched his arms back and inhaled deeply. "Anyway, it was a long time ago and I was an idiot, prone to overreaction. You can see not much has changed." He brought his arms down and drummed his fingers on the table like he was tapping a new theme. "So what about you? Ever been married?"

"Uh," I said. At least now I knew what I was supposed to say. "Once, when I was five, to my stuffed horse, Captain Oats."

"Didn't last?"

I shook my head. "My mom accidentally donated him to Goodwill. But we'd been growing apart for a long time."

"Sad," he said. He picked up the ball and tossed it to me. "So what's your last question?"

I was so surprised that I let the ball sail past. I heard it thwock onto the floor behind me. "Oh," I said. "I thought I'd asked three already."

"I didn't answer the first, so I'll let it slide," he said.

I looked at him. Why was he changing the rules? What did he want me to ask? "Right," I said. "Okay."

"Take your time."

Now that he'd given me a glimpse into his life, I wanted to know everything. I wanted to ask more about Rachel, about his past, about whether I meant as little to him as it seemed like I should. His life was so much bigger than mine.

But then I knew what I wanted to ask him. I knew that I couldn't, that I'd never be able to face him again if I did. But it pounded in my head again and again, and it crowded out every other thought.

"You look like you've got something in mind," he said.

"Mm," I said.

"Ask me anything. Really." His eyes were bright blue. I hated him for goading me—as if he knew what I wanted to ask and he was trying to pull it from me.

I was going to ask him. I didn't want to, or at least I knew I shouldn't want to, but suddenly I knew I would.

"Do you—do you think I'm pretty?" I said. My voice was barely above a whisper. I looked down at my hands. The pause was endless.

Finally he spoke. "Charlie, I can't—" He looked horribly vulnerable—young and confused. For a second I was disgusted by him. "I wish . . ."

I stood up abruptly; I hated that he was seeing me like this, that he knew how much I cared about his answer.

"I guess not," I said. I'd known he wouldn't say it. No one would ever say it.

"No, that's not—" He started to stand, but I shied away. He held his hands up, surrendering. "Okay. Sorry. You know I can't—"

"I shouldn't have asked," I said, before he could say something awful. "It was inappropriate."

"No, no, it was . . ." He trailed off.

"I'm sorry," I said. I didn't look at him again. I hoped the next time I did he'd be gone.

Finally he rallied. "Chuck," he said, his voice deeper and more confident. He was my teacher again. I felt a disappointing amount of relief. "Did I ever tell you to read Philip Larkin?"

I was so surprised that I laughed. "No. You skipped right from Heller to Shakespeare."

"Right," he said. "Well, I'm saying it now. Read Larkin. 'This Be the Verse.' "

"All right," I said.

"I've got to get home. Thank you for staying. I really appreciate it." He stood awkwardly, nearly tipping over until he balanced himself on a table. His chair clattered to the floor behind him and he had to stoop to retrieve it. "I'll see you on Monday, okay?"

"Okay." I froze by the window, waiting for him to leave.

"Okay," he said. He hesitated a moment. He moved toward me half a step, but when I backed up and sat down, he stopped. "Okay. Good night, Charlie."

I waited to leave until I couldn't hear his footsteps anymore, until I imagined he'd left the building, crossed the parking lot, gotten into his car, sat with his forehead on the steering wheel for a good ten minutes, checked his phone for messages, reached into the glove compartment for an Advil, found the bottle empty, and finally drove off. Then I heaved myself onto my shaking legs and went home.

When I got to my room, I looked up "This Be the Verse" online. I read it once quickly, hoping something would jump out at me, then another time, slower, when it didn't. "What does this have to do with anything?" I said out loud, and then I slammed my laptop shut and threw myself on my bed and cried.

chapter 26

When I arrived at his class on Monday, I slid into my seat with my head down. I didn't check whether he'd seen me.

"You okay?" Lila said. "I didn't hear from you all weekend."

"Fine," I said. "Just busy." I'd decided I couldn't tell her what had happened. It was too humiliating for her to know that I'd not only embarrassed myself by asking him such a stupid question but, even worse, that he'd rejected me for asking it. For her a rejection was a setback, but for me it was a verdict.

"Jason dragged me to a party this friend of his was having," she said. "He acted like such a moron, I nearly broke up with him."

"I thought you weren't together," I said.

"Yeah, well," she said, "he got drunk and decided it would be hot for me and this girl he knows to kiss."

I glanced at her. "Did you?"

She sighed in a put-upon sort of way. "I thought about it, I won't lie. I was pretty drunk, and she was cute."

"But?"

"Jason ended up . . . We got distracted."

"Ah," I said. "No breakup, then."

She smirked. "No."

"So this was basically your excuse to brag to me that you nearly kissed a girl."

"I'm not going to say it *was,*" she said. "But I won't say it wasn't either."

"Great," I said. I thought of telling her what had happened with Drummond: *He was begging me, but I told him we couldn't; he's my teacher and it would be too wrong. What would everyone say?* But the gap between that and reality seemed too depressingly wide to think about.

When the bell rang, Drummond didn't move from behind his desk. The class kept chatting. I doodled in my notebook, trying to blend myself into the paper.

Finally he said, "Okay, guys. I think it's time for a dramatic reading." When everyone groaned, he said, "It's this or a quiz. Which do you want?"

After a pause, Dev said, "Can I be Regan?"

Drummond sighed. "We're going to run out of female parts before you get tired of playing them. I see you forgot to bring your corset again."

Dev laughed. "It's at the cleaner's, dude. I'm not a slob."

"I have a spare if you need it," Katie said.

"That's at my house," Sean said.

It pained me to hear Drummond joking around with them. Wasn't he as upset as I was? Hadn't he also contemplated staying in bed for a month with immaculately acquired mono? As soon as I couldn't try to make him laugh, I didn't want anyone to.

"All right, who else?" Drummond said. "If you don't choose for yourself, I may assign you Edmund."

I kept my head down while people volunteered. Soon only one part was left. I willed Drummond to be afraid to speak to me. He wasn't.

"Charlie?" he said. "Feel like being Cordelia today?"

I looked straight at him. His eyes were hard. He was in one of his authoritative moods, that made him seem adult and unreachable. Normally I would have agreed, but this time I set my mouth and shook my head. I would run out of the room before I'd read a part that day. His eyes softened and for a terrifying moment I was afraid he was going to say something in front of the whole class. But he turned away, and finally he asked Katie.

I glanced at him periodically while everyone was reading aloud. He never looked at me, but he didn't seem like he was avoiding me either; it was only because he usually caught my eye during class that I knew something was wrong. But I got a small thrill knowing I'd affected him: I'd punished him and it had worked.

After school I thought about going straight home but decided it would look even more like he'd upset me if I didn't show up for the paper. He was talking to Frank when I went in, and as I sat down at the other side of the room, they both laughed and Frank shoved him.

I flipped open my notebook to the page I'd been drawing on in class. It was full of pictures of trees with knotted branches. I frowned at it.

I heard him coming but I didn't look up. He dragged a chair over so he was across the table from me. I tried not to let my hands shake.

"Chuck," he said. "How are you doing?"

"Great."

"You writing about our future adventures?"

"No."

"Not even *The Plums of Europe*?"

"No, not even . . ." I looked at his hands, and then out the windows, avoiding his gaze. I let a silence pass. Then I said, "What would I write about if I were?"

"Well, I don't know." I could feel him watching me, but I still didn't move. "Let's pretend," he said. My heart bobbled. "It's twenty years from now and I'm holed up in a garret somewhere muttering about the concept of the sublime in *Wuthering Heights*."

I tried not to smile. I didn't say anything.

"You kids drove me to drink." He paused, waiting for me to pick up the story. When I didn't say anything, he said, "Which wasn't difficult, admittedly. I got addicted to roofied Tang. Gateway drug."

I tapped my pen on my notebook and cleared my throat. "You went mad like Heathcliff."

"Sometimes I go wandering on the wild hills of Chatham Valley. Those edges they sometimes miss when they mow every week."

"Wearing a cloak made out of an ergonomic backrest you got on a teacher discount from Staples."

"Telling the lifeguards at the pool that they smell like they're made of disappointment."

"Showering with half-empty cans of Fanta."

"You come upon me one day. You have terrible memories of this, the most worthless and wasted year of your educational life, and you think of leaving me there to rot."

I paused. "But I don't. I give you a copy of *The Plums of Europe*."

"It changes my life," he said. "I'm freed of destitution and I only mildly stink."

"Back to normal, then."

He smiled, then looked down. "I'm sorry," he said.

I didn't say anything. "What's the sublime?" I asked finally.

"The idea of something being simultaneously beautiful and terrifying."

"Like Frank?"

He laughed hard, and I laughed too.

"If you're going to lie to yourself about our future, you could make yours a little better," I said eventually.

He shrugged. "Something to believe in, right?" He waited until I was looking at him before he said, "Thank you for putting up with me."

We watched each other for a long moment. As he stood, he put his hand on my head and pressed on it gently. A wave of heat rolled down my body.

"Keep that brain safe," he said. "You'll need it eventually."

"Dick," I said.

february

chapter 27

Asha had become my default partner for our team activities in gym. She was more athletic than I was, quick and observant, but more importantly, she was kind and she never blamed me when I missed a shot. Lila had always showed off in gym, and while she didn't laugh at me, she'd sometimes say things like "Get it together, Porter," or "Eyes on the ball." I'd been relieved when we'd gotten different schedules.

Asha and I were badminton partners now. We got paired with different boys every week, and that day, Valentine's Day, we had Mike.

For the first few minutes, he wouldn't meet my eyes. Dev was his partner, and I worried that Mike would embarrass me in front of him and Asha. But Mike was quiet and didn't look at me.

Asha sent a shuttlecock into the air. It came to me, and I was so nervous that I missed an easy shot.

"This is not making me trust your opinion on sports, Charlie," Dev said.

I smiled, afraid to say much in front of Mike.

"You're one to talk," Asha said. "You let that air ball go by a couple minutes ago."

"That was out!" Dev said. "Charlie, come on, back me up here."

I hesitated. Mike was walking toward the other end of the court. "Not after you insulted my badminton abilities so viciously."

Dev laughed. "I guess I deserve that."

Asha scooped up the shuttlecock and served again. Mike dove for it awkwardly and missed. He glanced at me and I looked away.

"You have a valentine tonight, don't you, Ash?" Dev said.

I would have frozen at the question, but Asha looked at me as if she was used to it.

"You giving me the leftover chocolates you don't like doesn't count as a valentine," she said.

"Mom always gets the ones with nuts," he said.

"That's because you'd eat them all otherwise."

Dev sighed and turned to Mike. "What about you, Mike? You have a date tonight?"

Mike looked startled that Dev had addressed him. "Uh, I'm not sure what I'm doing," he said.

"Charlie?" Dev asked. "Date?"

"What?" I said.

"Leave her alone, dummy," Asha said.

"Charlie's got the same plans I do, I think," Mike said.

I looked at him. He was smiling. My heart knocked. "I don't have . . . I don't know," I said.

Dev looked between us and then said, "You think Drummond does?"

"If you count reading Dickens as a date," Asha said.

Dev laughed. I glanced at Mike again; he was still

smiling. I frowned at him, and his smile faltered and he turned away.

"You think he's been different lately?" Dev said.

"Who?" I asked.

"Drummond."

"What?" I said. "How so?"

"I don't know," he said. "Just different."

"I hadn't noticed," I said. But he had been. It was subtle, but he was a little more distant, a little distracted. There was a pause before he laughed, a small hesitation before he made a joke. He didn't meet my eyes quite as often, and when he did, he looked away too quickly. I tried not to think about that night in the classroom, because if I did, I went hot with shame, but I worried that he was different because of me, that he couldn't think of me the same way anymore. But mostly I tried to pretend things were the same as they'd always been.

Dev batted at the shuttlecock again. "Do you guys think he's going to grade us for *Truth Bomb* this semester?" he asked. "Considering we haven't even put an issue out."

"I think we just get credit for participating," I said. "It's not our fault it hasn't come out. Well, except for the fact that only half the people have actually written their articles."

"I hope we get credit," Dev said. "Because Asha's article is terrible."

Asha threw her racket at him, and he laughed and let it hit him. "Asshole," she said.

"You'll be all right, at least, Charlie," he said. "He loves you." He said it guilelessly, as if it were indisputable.

I flushed. Mike made a noise and I looked at him. His face was red too.

"Less chatting and more playing, please," Mrs. Deloit said as she passed by.

"He loves everyone," I said.

chapter 28

That night as I stuffed my feet into my snow boots and strapped myself into my heaviest coat, my mother appeared in the hall.

"Walking Frida?" she asked.

"Looks like it," I said.

Frida panted and waved her tail at the word *walk*. She nosed her leash, which was still hanging on the wall.

"Mind if I come with you?" my mother said. She looked shy, like she was a child asking permission, afraid I would say no.

"I thought you were about to go out with Dad," I said. I stood up and pulled Frida's leash from its hook. She danced in a joyful little circle, her nails clicking on the tile.

"Change of plans," my mother said.

I looked up. "Not because of the park project?"

She nodded. "We're postponing. I thought maybe you and I could take a walk together."

"I'm backup?" I said.

She looked stung. "If you'd rather be alone, that's fine."

"Sorry, I didn't mean . . ." I fiddled with Frida's leash. "No. No, it's okay."

I always took Frida to the small clearing a few streets over. The snow had been melting into ash-colored rivulets for weeks, and I'd been worried that we were in the dregs of winter, those days when the sun couldn't push through the flat sky, and the slush was gray with tire tracks, and everything that showed through underneath was rotten and brown. But we'd had a storm the day before, and now the trees were crested with fat caps of snow, and the streetlamps' lights were soft and hazy.

"Did you have any plans for tonight?" she asked.

Pizza and masturbation, I thought. "I was just going to read," I said.

"We didn't ruin anything by staying home, then," she said.

I glanced at her. She was looking up at a roof that was heavy with snow.

"Like what?" I said.

"Just curious."

"No," I said. "Sorry to disappoint."

She paused. "You know, I'm aware that you don't care about makeup and haircuts and stuff. You think it's shallow. But, Charlie, I really am just trying to help."

"No, I— When—when have I said that?"

She ignored me. "Honey, why do you think you don't have a boyfriend?"

"I don't . . . what? Why do you want to know?"

"I'm just curious."

"Is it bad that I don't?"

"Of course not," she said. "But I think you could have one if you wanted to."

I laughed, but something in my stomach constricted.

"I'm serious," she said. "And I know you don't want to hear it, but I really think I could help. This is just the way the world works. I'm sorry to be the bearer of bad news, but appearances are important, especially to men."

When I didn't say anything, she said, "I know you think you shouldn't have to care about that stuff, that people should just see past it. I wish that were the case, I really do. I know you'd like to have a boyfriend." She stepped closer. Her voice turned soft. "If you'd let me in, I could—I could help. I want to— I wish you'd . . . I wish you'd let me help."

I hesitated. There was a hush over the street. "So you think I'm ugly," I said.

She stepped back, and her voice got hard again. "No," she said. "No, not at all. I think you are a beautiful girl who for some reason is determined to keep herself unattractive."

"Jesus, Mom," I said. I could feel a sob knotting up in my chest. I tried to say something else but I couldn't. Maybe she was right. Maybe I just needed to give in.

We'd reached the clearing. The snow was thick enough that the grass was covered, so it stretched out in a swelling plain, broken only by the deer tracks and footprints that littered the ground like little craters. The woods at the edge were dark and quiet.

I let Frida's leash play out as I tried to get my breath to stop hitching dangerously. I felt a buzz in my pocket. I pulled out my phone: a text from Lila.

Saw Drummond in ShopRite earlier. He was buying lotion & tissues & an issue of Shape magazine. :-(

I gave a sobbing sort of laugh. Frida tugged on the leash and I said, "Can you take her?"

"Of course," my mother said. As I handed the leash over, she said, "Something important?"

"Kind of," I said. I texted back: *Liar.*

She replied almost immediately. *All right, he wasn't. He did buy a single eggplant, though. Made me sad. Gotta go, Jason's here with some gas station carnations. Probably thinks he deserves a blow job for this. UGH.*

If that was what having a boyfriend was like, maybe I didn't want one anyway. I didn't need anyone. Screw my mom if she thought I did. I felt a tide of defiance rise where the sob had been. I was rereading the text when I heard Frida bark and my mother yell, "Dammit! Frida, come here!"

I looked up. Frida was scrambling across the clearing, kicking up clouds of snow like a stuck van. Toward a deer.

"Frida!" I said in my deepest, sharpest voice. She froze for a second, glanced at me, and then bounded after the deer again.

I turned to my mother and said, "Great." Then I started wading through the snow.

She kept pace with me. "I'm sorry," she said. "She startled me."

"Maybe if you walked her more often, this wouldn't happen," I said.

"If you hadn't been looking at your phone, you would have seen something was wrong," she said.

"I asked you to watch her for five seconds!" I said. "When I said I didn't have any plans, I didn't mean I wanted to be chasing after my dog in the dark."

"Our dog," she said.

"My dog," I said. "And I don't want a boyfriend, so you can stop trying, okay? Just give up."

"Okay," she said. "I give up. Good luck."

"Frida!" I shouted, and blundered into the woods. I didn't have to go far; Frida was sniffing frantically at a tree, trying to find the deer's scent. She whuffed distractedly. I grabbed the trailing end of her leash and pulled. She whined and then came away reluctantly.

"I'm sorry," my mother said as I walked past her.

"Thanks," I said, and kept walking.

chapter 29

One Saturday, while I was coming back from an errand my mother had sent me on, I spotted his car in the parking lot of the community center. I knew it was his from the license plate number, which I had memorized long before, and the way the black trim on the passenger-side door slumped downward like a line charting a bad stock.

"Ha," I said aloud. "So he does swim there."

I was stopped at a red light, and I watched the front door of the building, wondering if he was inside.

"I bet he's swimming now," I said. I tapped my fingers on the steering wheel. I laughed. "This is stupid."

The car behind me honked. I looked into the rearview mirror and saw that the driver behind me was making a *what are you doing?* gesture.

"What the hell," I said, and pulled into the parking lot.

I turned off the engine and sat there for a few minutes, listening to the radiator tick. Occasionally people walked past; the drumbeat of footsteps seemed magnified in the cottony silence of the car. I was sure they were all looking through the windows at me and knew what I was there for. I realized I had to either get out or leave, because the longer I sat there, the creepier I felt.

I walked up and peered through the front door. There was a reception desk in the lobby, and Katie from my

English class was standing behind it. She was flipping listlessly through the pages of a glossy magazine.

She looked up when I came in, and smiled in a perfunctory but not unfriendly way.

"Hi," I said. "This is going to sound stupid, but I'm looking for a friend of mine and I wondered if you could let me into the pool."

She frowned. "Are you a member?"

"Um, no," I said.

"Like I care." She grinned. "Yeah, go ahead."

"Thanks," I said.

"Drummond's in there," she said as I was walking away.

"Oh," I said. "Thanks for letting me know."

"No problem," she said. She raised an eyebrow at me and then turned back to her magazine.

The pool entrance was down a hallway and through two sets of double doors. A balcony ran around the outside of the pool, overlooking it from the floor above. The damp air clung to me as I watched from the corner, listening to squeaking and splashing and the occasional squalling laugh.

Then I saw him. He was at the edge of the pool, ready to dive in. He wasn't wearing a Speedo after all; he had on short brown swimming trunks that sat low on his hips and traced the curve of his ass. His torso was much more muscular than I had expected it to be. He looked good.

I'd been trying not to think about how awful it would be if he didn't, but now I let myself feel it: how pathetic he would have seemed; how embarrassed for him I would have been. It felt safe to think it now that it hadn't come to pass.

He dove into the water in a clean arc and came up like a seal with his hair plastered back. I had never liked swimming myself, so I hadn't realized how graceful it was: something about the explosive kick of his legs, the smooth muscular pull of his arms, the rhythmic power of each stroke, the way his body coiled and sprang open again at the end of a lap.

I watched him as he cut through the water like a blade slicing through a seam, back and forth, back and forth. After a while—I had lost track of time by that point—he reached the edge and pulled himself out in one quick powerful movement. He walked to a chair and started drying himself off with a towel. His chest hair looked darker now that it was wet. I followed the water's path down his torso, until it reached the band of his shorts. They were so low that I could see the indentations on his hips that led down to his groin.

"All right," I said. "Enough."

When I walked back to the front, Katie was texting someone. She ignored me until I was almost past her, and then she said, "You find your friend?"

"Kind of," I said.

I heard her laugh as I pushed through the doors.

I told myself I would leave after that, but I didn't. Instead I hung around in the parking lot, pretending to text someone. He came outside a few minutes later. His hair was still wet and slicked back, and he was wearing the brown leather jacket I loved. He looked so handsome it made my lungs hurt. I watched him leave from a safe distance, wondering whether I could plausibly pretend to bump into him. He walked around the side of the building and leaned against the brick wall, digging for something in his pocket. He extracted it with practiced flair: it was a lighter and a half-empty pack of cigarettes.

"No!" I said aloud.

He tapped a cigarette from the pack, lit it, and took a long, lingering drag. I had to admit he did look hot—nonchalant, somehow, and older. He let smoke pool out of his mouth and looked into the distance. Unbelievably hot, actually.

I shook myself and ran over.

"What are you doing?" I said when I got close.

He was in the middle of taking another drag, but when he saw me, he froze. "Oh shit," he said. Smoke curled between the words.

"You *smoke*?"

"No," he said.

"I don't believe this." I put my hands on my hips.

"I don't know, Charlie, I feel like 'hello' is more of a classic greeting."

"I thought you said you quit in college!"

"Listen, I've been under a lot of stress late— Hold on a minute, why are you here?"

"I work out," I said.

He eyed me as he took a final drag on his cigarette.

"I'm thinking about it," I said. "Anyway, you smoke."

He funneled the last of the smoke out of the side of his mouth and ground the butt into the wall. "Not anymore," he said. "*Some*thing put me off." He widened his eyes at me, but there was a teasing lilt to his voice.

"Sorry," I said.

"Ironic that you'd be the one to stop me," he said.

"Why's that ironic?"

He shook his head, looking amused. "No reason. You know anywhere around here that's good for lunch? I'm starving."

"Yeah," I said. "The Horseme—shoe. It's five minutes from here."

"Let's go, then."

I paused. "I'm . . . coming with you?"

"It's the least you can do after you shamed me into quitting, I think."

"Okay," I said. "You'll follow me?"

"As ever," he said.

It was odd letting him tag behind me, catching angles of his face in my rearview mirror, knowing I could have led him anywhere I wanted to, for a while at least. It was even odder being in public with him, not just because I was worried someone would see us together—a lot of people from school went there—but because it threw him out of context. I was used to seeing him talk to students and sometimes to other teachers, but I'd never seen him smile at a hostess or ask what was in the meat loaf ("You'd be better off staying ignorant," I said) or just exist outside of our school. It was almost embarrassing, to see him not be in charge, not know exactly what he was doing—even if it was just to ask an ordinary question or exchange a pleasantry with a waitress, things I realized only later he must do every day when I wasn't around—and I wasn't sure whether I liked seeing him this way or whether I couldn't stand it.

"So," he said after we'd ordered, "what's up?" He leaned back and rested his elbows on the edge of the booth. He looked far too comfortable for my liking, as if this wasn't weird for him too.

I fiddled with my straw, which was still in its paper wrapper. "Other than you being a secret smoker?"

"What can I say? I missed coughing up black tar every morning."

"Seriously," I said, "why would you do that to yourself?"

"I'll tell you when you're older," he said.

"It couldn't be to look cool, because you didn't."

"Honesty is not one of your better qualities, Charlie."

"It can't be part of your training regimen."

"It's actually an essential element of my training," he said. "Otherwise my lungs become too capacious from swimming. I was actually blowing houses down when I whistled."

"I think it's because of Ms. Anders," I said. "Peer pressure."

"Tracey smokes?" he asked. "I didn't realize."

"Yes, *Tracey* smokes," I said.

His eyes glinted. "Not a fan of her, huh?"

I pushed down the wrapper and stuck the straw in my drink. "What makes you think that?"

He shrugged elaborately. "Just a wild guess."

"I'll tell you why I don't like her if you tell me why you started smoking again."

"Ah," he said. "We seem to have reached a stalemate."

Our waitress arrived with our food, relieving me of the need to respond. We chatted a little while we ate—even watching him eat was strange—but mostly he was quiet, apparently lost in thought, though I caught him looking at me more than once. I wondered whether he was regretting this.

"How's the meat loaf?" I asked.

"It tastes like the inside of a mattress," he said.

"Hmm. Must be the good chef today." I looked at the counter, where a bearded man was slumped above his plate like an old jacket thrown over a chair. "Are you sure you're all right? You're being, I don't know, worryingly unobnoxious."

He smiled. "I'm fine, I promise," he said. "The smoking's just . . . I don't know. Maybe I'm having a midlife crisis." He laughed softly, like he thought he sounded ridiculous.

"You're a little young for a midlife crisis, aren't you?"

"An existential crisis, then. Something profound."

What kinds of problems did adults have? Unfathomable things, full of lust and envy and rage—all the sins, probably. He had a whole life outside us, almost certainly filled with sex in grubby bathrooms and arguments where plates smashed against the wall and thrillingly dark depressions and *Doonesbury* and mortgages. The number of things I didn't know, hadn't experienced, seemed like a gulf I'd never be able to bridge.

"What's wrong?" I asked, though I knew he wouldn't tell me.

He rubbed his eyes. They were bloodshot from the chlorine, veined like marble. "It's not important," he said. "But thank you for asking. I'm more curious how you're feeling about Oberlin."

"Oh," I said. "It seems very far away." *Please stop talking about college,* I wanted to say.

"Well, you still have a few months left to enjoy the humorous stylings of Sean et al." He balled up a napkin and put it next to his plate.

"Your class is what makes me worried," I said. "I'm starting to realize how much I don't know."

"All intellectually curious people feel that way," he said. "Only incurious people feel comfortable with how little they know."

"You're confident about your intelligence," I said.

"Charlie, I'm an idiot. That's the only thing I'm confident about."

"You have whole passages of *King Lear* memorized."

"I also have the Ewok song from the end of *Return of the Jedi* memorized."

"The 'Yub Nub' song?"

His eyes lit up. "Yes! How do you know that?"

"My dad's a dork," I said.

He laughed. "I only have it memorized because I'm reasonably sure it's the nadir of human existence. Worse than Las Vegas." He tapped his finger on the table for emphasis. "But the thing is, the more you learn, the more you realize how much there is that you'll never know. The point of education is not to teach you everything there is to learn but to teach you *how* to learn—how to interpret meaning."

"Good meaning or bad meaning?"

"Stories create meaning," he said. "The only meaning anything has is what you give it."

"Hmm." I traced the map of the states on my paper place mat. "Can I ask you something weird?"

He raised his eyebrows.

"Do you ever think about her?"

"About who?" he asked. He was smiling, like he was ready to be pleased at whatever I said next.

"Rachel," I said.

He kept smiling, laughed even, but the worry lines between his eyebrows folded in. "Rachel? Why do you . . . Why would that occur to you?"

"I just wondered," I said.

"I'm surprised you even remember that." He looked away, out the window at the gray parking lot. "No, not really. It's not exactly a part of my life I want to dwell on."

"You don't ever wonder what happened to her or how she's doing, or, like, you know . . ."

"Like, you know . . ."

"Like, you know, wonder if you missed out on something that could have been great. Or think about getting back in touch and apologizing."

"No, I don't. . . ." He sighed. "She doesn't want to hear from me. It would be arrogant to intrude on her life now."

"You don't know that."

"I know *her.*"

"Okay, but don't you—don't you wonder if she was the love of your life or something?"

"No," he said. "And I wasn't the love of her life either."

"Maybe you're just telling yourself that."

"Oh really?" he said. "How wise." His voice sounded sharp. He looked annoyed for a moment and then softened. "Sorry. It's just— I mean, yes, maybe I am, but if that's what I need to do, then . . ." He shrugged. "We all lie to ourselves. Even you, Yoda."

"I guess I do, Doc Daneeka," I said.

He smiled. "How do you remember all the idiotic things I say? God, of all the characters to be. A coward who can't even fake his own death."

My phone buzzed and I pulled it out of my pocket. "Oh good," I said. "My mom wants to know where I am."

"This is why I keep my phone turned off at all times," he said.

"Your mom tracks your movements too, huh?"

"She would if I kept it on." He raised his eyebrows in a question and reached for my phone. I let him take it. He ran his fingers over it as if it were studded with Braille. "Mine's practically rotary."

"You open it here," I said.

He flinched as the home screen came up. "Nuts."

I laughed.

"What?" he said, looking up at me guilelessly.

I swallowed and shook my head. The phone buzzed, and he dropped it as if it had shocked him. I laughed again and took it back, running my thumb over the screen.

"You haven't used a smartphone before?"

"God, no. They're witchcraft," he said, waving his hand dismissively. "All that bleeping and blooping. Give me numbers on a matte screen."

"How old *are* you?"

He laughed. "Old enough to know you should get back home before your mom gets me fired."

I paused. "Right," I said.

He looked down and cleared his throat. He took a minute to say "So do we go up to pay?"

I nodded. I followed him to the till, where he paid for both of us and joked with the hostess again, and I stood there thinking she must wonder what our relationship was, and then we went out and faced each other in the parking lot.

I bounced on my toes. "So," I said.

"So now that I've paid you off, you'll keep the smoking thing under your hat," he said.

"As long as you don't tell Ms. Anders I don't like her," I said.

"Mutually assured destruction," he said. "Let's never get drunk together."

"Deal," I said. "You did look a little cool. You know, smoking."

He smiled, and the lines around his eyes fanned out. I felt something knot up in my throat, and I had to stop myself from throwing my arms around him, looking so big and warm in the cold. It was getting too hard to constantly hold myself back from him.

"I appreciate your pity," he said.

“It wasn’t pity,” I replied. I crossed my arms over my chest. “And thank you for the meal.”

“Thank you for the company,” he said.

I hesitated, waiting to see whether he would move toward me. He wavered for a second, and then he jammed his hands into his pockets and stepped back. We nodded at each other, and then he turned and walked off. I watched him until he was out of sight, and then I slouched my way to my dad’s car and slumped there with my head on the steering wheel to wait until my phone buzzed with my mother’s messages again.

march

chapter 30

Every spring there was a senior class trip. The previous year's class had organized an ambitious but ill-fated camping trip that, rumor had it, ended with one kid almost losing a hand to a smuggled firecracker and a chaperone in tears over the condition of a student-abused Porta Potty. This year's trip was decidedly less adventurous: we were going to a theme park and then a hotel, where we could be corralled and monitored. I'd vaguely wondered for years how I was going to get out of it when the time came, but then Drummond told us he was going.

Lila and I stood together as we waited for the bus to arrive one cold Saturday morning. The chaperones—a group of half a dozen teachers who looked partly dismayed by us and partly relieved to be wearing jeans—were talking together, bobbing with suppressed laughter. Asha was huddled next to Dev and a few kids from our English class, and Jason was entertaining his acolytes with a story that apparently involved a lot of shouting. Lila had been spending more and more time with them lately. She usually invited me to go along, but I always had an excuse not to.

"He dressed up for the occasion," she said, inclining her head toward Drummond, who had broken away from the other chaperones but then got pulled over by a group of kids to talk. He was in jeans and a gray hoodie and he didn't seem much older than them. Also, his ass looked fantastic.

"I like that he's comfortable enough with us to not make any kind of effort," I said.

Lila watched him over my shoulder. "He's coming this way," she said. "Why don't you tell him how hot you think he looks?"

"What, like 'I just want to rip that elastic right out of your sweatshirt'?"

He stopped in front of us while we were still giggling.

"This happens much too often when I come to talk to you guys for it to be a coincidence," he said.

"Lila's drunk," I said.

He squinted at her. "Sorry, I couldn't tell the difference."

She punched his arm, and he winced exaggeratedly. "I have to take it where I can get it, since Charlie won't join in," she said. "Don't tell me you're not drinking either. You're on a trip with a bunch of idiotic seventeen-year-olds."

"I'm afraid I have to stay sober," he said. "There's been far too much imbibing among the faculty lately."

"What, like at staff meetings?"

"That's just the organized stuff," he said. "You would not believe the amount Papakostas can put away."

"I knew it," Lila said. "There is no way he's sober during our class. He—"

"Are they still bugging you about the paper at staff meetings?" I asked. I shot Lila an apologetic look. I had been so impatient to speak I hadn't realized I'd interrupted her.

"Yes," he said. "I've been informed we technically have not produced one."

"Unbelievable."

"Well, I told them you can't rush these kids and hadn't they ever seen *The Agony and the Ecstasy*, but they weren't swayed."

"Frank says he's finished a whole word search."

"What, writing one or solving one?"

"What do you think?"

"I think I don't believe him."

We both laughed. I glanced at Lila, who was frowning at me.

"I'm going to need you to tell Frank he has to learn how to spell words before he puts them in a puzzle," he said.

"You're the teacher!"

"I'm teaching you how to tell someone they're incompetent without hurting their feelings," he said. "Believe me, you will need it in your working life."

The bus pulled in with a weary sigh, and a cheer went up among the crowd.

"I should supervise in case anyone tries to run," he said. He made a gesture that was something between a wave and a salute. "See you guys on the other side."

Lila turned to me. "You two have gotten chummy."

"I guess," I said.

Lila chose a row of seats halfway down the bus. She let me sit on the inside, next to the window. After a minute, she pulled a bulky pair of headphones from her bag and turned on her music. She waved at Jason, who was sitting in the back with his group of friends, and blew him a kiss. He grinned at her and made a gesture I wasn't sure I wanted to figure out.

I spent the first half hour watching as the tightly packed suburban houses of our town unspooled into the occasional dilapidated farm. Sometimes I looked at Drummond. He was in front with the other chaperones, sometimes chatting with them but most often reading a paperback.

"What's he reading?" I asked Lila.

"What?" Lila pulled a headphone off her ear.

"What's Drummond reading?"

"Oh." She looked annoyed, but she craned her neck to see if she could tell. "Sorry, no idea." She readjusted her headphones and clicked the volume up.

I sighed and looked out the window.

"Are you guys talking about Drummond?"

I turned. Two girls I knew vaguely, Irina and Maddy, were sitting behind us. They were both passably popular and shared a kind of spackled beauty born of extensive product knowledge. They had all the signifiers of attractiveness—clear skin, long glossy hair, short skirts—but their faces still looked unfinished, plump with baby fat.

"Yeah," I said eventually.

"You know him, right?" Irina said.

"Uh, he's my teacher."

Maddy crossed her arms over the back of my seat. "You know he's not circumcised?"

Lila took off her headphones and turned around. "Sorry, what?"

Maddy smiled, knowing she had something we wanted. "A girl on the swim team told me."

"A girl on the swim team told you?" Lila said. "What, did it fall out of his Speedo while he was swimming?"

"No," Maddy said as if this was a ridiculous suggestion. "She said she could tell through the fabric."

"Oh Jesus," Lila said, and sat back down.

Maddy rolled her eyes at Lila and turned to me as if in confidence. "They're really tight Speedos, apparently."

"Kind of a product feature," I said. I decided not to mention that he hadn't been wearing a Speedo when I'd stalked him. "So are you guys in a class with him or what?"

"He's our study hall monitor," Irina said. "Everyone in there wants to have sex with him. Even the guys."

"Uh," I said, but I couldn't think of anything to say after it. I was never sure what to think when I heard someone else liked him. There were a lot of attractive girls in our class: at the crest of their youthful beauty, eager to test out their power, knowing he wouldn't reject them. I was happy they saw what I saw in him—even if I knew I saw it more deeply—but they were competition too.

"Are you, like, friends with him?" Irina said.

"Charlie loves him," Lila said. I hadn't realized she was still listening.

I shook my head. It seemed cheap somehow to align myself with them, as if I too were just a schoolgirl with a crush.

"He is hot," Maddy said. "I don't blame you."

"I swear he got a semi once," Irina said.

"He did not," Maddy said with a tone that implied it was not the first time they'd had this argument.

"He *did*," Irina said.

"He was wearing pleated pants," Maddy said to me.

"And we were talking about my pool party," Irina said.

"This collective obsession with Drummond is getting pathetic," Lila said without turning around.

"Hypocrite," I said.

"I liked him before it was cool," she said, and put her headphones back on.

When we got to the park, Lila pulled her headphones off and tumbled down the steps with Jason without waiting for me.

"I'll see you at lunch, okay?" she called back.

"Great," I said.

I went to where Asha and Dev were sitting. They'd been directly behind the chaperones; I'd seen them talking to Ms. Anders occasionally.

"You guys mind if I tag along with you?" I asked.

"Course not," Dev said.

"I don't do roller coasters," Asha said. "But I'll watch while you puke."

Dev and I got in line for a ride called the Terminator—*Twenty stories of terror!*—with a rowdy group of kids from our school. The boys were laughing and shouting and shoving each other; the girls were giggling and hopping in little excited bursts. Sean and Katie from our English class were there, and so were Irina and Maddy. Maddy waved at me, and I smiled and waved back.

"You know her?" Dev asked.

"A little," I said. "The way you know the people you grew up with, I guess."

"Not exactly familiar with that experience," he said. He rubbed his jaw and grinned at me.

"Oh, right," I said. "Well, I guess I know all these random facts about her, but it's all surface stuff. Like she used to be obsessed with Lisa Frank and she went through a biting phase in kindergarten and she had purple braces when she was twelve. But I don't really *know* her."

"Yeah, but you know her in a way a lot of people never will," he said.

"I guess," I said. "But I don't, like, know her secrets."

"I think you can know someone without knowing their secrets," he said. He looked over at Asha, who was taking pictures of people as they waited in line. "I wonder about Asha sometimes, though. I mean, I know everything about her, but I don't know what's going on in her head half the time."

"She just keeps her cards close to her chest," I said.

He laughed. "Not with me. But I didn't mean like that. I just . . . I don't get girls sometimes."

I squinted at him. "What's to get?"

"You're a mystery," he said, looking at me thoughtfully.

"We're no more mysterious than guys are," I said. "We don't want anything different." I turned to Asha and she glanced up and waved. When I turned back, he was still watching me.

"I wish I knew what you did want," he said.

I was trying to think of a response to that when the group of boys bellowed, *"Drummond!"*

I spun around. He was walking by us with Ms. Anders. She was laughing at something he'd said and her hands were fluttering in the air, threatening to land on him.

"Ugh," I muttered.

Drummond looked up. He had been laughing and the smile was still on his face, like an afterimage burned into a screen.

"Get over here, dude!" one of them called. I realized it was Frank. "Come ride *the Terminator*!"

Drummond waved at them dismissively, and Frank yelled, "Come on, what else are you going to do?"

"No thanks, kids," he said. "I paid for my lunch."

The group booed at him and he laughed. He was enjoying this, I could tell. Dev and I looked at each other.

"Five bucks he comes on," I said.

"I'll take that bet," he said. He stuck out his hand and I shook it. His skin was warm and for a second I felt something prickle in me, a small pleasant shiver. I let go.

"Come *on,* Drummond," came another voice. Sean's. "Stop being a girl."

"Well, if you're going to impugn my masculinity, I guess I have no choice," Drummond said. But he stayed where he was and glared at them.

There was silence for a moment, and then they booed him again. He turned to Ms. Anders, who stood back with her arms crossed, looking uncomfortable. "You all right on your own, Trace?" he asked. "Or you want to come on this wretched thing?"

"Go, go," she said. "I'm sure it will be thrilling." She looked like she was trying to frown at him, but he was grinning now, excited despite himself, and the corner of her mouth kept tugging upward in response. She scanned the crowd and her gaze landed on me. She raised an eyebrow. *Trace,* I thought scornfully.

Drummond walked toward the crowd and everyone cheered. "None of you have cameras on your phones, correct?" I heard him say as he joined them.

"Guess I owe you," Dev said.

"What?" I said. "Oh, right. You can buy me a slushie if we make it off this thing without puking."

"Deal," he said.

The bright day closed down as we went inside to the dark, damp loading area. Dev and I moved toward the back, where the line was shorter. Each car—a smooth green bullet-like thing with fangs at the front and purple flames up the sides—had four rows of two bucket seats, so we would be able to sit next to each other.

The group was jittery with excitement now. Some of the guys had started jeering, and I realized they were laughing at a couple who were wrestling each other: Sean and Katie. At first I thought they must be together now, but then I realized Katie was struggling against him, half laughing and half pushing him away.

"Come on, get off," I heard her say, but Sean grabbed her again and the crowd laughed. "You love it," he said. He let go and she bolted, and he chased her backward out of the line until he caught her from behind and swung her around as she kicked and squirmed like an upturned beetle.

There was only one ride attendant, a college-aged

guy with a long greasy sweep of hair, who sat behind a scratched-plastic booth, watching them with a bored expression. He looked like he saw this a lot.

I glanced at Drummond, who didn't seem amused anymore. "Sean," he said, "Katie clearly doesn't want to be held. Please put her down."

"Sorry," Sean said, but he was smirking.

Dev and I were up next. I stood back a little as a car full of laughing, dazed-looking kids clattered into the landing area. Once the riders had unbuckled themselves, the barriers opened and we were allowed on. Dev and I got into the two seats at the back and strapped ourselves in.

Sean moved toward the front car, dragging Katie after him. "Don't even try it," he said as she squirmed. He lifted her so she was tucked under his arm like a package. She shrieked as he carried her toward the car.

"Sean!" Drummond said. "What did I tell you, man? Put her down, *now*." He stepped out of the line and stood in front of the car, blocking Sean from it.

Sean stopped. His expression darkened. "When did you turn into a narc?" he muttered, and put her down. He walked back toward the line, shaking his head at Drummond.

Katie wobbled as she regained her footing. She was breathing hard, but she smiled at Sean and then at the crowd.

Suddenly Sean spun toward her again. The crowd whooped as she realized he was coming after her. She screamed again, and a ghost of it echoed in the loading area. She was standing in front of the car next to

Drummond now, and I worried Sean would barrel into her and knock her into the row of empty seats. Sean was only a few feet away when Drummond stepped in front of her and directly into Sean's path. He took the impact on his shoulder, so when Sean hit him, he only had to step back to keep his balance, but Sean slewed to one side, stumbled toward the car, and nearly hit his head on the upraised safety harness of one of the bucket seats.

"Jesus Christ!" he yelled. Suddenly the loading area was silent except for his voice. "What the hell, Drummond?"

"Sean," Drummond said, "go back to the bus."

"You nearly put me in a coma," Sean said, rubbing his head at the site of the phantom injury.

"You nearly assaulted your classmate," Drummond said. "Since you're unable to handle the privilege of being here, you need to leave."

Sean didn't move. "Fag," he muttered.

"Leave, Sean," Drummond said. "Now."

Sean said, "Fuck this," and shoved his way to the exit.

Katie hugged herself and tottered toward the group of kids. Drummond stepped forward, and she shied from him and said loudly, "I didn't need your help!" He moved back, looking flustered, as she followed Sean outside.

Finally the attendant came out from his booth, where he'd been watching the whole thing with an expression of detached amusement, and said, "Everyone okay?"

"Yes," Drummond said. "I'm sorry for the, uh, excitement."

The attendant shrugged and turned to the rest of us. "Can everyone who's going on the ride please get in and everyone who's not get behind the barriers? We're experiencing a little bit of a backup here."

Drummond ushered a couple of people into seats. Frank tried to grab his arm as he went past, and said, "Come on, want to go?"

Drummond still looked annoyed. "Thanks, but I'll pass, Frank," he said. He leapt over the barriers and into the group of kids, where everyone crowded around, wanting to talk, to touch him.

Dev and I sat in silence for a minute, watching him. Finally Dev said, "You okay?"

I glanced at him and shook my head. Then I looked down and saw that he was gripping the handles on his safety harness.

I took in a breath. "Don't worry," I said. "I won't puke."

He laughed uncertainly. As the ride started I grabbed his hand and squeezed it. He smiled at me and I smiled back, and it was only as we came to the drop that I raised my arms and let go.

chapter 31

Everyone started drinking as soon as we got to the hotel. I'd brought one of the Austen books my mother had given me and decided to start it in the hour before we had to get ready for dinner, but Lila dragged me down a floor into Jason's room, where a bunch of people had gathered. They were stuffed in, spilling onto the two twin beds and draped over the toilet. Someone had smuggled in speakers, and music warbled out, tinny and thumping.

Lila led me over to Jason. "Remember Charlie?" she said.

Jason grinned at me. "Hey, Chuck!"

"It's *Charlie,*" I said. I wasn't usually so brave, but Lila's frequent tales of Jason's idiocy had made it seem like I knew him. I felt a fierce wave of protectiveness toward the name: Drummond had given it to me, and this clown wasn't allowed to use it.

"Sure, sure, Charlie," he said. "I can't believe we haven't hung out before now. It's been, like, five months."

"It's almost like Charlie deliberately turns down invitations that involve you," Lila said, smiling sweetly.

I glared at her. "Five months, huh? I guess you guys are official, then?"

Jason laughed and squeezed her shoulders. "Lila gets

to decide those things. She's the smart one. Aren't you, Stanford?"

She gave him the finger. "I haven't gotten in yet."

"Ah, Lila's not that smart," I said. "She just likes feeling superior to people."

Jason's face lit up and he held out his hand for a high five. I stared at it and then tentatively touched his palm. It was hot. "She did well picking me, then. Didn't you, Boorman?"

Lila grimaced. "A) Screw you both. B) It's not hard feeling superior to this dumbass."

Jason kissed her on the temple. "You're a good kid," he said. She narrowed her eyes, but I could see she was pleased. I realized that I was smiling at them.

"Lila," said one of the girls, "what were you going to tell me about Sean?"

"Oh my God," Lila said as if she'd just been waiting for an opportunity to tell them whatever the gossip was. She pulled Jason behind her—he waved and gave me a last golden retriever smile, and I laughed and waved back—and they all wandered off in a huddle, giggling.

Now that they were gone, I had no one to talk to. The heat was uncomfortable, the result of the endless friction of bodies touching, rubbing, talking. I looked around to see if Asha would rescue me, but I couldn't find her anywhere. Of course she wouldn't be invited to a party like this. I glanced at Lila, who was deep in conversation with a pack of girls, and decided she wouldn't miss me.

I escaped into the hall, which was covered in peeling wallpaper and pocked with water stains. I went to our floor and found Asha's room.

"Hey," I said when she opened the door. "Want to take a walk?"

"Please," she said. "Where are we going?"

"Somewhere that I can't hear someone puking every five minutes," I said.

The hotel was moored in the middle of an expanse of Tarmac, but behind it was a long stretch of woods. The path at the edge looked like it had been used recently. I pointed to it silently and Asha nodded.

"Where's Dev?" I said after a minute.

"Out with Frank and those guys," she said.

"No invite for you?"

"Kind of a guys-only thing. Plus I think he's kind of sick of me."

"Sick of you?" I said. "No, I doubt that."

She smiled. "I think maybe we've . . . I don't know, maybe we rely on each other too much." I thought she might say more, but she went silent.

"Sorry if . . . ," I said.

"No, it's okay," she said, but she didn't say anything else. Eventually we had to climb over a big log to follow the path. Asha's shoe caught on a branch and I steadied her by the elbow so she wouldn't fall.

"Thanks," she said. She paused. "I think he . . . you know, we've always been close, obviously, because we're twins and because we moved around so much. But he and I didn't apply to any of the same colleges, which I thought was just an accident, but . . . I don't know, I just get the feeling he's trying to push me away."

"Dude, I just left a party where Lila ditched me for a bunch of cool kids," I said. "I know the feeling."

"Yeah, but we're family, you know? I realize it happens, but I think I wouldn't mind as much if I had other . . ." She trailed off.

"I bet you do," I said. I stared down at the budding flowers at the edge of the path so I wouldn't have to look at her.

She didn't say anything back, and we walked in silence down a small hill. The path narrowed and Asha's shoulder bumped mine, once and then again. I felt a laugh bubbling up in me.

"What?" Asha said.

"Nothing," I said. "I just . . . How stupid do Lila and I sound when we talk about Drummond?"

"Like on a scale of one to ten?"

"God, are we that bad?"

"Nah," she said. "It's just silly sometimes. You know, like all crushes are."

"You think it's silly?"

"I don't think *you're* silly," she said. "Him, well . . ."

I snorted. "Thanks."

"Just him and his little cult of personality is so ridic—" She looked at me. "Sorry. I just think there are nice guys our own age."

"Name one."

She paused.

"Yeah," I said.

She laughed. "What about Dev? I mean, I hate him, obviously, but . . ."

I laughed too. "I'm glad you think he'd be interested."

"Why wouldn't he be?" she said.

I shook my head. I didn't want to run down the list of reasons.

"I wouldn't say it if I didn't think it was a possibility," she said.

"All right," I said, but I didn't believe her.

We walked in silence for a while longer. The path was cool and stippled with shade. I felt better now that we were outside, away from the crush of people.

"Just be careful, okay?" Asha said finally.

"You don't trust him?"

"No," she said, "I don't trust you."

I shoved her and she laughed.

The path veered sharply and ramped up a little hill, and then the woods opened onto a clearing that shuddered with waist-high grass. It looked like the surface of a lake, unstable and rippling. At the end of the meadow the ground sloped away into a valley ridged with soft hills like knuckles. The sun was fat and blurred at the edges, and it was so low that it skimmed the trees, which were stubbled with new blossoms.

"Should have brought my camera," Asha said.

I realized with a start that Drummond was sitting at the edge of the clearing. He was on a bench, but the grass had grown up around it so it was half hidden.

"Hey," I said as we walked up beside him.

He turned as if he'd been expecting us. "Hey," he said. "I was just trying to figure out how to write a poem about this sunset without using the word *limned.*"

I moved to sit on the ground but he got up and said, "You guys have the bench. I can commune with nature."

He found a large rock near our feet—my shoes nearly touched him—and settled himself on it. The breeze ruffled his unruly hair, and golden filaments of grass shivered behind him. He looked like he was in an old overlit photograph, warm with age. None of us spoke as we stared at the sky.

"You guys doing okay?" he said after a minute. "It seemed chaotic in there when I was doing my round of bedroom checks."

"Yeah," Asha said. "We both just needed a break."

"Likewise," he said. "I warned Papakostas he might need to break up a party or two. But if you need someone to crack some skulls, I'm always available."

"You've done that a lot?"

"Not as such," he said. "But I'm really good at opening jars."

Asha laughed. I was pleased; she hardly ever laughed at his jokes. "Same principle?"

"Yes, and usually much less messy." He turned to me. "You're quiet. You need any skulls cracked?"

I had to look down before I could answer him. "Sean's, maybe."

"Ah," he said. "You heard about that?"

"I was there," I said.

He frowned. I couldn't tell if he was upset that I had seen it or that it had happened at all. "I'm sorry about that," he said. "I didn't mean to get so . . . forceful."

"It's okay. I liked seeing your action-man side. You almost did give him a skull cracking."

He shook his head. "I overreacted."

"He was taunting you," I said.

"It didn't matter. I shouldn't have let it get to that point."

"He's the one who wanted you to go on it in the first place. They all did. It's not your fault people like you."

"Hmm," he said. He stared at the rock he was sitting on, where he was absentmindedly scratching away at some moss.

I didn't know what to say in the silence. "It was weird, though, right?" I said eventually.

He laughed. "Yes," he said. "It was."

"What happened to Sean?"

"He's spending the evening in his room with a chaperone."

"Who?"

"Ms. Anders," he said.

"Ha!" I said. When he glanced up, I said, "Sorry. Just an odd pair."

He cocked an eyebrow at me. After a few minutes he said, "You guys know it's not always going to be like this, right?"

"It's still like this for you," I said.

A frown flicked across his face. "No, it's— That's not—"

"Chuck!"

"Great," I said.

"Who is—" Asha said, turning to see. "Oh."

Lila was bounding across the field with a demented gleam in her eye. As much as I hated to admit it, she looked beautiful, her hair spilling out behind her, her whole face a grin, her body bronzed by a corona of sunlight. She was carrying a blue sports bottle in one hand—presumably the source of her energy.

"Charlie!" she shouted as she got closer. "Charlie,

guess— Oh." She pulled up short as she noticed Asha. "Hi." Then she noticed Drummond, and she beamed. "Well, hello to you too."

"Perfect," I muttered.

She heaved up next to me like a boat coming in to dock too fast and pasted her arms around mine. "Why did you leave? I thought we were having fun."

I tried to draw back but she clung to me. "I just needed a break," I said.

"From *me*?" she said, exaggerating a pout.

"From everyone," I said. "Are you okay? You look like you need a nap. Why don't we—"

"Oh, please, I'm fine. So guess what?" She said it in a drunken shout of a whisper. I heard Drummond make a sound between a sigh and a laugh behind me.

"Are you sure you want to say whatever it is right now?"

She looked dubiously at Asha and then leered at Drummond. "I'll be quiet," she said loudly. "Anyway, he won't mind. *She* might."

Asha and Drummond exchanged amused looks.

"So what is it?"

Lila leaned in close, bumping into my ear. Her breath was sticky with heat and alcohol. "I'm gonna have sex."

"You're *what*?" I said, pulling away from her.

"Shhh!" Lila said. "I thought we were supposed to be discreet." She grinned at Drummond again, then took a sip from her sports bottle. She offered it to me and I shook my head.

"Are you sure? Is this with Jason?"

"Of course it's with Jason. I'm not a slut." She dragged out the *s* as if she were pressing an accelerator.

"I wasn't saying you were!" I said, much too loudly. I glanced at Asha, who was pretending not to listen, and lowered my voice. "I just . . . You don't even like Jason half the time."

"I like him," she said. "I like him more than I like you right now."

"Nice."

She kissed me on the cheek with a wet smack. "Sorry, that was mean," she said. "I do love you, Chuck. Almost as much as he does." She inclined her head toward Drummond.

"Shut up!" I said.

"Oh God, everyone knows you love each other," she whispered, leaning close to my ear again. "Look at you out here watching the sunset together."

"Asha's here," I said.

"Hmm. I bet she's contributing a lot."

"Lila."

"Charlotte," she said. "We're getting off the point. Jason's going to fuck me and I'm going to get it over with."

"Lila," I said. "Please listen to me for a second. Are you sure you want it to happen like this? I'm not trying to judge, I promise. I just don't want you to do anything you'll regret."

"Yes," she said. "I'm done being a virgin. I feel like I'm wearing a straitjacket and I want someone to untie it."

I laughed despite myself. "That's awfully poetic."

Lila gestured grandly. "Nature is inspiring!"

"But," I said, "are you really—"

"Jesus, Charlie, why are you trying to cock-block me? You're a sexist, you know. You can't stop this woman from making a choice."

"I'm just not sure you're in the best state for judgments on important issues right now, okay?"

"Thanks, Mom. I thought you'd be happy for me. Instead you're just jea—"

"Lila," Drummond cut in. "I think maybe you need to turn in for the night."

She grinned at him. "You think so, Tom?"

"Yeah, I do," he said. "It'll be a lot less painful than getting suspended."

"Oh my God, Thomas. Is everyone here just not getting any? You're really going to suspend me? I thought you were the cool teacher."

"I'm trying to prevent you from getting suspended," he said. He got up. "Let's go back. I'll walk you to your room."

Lila considered his offer. "What do I get out of this?"

"Probably a lot of barfing into the toilet," I said. I turned to Drummond. "I can take her if you want."

Lila glared at me. "No thank you."

"It's okay," Drummond said to me. "You guys enjoy the evening. Come on, Boorman. Let's get you some coffee."

She nearly tumbled against him, but then, remembering herself, she lagged a couple of steps behind. I wanted to follow them just in case Lila . . . I didn't know what. I didn't want them having any intimate moments with each other. She was even looser and more dangerous than she usually was.

Asha and I watched them disappearing into the distance, dark shapes against the fading sky.

"Lila's a fun drunk," she said.

"I'm sorry about that," I said. "You think she's okay? She looked really wasted."

"She's fine," Asha said. "I've seen way worse. And remember how you're not supposed to apologize?"

"I know, but I feel like I unleashed this on the world somehow," I said. "I know this is stupid, but did it seem like they were going to . . ."

Asha looked at me and raised her eyebrows. I raised mine back.

"Ew," she said. "No."

"Are you saying that 'cause the thought's gross or because it seemed unlikely?"

"Both," she said. "Both reasons."

"I hope so."

"He's not going to fall in love with her because she's drunk," Asha said. "He was just being a good guy."

"I know," I said. "But— Hold on, did you just say something nice about Drummond?"

"I'll deny it if you tell anyone."

"You like him," I said in a singsong.

She hit me playfully. "Not like you do."

I hesitated a moment, and then I leaned my head against her shoulder. I was worried she would pull away, but she didn't. After a moment she put her head against mine and let out a long breath.

"We should probably get ready for dinner," I said.

"Yeah," Asha said.

But neither of us moved, and we sat like that for a long time, until the sun blazed out of the sky and the stars wheeled on top of us. Then we got up and started the long walk back.

chapter 32

When I went to our room after dinner, Lila was passed out on my bed. At first I thought I'd let her sleep, but suddenly the idea of her and Drummond alone together felt catastrophic.

I used the bathroom loudly, banging the toilet lid up and down, slamming the door, humming as I brushed my teeth. When that didn't work, I tested out ringtones on my phone and switched the lights on and off a few times. She still didn't stir.

Finally I stood over her. "Lila."

She didn't move.

"Lila!" I grabbed her arm and shook it.

"Mmmm," she said. She turned toward me, but her eyes stayed closed.

"Are you okay?"

"Oh yeah," she said. "I feel fantastic."

"So what happened?"

"With—how?"

"With Drummond," I said. "What happened?"

"What are you— Where am I?" She cracked one eye open and looked at me blearily. "What's going on?"

"You're in my bed," I said. "What happened with Drummond?"

"Kissed him," she said.

"You *what*?"

She smiled lazily. "He's hot, Charlie."

"Tell me what happened."

"Hot for teacher."

"Lila, I need to know."

"Why, so you can have your shot?"

"Please, Lila?" I said.

She sighed deeply, as if she were preparing to do me the world's biggest favor. Then she rolled over so half her face was still submerged in my pillow. "No, we didn't kiss, okay? I tried and he turned me down."

"What happened?" I said softly.

"He walked me here and I went for it, and he pulled away so quickly he probably sprained his neck. He humiliated me. Took my vodka off me too, the prick."

I sagged onto her bed.

"Why don't you go see him, Charlie? I'm sure he's got blue balls after that, so he should be up for it."

I gaped at her. "What the . . . I'm going to pretend you only said that because you're drunk."

She squinted at me. "Go tell him how I'm an embarrassment and you guys can laugh at how superior you are to me."

My jaw tightened. "Happy to," I said.

He answered his door almost immediately. "Chuck," he said. He smiled, but he didn't look happy. "Perfect. Should have known it would be you."

"Uh, hi," I said. "I was just— I wanted to make sure—"

"How did you know where I was?" he said. His voice was jagged around the edges, as if he'd just woken up. His hair was damp and spiky like he'd been sweating.

"They told us where the teachers' rooms were in case we had an emergency," I said. This was true enough.

"Ah," he said. "You might as well come in." He stood back and after a second I tentatively stepped past him. His bed was made, but the comforter had crumpled where he'd been lying on it. I recognized Lila's blue sports bottle on the nightstand and realized that he reeked of alcohol.

I turned to him. "Have you been drinking?"

He let the door bang shut. "Just a little."

"Did you . . . drink Lila's vodka?"

"Some of it," he said. "Though there's only so much pineapple-flavored alcohol you can take even if you're desperate."

I watched him as he sat down shakily on the armchair across from the bed. It let out a series of squeaks as it took his weight.

"Are you okay?" I asked.

He laughed and pressed the heels of his hands to his eyes. "Not really."

"What's wrong?"

He lowered his hands. His eyes were rheumy. "Sorry, Chuck, but I'd rather not talk about it with you."

I swallowed. "Oh," I said. "Okay." I sat down on the bed. "Not that I'm judging or anything, but aren't you supposed to, I don't know, not drink, since you're a chaperone and all?"

"Ideally," he said. "But today was not ideal."

I took a breath, preparing myself. "Lila—"

He shook his head. He looked annoyed. "Don't worry, Chuck, I didn't get any ideas." He said it like I was ridiculous to have even considered the possibility.

"I didn't think you—"

"It wasn't that, all right?" he said. "It wasn't just that, anyway."

Relief stopped me from pressing him about it. "The thing with Sean?" I said.

He sighed. "Charlie, don't bother trying to figure it out, okay? In fact, I'd appreciate it if you'd stop trying to figure me out at all."

I paused. "Okay," I said.

He slumped in the chair and covered his face with his hands. "Couldn't you just have left me alone for one night?"

I was still reeling from the last shock and didn't know what to say. Was this who he really was? Maybe he was cruel and the alcohol had revealed it, like a lenticular picture that changed when you flipped it back and forth. "I'm sorry," I said. "I was worried about Lila."

He laughed. "Sure. You seemed really concerned for her well-being."

"I seemed— What does that mean?"

He looked at the ceiling. "I do wonder sometimes if I am Doc Daneeka," he said.

"Wait. We're talking about *Catch-22* now?"

"You read a book like that enough times and you start to wonder if there's any meaning to anything."

"I think, um, yes? Where is this . . . where is this going?"

He rubbed his hands over his face. He'd let his stubble grow longer lately and his jawline was ragged with hair. "When I was young, I thought I wanted to be a writer. But as I got older I realized I just loved stories; it didn't matter whether I told them or not. I decided to be a teacher because I liked sharing them with people—taking them apart, unpacking their meaning. I thought they could, I don't know . . . explain something to me about my own existence, I guess, and I liked the idea of giving that to other people.

"But there is no meaning really, is there? All our stories are just rationalizations. Making meaning where there isn't any. You think there must be some significance behind why things happen the way they do—some moral or purpose—like that would justify your own idiocy or give it a point or elevate it beyond the stupid, petty bullshit you see every day. Why is it so easy to see that other people's lives are random and pointless and so hard to see that your own is too?"

"Um . . . I don't— That's a tough one," I said, but he went on as if he hadn't heard me.

"Then you meet someone and you think they're special and they bring some meaning to your life and they make you feel understood and you start creating all these— But it's just your excuse to do what you wanted to all along. No one's that special. No one's meant for you. It's not ill-fated or star-crossed or unjust. It's just desire, stupid and meaningless and base. I wish I had as much meaning as Doc Daneeka did."

I was terrified of what he would say next, but he

abruptly stopped talking. He exhaled in a long sweep like he was clearing his lungs of the words.

"He kind of got redeemed," I said. I kept my voice low so it wouldn't shake.

He finally looked at me. His pupils were huge, as dark as carbon. "Exactly," he said. "That's exactly why I can never be him. The story itself created meaning for him. You can't . . . Things don't actually work that way."

"I guess . . . ," I said. "I guess we're not still talking about me and Lila?"

He huffed. "No, about me and Rachel—according to you, anyway."

I blanched. "You and Rachel?"

"Well, apparently I screwed up my life with that one, so why not do it again?"

"What are you . . . what are you saying?"

"I've been alone all year," he said. "And for what? I could have been with somebody. I've had offers." He looked at me. "Okay, one offer."

"I'm not sure I'm following you here," I said.

"You probably have good reason to hate her."

"Lila?"

"No," he said. "Tracey."

"Tra— Ms. Anders?"

He smiled in a way that made me feel very young. "Yes, *Ms.* Anders."

I stared at him. "She . . . wanted to be in a relationship with you?"

He laughed deep in his throat. "Something like that. But I turned her down. I thought I . . ." He glanced at me and then looked away. "Thought I was a real hero too."

I realized I was shaking my head. The whole conversation felt surreal. "Why are you telling me this stuff?"

"I don't know, kid," he said. "You're not taking it as well as I had hoped."

"Then why are you acting like this?"

He held up his hands. "You'll have to get used to bullshit like mine eventually. This is the thrilling world of adulthood."

I finally bristled. "Not all adults are full of bullshit," I said.

He blinked at me slowly. "Most of them are," he said, "but I take your point. I'm not exactly an ambassador for the brand, am I?"

"I guess not," I said. I stood up. "I shouldn't be here."

He let me get to the door before he stood up too. "Charlie, hold on," he said.

I turned around, ready to yell at him. "What?"

He paused. "Can we just— Let's pretend."

"No," I said. "Don't you dare. You cannot use that for this. This is—"

"Okay," he said. "No, you're right. You're right. I'm sorry. Please just stay."

Even though I was mad, the word *stay* was irresistible. He was begging me. I felt flush with power. "Why should I?"

I wanted him to say something like *Because I need you* or *I can't be alone tonight,* but instead he repeated, "Just stay, please."

I went back to the bed and sat down. He was still standing by the chair opposite. "You look like shit," I said.

"Strangely enough, I feel like shit."

"So you're not going to be drinking pineapple-flavored vodka again?"

He flopped onto the bed next to me and groaned. "No," he said. "No more alcohol talk, please."

"Maybe I should take it away from you just in case," I said. I started to get up, but he grabbed my sleeve and pulled me down next to him on the bed so we were lying only a few inches apart.

"I'm sorry," he said. "I'm so sorry."

I didn't say anything.

"There's no excuse," he said. "None of that was true. Well, except the part about Ms. Anders. I really should not have told you that."

I was afraid I was going to start crying. "Why did you say it, then?"

"I'm an asshole," he said. "I was angry at myself, so I took it out on you."

"What is going on with you?" I said. "Please tell me."

He looked at me for a long time. "You know what's going on," he said finally. He reached up and tucked a strand of hair behind my ear. His fingers brushed my temple. "I'm just a person, Charlie. I'm not special."

My mouth went dry. My heart felt like it was going to crack my ribs open. "That's not true," I said.

"It is," he said. "I'm not mysterious. I'm such a— I don't deserve this . . . attention you've given me. As lovely and flattering as it is."

I was embarrassed it had been so obvious and pleased that he'd noticed. I hesitated for a moment, and then I reached out my hand and brushed the damp hair off his forehead. A few strands stuck there like dark corn husks. He had a sad smile on his face that looked like he was getting further away from me the longer it went on.

"But you like it," I said tentatively.

He blinked, and I watched color spill over his cheeks. I was terrified he would deny it and humiliate me, but he didn't.

"You're so young," he said softly, as if he were saying it to himself.

"You're so old," I said.

He laughed.

"What are we going to do?" I said. I liked being able to say *we,* like we were in this together.

He was silent for a while. I studied him more closely than I ever had: the fine lines on his forehead that looked like hairline fractures, the dark raised mole on his neck, the pothole of an old acne scar in his cheek.

Then he said, "I don't know."

chapter 33

The next morning Lila didn't wake up until eleven. She hadn't moved all night—I knew because I was awake for most of it—and when she finally stirred, it was with a sound that seemed like it came from inside her bones.

"Oh Jesus. Am I alive right now?" she said.

I didn't look up from my book.

"Charlie?"

"You are," I said. "And you missed breakfast."

She groaned. "Please don't remind me about food." She closed her eyes and rubbed her stomach delicately, as if it could pop at any second. After a minute she glanced over. "Are you mad at me?"

I put my book in my lap. "Just because you told me I should go have sex with Drummond? Or, wait, I guess you told me to go laugh about you with him and *then* have sex with him."

"Oh shit," she said. She started to laugh, and then she saw my face and her lips compressed like she was biting down on the smile. "I'm really sorry. I wasn't myself, I promise. I don't even remember saying that."

"In vino veritas."

"Ugh, no Latin right now, Charlie." She sat up and then went gray. "That was a bad idea." She clutched at her head like she could claw out the headache. "So did you kiss him?"

My heart lurched at the thought.

"Sorry," she said. "He— Oh. Oh, no." She looked at me. "*I* tried to kiss him, didn't I?"

"Mm-hm."

She blew out a long breath. "I'm going to have to drop out, aren't I?" I watched her as she looked at the blank TV, where a negative of her reflection leered in the screen.

"You could get suspended."

"You think he'd turn me in?"

"No," I said. "He's not like that."

"I hope not," she said.

"I know he won't," I said.

I could tell she noticed my tone. She narrowed her eyes at me the way she did when she knew I was keeping something from her. "Did anything happen last night?"

"No," I said. "Other than you insulting me."

Her face softened. "I really am sorry about that. I don't remember saying it, but if I did, I was out of line."

"It's fine," I said. I was too distracted—excited and confused and looping back to the night before over and over—to be angry anymore anyway. "Were you really thinking of having sex with Jason last night?"

"Oh God," she said. "That happened? I thought I dreamed it."

"More of a nightmare, I think."

"Ugh," she said. She peered at the TV again, as if she'd forgotten I was there. She looked guilty for a second, and then amused, and then pleased. "I really was going to."

"I don't blame you, actually," I said. "You know how you said it felt like a straitjacket you wanted to take off? I feel like that too."

"I don't know," she said. "It's not that bad."

"It is that bad."

She looked back at me. Her eyes were serious. "Yeah, it is."

We laughed.

"Are you sure you're all right?" she asked.

"Yeah, I'm fine," I said. "I just had a weird— Yesterday was weird."

I hated that I couldn't tell her about Drummond. When it didn't mean anything, when you knew nothing was going to happen anyway, it was easy to talk about crushes or kisses—to use the guy as a shared secret. But to say something now meant it would become a secret between me and Lila, and the one between me and Drummond would slip away. The fact that it was wrong for it to have happened—that he wasn't supposed to have said any of that to me—made it seem more special.

"God, I'm horny," Lila said. "I mean, like, in general. Not at this exact moment."

"Why don't you get it over with?" I said. "Jason is as good as any."

"If it's with him, I might have to get drunk," she said. "What about you?"

"I figured out how to . . . um . . ." I made a vague gesture like I was priming a pump.

"Lift weights?"

"No! The . . . thing that makes God sad."

"Holy shit! You didn't tell me!"

"It's never really the right time to announce I learned how to abuse myself, is it?"

"Depends on the company," Lila said. "Was it good?"

"Yes," I said. "I'll leave it at that, because I'm a lady."

"Who was your material?"

"Who do you think?"

"Ha! Was it weird seeing him the next day?"

"Yes."

"Have you done it since?"

"I'm doing it right now." I waggled my eyebrows at her.

"Stealthy," Lila said. "Man, I've got to get on that. I've fallen behind."

"Too bad it didn't work out between you and that toothbrush."

"I threw it away," she said. "I couldn't take it staring me in the face every day, judging me."

"I fear for Jason."

She laughed. "That toothbrush cared way more about my health than he ever has. And it was much more skilled orally."

"I wish I could use it to scrub out my ears."

After Lila left to check if they were still serving breakfast, I decided that I should take my chance to see him alone one last time. We'd left on an uncertain note the night before—he'd said we should both probably get some sleep—and I was excited to see him again, to have a whispered conversation where we alluded to all the secret things we'd said in private.

I snuck to his floor, to his room, making sure that no one saw me. I had prepared what I would say if I ran into anyone: *I was just going to ask what time the bus leaves.* I'd deal with the rest later.

I knocked on his door. There was a pause, and then he opened it, looking back into the room and saying laughingly, "Just put it in the suitcase!" He turned to me, looked slightly startled, and said, "Oh, hey, Chuck."

I paused. "Hi," I said. I suddenly felt small and stupid and like I'd misunderstood everything.

He smiled like he wasn't sure what I wanted. "What can I do for you?"

"I just . . . ," I said. "Who is—"

"Oh," he said. "Tr—Ms. Anders and I were just getting ready for the trip back."

She appeared behind him. She was in high-waisted jeans and a sweatshirt with a dog on it. My heart seized up. Oh God, had they had sex? Had she been wearing that shirt?

"She just came over a few minutes ago," he said, as if he knew what I was thinking.

"Ah," I said, "how nice."

"What can we do for you, Charlotte?" she asked.

We. "It's . . . nothing," I said. "Not important." I felt even dumber with her looking at me while she was ensconced in his room, touching his clothes, putting things into his suitcase.

"You sure?" he said. Was he trying to signal something to me? Could he not say anything in front of her? Or had he completely forgotten the night before?

"I just wanted to ask when the—when the bus was coming."

"Oh," he said. He turned away. "Trace, do you know? The bus?"

"One," she said.

He turned back to me. "One, apparently."

"Great," I said. "Thanks. See you then, I guess."

"All right," he said. He smiled again. I tried to see if there was anything behind it, but I couldn't tell for sure.

He waited until I turned to leave before he shut the door.

chapter 34

"I can't believe I let you drag me to a game," I said. We were outside, at the edge of the bleachers, waiting for Jason's lacrosse team to play.

"What did we say?" Lila asked.

I sighed.

"Come on."

"I don't complain about games and you don't complain about books."

"Exactly," she said. "And I think the fact that I accompanied you to the library *again* without shooting myself should count for something." She rummaged in her bag and extracted a pack of red licorice. She pulled one out with her teeth and offered me the rest.

I grimaced and shook my head. "That's a complaint."

"That's an expression of restraint."

"You have no idea what it's like to feel joy, do you?"

"Look," she said, "I know we both make fun of Jason—"

"And rightly so."

She wrapped the licorice around her finger and ripped off a bite. "But I want my best friend to get to know my . . ."

"Boyfriend?"

"Let's say . . . guy friend."

I snorted. "You can't like him that much if you won't even call him your boyfriend."

"Fine, *boy*friend. I just want you to get to know him a little."

"I told you I like him," I said. "Why isn't that good enough? Anyway, you don't talk to Drummond anymore." I hadn't talked to him much lately either, but that was beside the point.

Her head snapped toward mine. "What does that have to do with anything?"

"Why should I make an effort if you—"

"You're not seriously comparing the two, are you?"

I felt my skin blotching with humiliation. I looked down at the field. "I guess you haven't told Jason about the, uh, incident."

"No, I haven't," she said sharply. "It's not his business. And it's not yours either."

I looked at her; her lips were set in a line like a closed slot.

I sighed. "I'm here, aren't I? After it's over we can talk about 'rad' bands together."

"God, you're such a dork," she said quietly, as if she didn't intend for me to hear it.

"Thanks," I said. We sat in silence for a few minutes. What she'd said vibrated through my head like a bell being struck.

Lila could put up with angry silences much longer than I could. I knew she would be able to stay pissed off at me as we waited for the game to start, through the game itself (pretending the whole time that she was enjoying it), and all the way back home. The thought of that much uncomfortable silence made my forehead bead up in anxious sweat.

"I'm sorry," I said finally. "Sincerely."

"Me too," she said. "This is stupid. What are we even fighting over?"

"Hey, guys." I turned around and saw Asha standing behind us, her camera slung over her shoulder.

"Hey," I said. I smiled at her, into the sun.

"What are you doing here?" Lila asked.

"Lila," I said.

Asha laughed. "My brother's on the team."

"Oh yeah," Lila said. "Come sit down, then." She moved over so Asha could sit between us.

Asha looked at me. I shrugged. She sat down.

"So," Lila said, "what position does he play?"

"What's the one where they don't let you onto the field until they're winning?" Asha said. "Whatever that one is."

Lila hesitated for a moment, and then she smiled. "Jason's told me he thinks he has potential."

"Don't let him hear that," Asha said. "You heard about that goal he scored at the game last week?"

"I was there," Lila said.

"He hasn't shut up about it since. I'm surprised it didn't make the local news."

Lila laughed. "It was a good goal. He should be proud." She held out the licorice. "Want?"

Asha pulled one from the pack. "Thanks," she said.

She took pictures all through the game, and let me look at them during a break.

"These are amazing," I said. "You're really talented, lady."

She grinned and looked away. "The camera does most of the work."

"Come on," I said. "You made Jason look good. That's some kind of miracle work."

"I heard that," Lila said. "And I reluctantly agree."

"You want me to take a picture of you?" Asha asked. I looked up and realized she was talking to me.

"Oh God," I said. "No, that's okay."

"For the yearbook," she said.

"That sounds like a threat."

"Okay, just for you."

"How about one of you and me?" I said.

"I can try that," she said. She leaned in next to me and we grinned at the lens. The sun was warm and bright and the wind whipped our hair around our faces. Asha pressed the button for the shutter and it blinked, closed and open, like an enormous black eye.

She turned it around to look at the view screen. "Oops," she said. "Just got me." She showed me. It was an arresting picture: the camera was looking up at her as she gazed into the distance, a slice of blue sky behind her, her hair flying out like a flag.

I passed it back to her. "You should keep that one. Put it in the yearbook."

She looked down at the picture for a long time. "Yeah," she said. "Maybe I will."

april

chapter 35

"I'm organizing a party for your birthday this year," Lila said as we waited for the bell to ring. "Don't protest."

"Fine," I said. "As long as it doesn't involve other people."

"You're turning eighteen," she said. "It's time we got you a hooker."

"I'd prefer a cake," I said.

"Guys, let's get started, shall we?" Drummond said.

Things were sometimes different and sometimes the same with him now. At night I would replay the conversation we'd had in the hotel—more than any other conversation I'd had with him, which was not an easy accomplishment—going over each word and gesture with the thoroughness and precision of a surgeon rooting out infected cells, probing each syllable for some hidden meaning. He *had* admitted that he had feelings for me, hadn't he? I'd been sure I hadn't misunderstood him—it had seemed very clear at the time—but the longer we went on without mentioning it, acting as if nothing had happened, the more I felt I must have been wrong. I had always imagined that when—if—he did, it would be under duress, when we were both tormented by longing, in the middle of a violent argument, and he would finally confess while standing outside in the rain, crying and bearded and broken. Then we would kiss, repressedly. I hadn't expected that he would just say it, quietly, freely, that it wouldn't seem like a surprise to either of us, and that I wouldn't even get a hug out of it.

That it had happened so easily made me doubt my memory of it; he had been drunk, after all, and while he had seemed lucid, he had also been tired and we'd argued and maybe it was all a misunderstanding. Hadn't he been telling me how ordinary he thought I was, how little I mattered to him, how he only liked me because he was lonely? Or had he been saying the opposite—that I was so special he couldn't admit it to himself and had to pretend I wasn't? Or maybe he had been talking about himself, or Lila, or Ms. Anders, or Rachel. I worried it over and over again and never hit on an answer that would allow me to bury the question for good.

I thought about Rachel sometimes, and what she looked like, and how she acted, and whether he still thought about her. I wished I could know how he felt about her, dig around inside his brain and scoop out his memories and squeeze them for information until they popped. I felt sure that this somehow held the key to how he felt about me. Maybe I had read too many books.

Usually he treated me like he always had, with a mixture of affection and distance, and he was still careful not to touch me. I felt like I was always trying to get more from him than he wanted to give me, like I was looking at him underwater and constantly misjudged the distance; he was always farther away than I'd thought he was. Sometimes I would catch his eye in class, or he would catch mine, and I'd try to see if there was anything more behind his look. But he would always turn away first, so I could never quite tell.

I never knew how to act or feel on any given day, or even from moment to moment; I careened from giddiness to terror to anger to lust to frustration. At night I'd decide I was going to confront him, to tell him how I hated that he pretended that evening had never happened, to tell him how angry I was, and then in the morning I would see him and he would smile at me and the words would drop out of my head. It seemed ridiculous, being so angry at him when anyone would think we were just teacher and student. The beige halls of our school didn't allow for it; the context seemed to push out any interpretation other than benign friendliness.

I couldn't talk about it to anyone, and while sometimes I liked having a secret, and imagined enjoying clandestine trysts in a back stairwell while people thundered over us, oblivious; or having whispered urgent arguments with him; or getting coded messages that confided his unbearable lust, none of that ever actually happened. Instead there was silence, and in that silence I could fill in any story I wanted, and did.

"Charlie," he said, "your thoughts?"

"What?" I said. I'd been staring out the window.

"Your thoughts about Mr. Rochester?"

"Oh," I said. "I think he's creepy."

The class laughed. I liked that.

"Really?" he said. "Why?"

"He hides his wife—his foreign wife, from *Jamaica*—in his attic and then acts like this poor tortured soul about it, like *he's* the one with the horrible life. Jane only finds him interesting because she thinks he's so dark and troubled."

"True," he said, "but there were very few other options for the mentally ill at the time."

"Maybe she was fine before he locked her up—maybe she just cheated on him or something because she couldn't stand him—but he got sick of her and she had a mental break after he stuffed her in an attic by herself. As most people probably would."

"Fair enough," he said as the class laughed again. He smiled in deference to their laughter, but the arc of worry lines between his eyebrows furrowed. "That's certainly a valid line of interpretation. But let's not forget that Jane calls him on that. And on everything else. It's only when he's humbled and she's independent that they come together as equals."

"Yeah, but the whole relationship reads like fan fiction," I said. "She's this ordinary girl who gets a handsome, loaded guy to love her for who she really is. It's bull—BS."

"Okay," he said. "But we could read it as a critique of the trope. It's only after he's terribly injured and his house burns down that she forgives him. And it's her forgiveness alone that gives him absolution."

"Why does he even deserve to be forgiven? He's a dick."

"Good question," he said. "Anyone want to take a crack at it?" No one said anything. "Great. Okay. Well, what if the forgiveness is less about him and more about Jane not allowing him that control over her anymore? Forgiving someone is a powerful act."

"Or it's letting the person who has power over you off the hook for what they did."

"Do you not think that he genuinely loves her? Or that, at least, we're meant to believe he does?"

"I don't know," I said. "I just don't get why you're defending him."

That stopped him for a minute. "Right," he said eventually. "So you think the book can be read as a female fantasy of male desire."

"Yeah," I said, "sure. I guess I don't see why you thi— you all think it's such a great love story. It's just Brontë's wet dream of getting some hot guy to go through hell just to marry her."

The bell rang.

"Okay," Drummond said, "I guess that will have to stand as the last word on the subject until tomorrow."

I got up to leave with the others, but he said, "Hang on a sec, would you, Chuck?"

He waited until everyone had left and then shut the door softly. I shivered as he sat down on the table near me.

"Is everything okay?" he asked.

"Yeah," I said. "Why wouldn't it be?"

"Hmm," he said. "Well, I try not to make assumptions where you're concerned, but you don't often use the words *wet dream* in class discussions."

"Sorry," I said. "I won't do it again."

"That's not quite what I was getting at," he said.

I crossed my arms over my chest. "I'm okay."

"All right," he said, though he clearly didn't believe me. "Anyway, the reason I kept you here was because I wanted to ask you for a favor."

"What kind of favor?"

"I'm covering Ms. Anders's study hall tomorrow. She's got a meeting with Dr. Crowley, and in case it runs late, I wondered if you wouldn't mind starting the class discussion without me."

"Me?" I said. "What— Why?"

"Because I think you can do it," he said. "It'll be five, ten minutes at most."

"Is that . . . allowed?"

"You think our lit class seems likely to riot?"

"Who knows what Frank gets up to in his spare time?" I said.

He smiled. "It'll be fine. I trust you."

I looked down. It was true that he'd basically stopped grading me in the past few months; I got As for nearly everything. I'd always done well in his class, but we both knew how strange it would be for him to give me anything less now. "I guess this means I'll actually have to read the book."

"Who needs sleep, right?"

"Can I have your notes?"

He laughed. "I love that you think I ever have notes."

I looked out the windows; the only view was of the other walls of the building. I thought of that night when I'd asked him if he thought I was pretty, when I'd sat there feeling nervous and sick. Then I thought of him in the hotel telling me I wasn't special. I knew I was frowning.

"You don't have to say yes," he said. "In fact, you're entitled to tell me to fuck off."

I looked back at him. "You know I won't do that," I said quietly.

It struck his eyes first—guilt, then shame, then sadness—and then it spread across his face like a stain. For a moment I enjoyed it: that I had gotten him to acknowledge it, that I did have some power over him after all.

"I know," he said.

I looked away, guilty that I'd made him feel bad. "So you think I'd be a good teacher."

He cleared his throat. "If you want to be," he said. "You can see the many rewards." He gestured toward the bare cinder block walls I'd been looking at.

"I thought you regretted it." I felt tense bringing up anything we'd talked about that night, even the edge of it, like a thread that would unravel the whole carpet if I pulled hard enough.

"No," he said, "I don't."

"You must have had other reasons besides the . . . thing you mentioned."

"Well," he said, "the money, obviously. The recognition. The respect. The unbridled power." When I didn't say anything, he said, "The cafeteria food. I love square pizza."

I looked out the window again. "And Tater Tots?"

"Did I ever tell you what we found out about them?"

I shook my head.

"The potato flakes are twenty percent lye."

I looked at him. "No," I said.

"No," he said. "But they do have ten grams of saturated fat per serving, which is probably worse."

I looked down to hide my smile, but he knew he had me. Out of the corner of my eye, I could see one of his dimples fatten, like someone was tugging a string inside his cheek.

"You teach me something invaluable every day," I said.

"I haven't taught you anything you didn't already know," he said. "And you know plenty."

I watched my legs as they swung. "Not enough."

I could feel him looking at me. "You really want to know why I teach?" he said.

"Why?"

"Because I remember what it was like," he said.

I swung my legs again and they hit his, gently. "I thought you hated it."

"Yeah, I did," he said.

"That seems like it's worked out well," I told him, but I laughed as I said it.

"Charlie," he said. I looked up. That sweet, sickening, queasy feeling was back, the one that came at the moments when I thought my feelings for him would rip me apart. It was like loosening your grip on the handles while your bike careered down a hill. You couldn't sustain a feeling like that. The center wouldn't hold.

"What?" I said finally.

We studied each other for a long time, and I kept thinking he was about to say something—he looked poised on the edge of a word—but in the end he only said, "I have a meeting to get to."

"Okay," I said.

"So," he said. He stood up and held out his hands. "Come on. Up with you."

I didn't move for a second, I was so surprised, and then I held out my hands and he pulled me up, although I didn't need any help. His hands were warm. Mine were sweaty. He pulled too hard and I had to rear back before I tumbled against him. Once I was standing firmly, he put his hands on my shoulders, as if to keep me from falling into him again.

"See?" he said. "It's not so hard."

chapter 36

Every year on my birthday, my dad woke me up by bringing me cake in bed. After that my mother brought my presents in and I opened them amid the bedsheets, all of us still rumpled, with crumbs and paper spilling everywhere.

On my eighteenth birthday, I woke up to silence. I listened for the rattle of plates downstairs or the gush of water in the walls that meant my dad was using the sink, but all I could hear was the swish of an occasional car outside. I looked at Frida, who slid open one blue eye and thumped her tail, then sighed and closed her eye again.

"Loser," I said. I lay back for a moment and looked at the ceiling. "This sucks."

Frida huffed at me, then got up and pushed her wet nose into my arm.

"Come on, Frito," I said. "Let's find out what's so important that they forgot my birthday."

I peered into the hallway. My parents' bedroom was at the end. The door was closed and the corridor looked gloomy; the only light came from the window in our shared bathroom.

My parents usually kept the door open a crack so Frida could wander in if she wanted. I knocked softly but there was no response. My mother sometimes went running in the morning, but if she did, she was usually in the shower by this time. She'd be late if she didn't get up soon.

I decided to shower and get dressed and see if they'd get up on their own, but when I came out of my room again, their door was still closed. I was annoyed now: not only had they forgotten my birthday but I had to wake them up?

I knocked again, not loudly, because I wanted to punish them by standing over them as they slept. I wished I had a party blower to wake them up with. I cracked open the door. I could hear heavy breathing, but not the deep, regular breaths of sleep; these had a suspiciously jagged staccato rhythm. In that instant I knew that I should stop, that I should shut the door, but I didn't. I let it swing open soundlessly, and I saw my parents on their bed, my mother naked, her body taut like a cable, her mouth red and wet and working, my father with his head in her lap, looking like a dog eagerly lapping up water. Looking debased.

"Oh," I said before I realized I was going to say anything.

My mother's head snapped toward me, and before she could look shocked, I saw the imprint of pleasure on her face, the flush on her cheeks, her frayed hair, the way her eyes still hadn't quite focused and stared at some point in the distance I had never known.

"Charlotte," she said. Her voice was husky.

I turned and stumbled downstairs, stopping only for my keys—and then I threw them down and found my mother's bag and dug out her keys instead. I heard my father call, "Charlie, wait!"

"I'm late!" I called back. "But thanks for the great birthday present!"

I ran outside, hoping they were watching me from the

window. My mother's car was an Audi, an older model but still red and slick. I had never driven it. I wrenched open the door and slid into the driver's seat. It was immaculate inside. I took a long time adjusting the seat and mirrors; then I sat there until I had stopped shaking. I had hoped my father would run after me and plead that I come back inside, but even though I waited and waited, he never did.

By midmorning my mother had called me twice and my dad had sent me several apologetic texts, promising to make it up to me that night. I ignored them both. I was desperate to see Drummond and let him make me feel better, but as soon as I got to class I could see he was distracted.

"Guys," he said after we'd settled down, "I'm going to need you to split up into groups to analyze a poem today. I have to prepare for a teacher conference, but I'll come around in a few minutes to check on how you're doing."

He didn't make eye contact with me as he passed around the photocopies—"The Flea" by John Donne—and as soon as we were in groups, he started working amid a pile of books. Halfway through class Ms. Anders came in and they talked together for long minutes, quietly enough that we couldn't hear but laughing loudly enough that we had to notice. The longer she stayed, the more annoyed I got.

"This poem is obscene," Asha said.

"No, it's not," Dev said.

"'It suck'd me first, and now sucks thee, / And in this flea our two bloods mingled be'? That's gross."

"I like it," Dev said.

"You would," Asha said.

"Harsh," Dev said.

I watched out of the corner of my eye as Ms. Anders finally left and Drummond came around to check on people.

"You like it, Dev?" I said.

"Yeah, I think so," he said. "It's kinda sweet in a way."

"Isn't he talking about how the flea biting them is like them having sex?"

"Yeah," Dev said. His eyes darted from his desk to me and away again. "But he's doing it to say how much he loves his girlfriend."

"Or to guilt her into having sex," I said.

"Well, uh, I guess wanting to have sex isn't bad in itself," he said. He was flushed now.

"How's it going, guys?" Drummond said as he came up behind Asha and tapped her chair with a pen.

"Fine," Asha said. "We think it's dirty."

"Dev likes it," I said, making my voice lilt. I ignored Drummond and looked straight at Dev.

Dev looked up. When he saw me smiling at him, he smiled back and looked down again.

"So you think it's about sex?" Drummond said.

"Of course it is," I said, still looking at Dev. "He's saying it's not such a big deal, so why is she objecting so much?"

"He sounds like a date rapist to me," Asha said.

"I'm sort of inclined to agree with Asha here," Drummond said.

"I think he just likes her a lot," Dev said.

"I think so too," I said. "What's wrong with that?" I held Dev's gaze until he glanced away.

The bell rang, and Dev immediately stood and said goodbye to us. Drummond tapped his pen on the table. I looked up. He frowned and mouthed, "You okay?"

I nodded, and then I quickly got up and left. Lila caught me in the hallway.

"Hey," she said, and I spun around, ready to snap. "Whoa. You okay?"

"I'd be better if people would stop asking," I said.

She gave me a suspicious look and said, "Okay. Sorry. I was just going to ask if you wanted to come over after school. You can help set up if you want."

"What— Oh, the party."

"You're not going to bail on your own birthday party, right?"

"No," I said. "No, this is good. Yeah, I'll come straight over."

"All right," she said. "You sure you're okay?"

"Fantastic," I said.

Lila's family lived in a gated neighborhood up the hill from ours, each generically imposing house more glittering and opulent than the one before. Lila's house stretched out on the ridge of the hill like a cat sunning itself. When I pulled into the forecourt, Lila ran outside and bounced toward me.

"Happy birthday!" she said. "Sweet ride."

"Oh yeah," I said. I slammed the door. "On loan for my birthday."

"Come inside," she said. "Parents and sister have been expelled and we're setting up."

Jason barged out through the garage. *"Chuck!"* he bellowed. "Happy freaking birthday!"

Lila rolled her eyes. "Sorry. He raided the vodka. Watch out, he gets affectionate."

He cantered toward us with the giddy expression of a dog who had slipped his collar. As he neared me I realized he wasn't slowing down. I braced myself. When he reached me, he swept me up into a sideways hug and spun me around. I couldn't help laughing. It felt good to let someone touch me, to be so bodily embraced.

"Jase," Lila said, "have you thought that maybe Charlie doesn't want to be swung around like a rag doll?"

He stopped spinning but he kept his arms wrapped around me. I relaxed against him. Something about his maleness, his willingness to touch me, filled me with happiness.

"Is this true, Charlie?" he asked.

"I'll make a birthday exception," I said.

"Ah, I knew you would," he said, and kissed the top of my head.

"Sorry," Lila said. "I can't take him anywhere."

"You love it," he said.

"I tolerate it," she said, but her mouth crooked into a smile. It struck me that they were happy. I gently loosened myself from Jason's grip.

"So you've got alcohol?" I said.

Lila raised an eyebrow. "You're drinking?"

"Seems like the right time to start," I said.

By the time people arrived, Lila and Jason had given me something they called a screwdriver and we had been dancing wildly in the vaulted great room, which echoed with music, until we were sweaty and flushed and laughing. Drinking was much more pleasant than I had imagined: the alcohol tasted like paint-stripping fluid in my mouth, but it went down hot and the warmth lingered like coals glowing in my stomach.

I didn't shy away when Jason started to grind on me and Lila. It started as a joke, but the more they drank, the farther they got from me and the closer they got to each other. At first I tried to get in between them, and then I started to look away when they whispered to each other and giggled and kissed, and then I retreated to the vast kitchen, panting and red as a rash, and waited to see if they'd notice.

Once the house started to fill up, I realized how few of the people I knew. They were mostly Jason and Lila's friends, and though I felt warm and lubricious from the alcohol, the more people I saw, the more I wondered how much this party was really about me at all. I knew Lila had invited Asha and Dev, but they'd had a family party they couldn't get out of. She hadn't invited Katie or Frank or anyone else from our lit class. Who was I kidding, though? I wasn't even friends with them. We were friendly—that grazing, noncommittal word—at best. Lila was all I had, and she was with him. I watched the throbbing mass of dancers from the edge of the room and saw that Lila and Jason had slipped into a corner and started making out. For a second the warmth in my stomach fanned into a hotter anger. Lila leaned into his ear and whispered something; he raised his eyebrows and she nodded. She took his hand and led him into the hallway.

I knew I shouldn't follow them. I knew I would only regret it. But I did, and they went up to Lila's bedroom suite, and I could hear giggling and then moaning and then I ran back downstairs. I grabbed the first drink I could find—someone had brought Pabst Blue Ribbon—and chugged it as fast as I could, which wasn't fast at all. When I was finished, I stood in the corner of the great room again and looked at all the people dancing and thought about what it would be like if Drummond were there. Then I made myself stop. He wasn't there and he wasn't going to turn up and claim me and he wasn't ever going to finish what he'd started that night in the hotel. He was gutless, and he didn't give a shit about me.

I barged onto the patio. There was a couple making out by the pool, but otherwise it looked deserted. Except for Mike. He was hunched against a wall, looking intently at his phone.

"Oh, great," I said. "You." On his own, outside school, he looked smaller.

He looked up. I wasn't sure what to expect when he recognized me—laughter, maybe, or scorn—but he seemed worried. "Uh," he said, "hi."

I realized I didn't care what he thought of me anymore.

He couldn't scare me. "You realize this is *my* birthday party, right?"

"Yes," he said. He held a red plastic cup in one hand and he looked around as if he wanted to set it down but couldn't find a place for it.

"So why were you invited?"

"Uh," he said. His face stuttered into a smile. He looked like a dog who knew he'd done something wrong. "Jason invited us, and Austin—"

"Austin?" I said. My head filled with anger. "Is he here?"

"No, he left. Said it was lame."

"And you stayed? I thought you were his shadow."

He laughed. It was high-pitched, like a balloon leaking air. "No shadows at night."

I stared at him. "You made a joke. Not a very good one, but a joke."

His eyebrows rose and he smiled as if he was embarrassed.

"Why would you come to my party?" I asked. "Did you just want to torture me?"

"No," he said, shaking his head for emphasis. He was still clutching his drink. He looked too nervous to take a sip.

"You realize you made me feel like shit. More than once."

"That was Austin," he said.

"No," I said. "You were there and you didn't stop it. I can remind you what he said if you want."

He glanced at me and then away again quickly. "I remember," he said.

This felt so good that I kept going. "Did it make you feel like a man? To make me feel like I was ugly? Do you think I don't know what I look like?"

He stared at the ground. "I don't think you're ugly."

"Don't lie now that I've cornered you."

He looked up at me again. "I don't think you're ugly," he repeated. He said it slowly this time, and he didn't look away.

"Well," I said. "That's not even . . . that's not even the point." I looked at the pool. The couple was still there, making wet smacking noises. "Ugh. Who invited them?"

Mike shook his head.

"This is the first time I've ever gotten drunk," I said. "It's turning out pretty awesome."

The song ended, and a new one blasted from the speakers so loudly that for a second I forgot where I was. I stumbled against the wall, feeling sick.

Mike leaned close to my ear. "Are you okay?" he asked.

"I'm fine!" I said. "I'm fine." I groaned as my stomach lurched. "Why is music always so loud?"

"Come on," he said. He tried to take my arm and I pulled back. He waited a second and touched my shoulder, and I shrugged him off again but looked up at him and said, "You can take me inside, but don't touch me again, okay?"

"All right," he said.

I followed him into the house, down the hall through clots of people, and into one of the downstairs guest bedrooms. He shut the door and the noise became distant and muted, softened by the thick carpet, the acres of soft curtains and sheets and fabric.

"There's a bathroom in here," he said. "If you, um, need it."

"I know," I said. I slumped onto the bed. "You can go now."

He hovered against the wall, but he didn't leave.

"Did you need something else?"

"No," he said. "You just look really— You look like you might puke. I think I'm going to get Lila."

"She's busy having sex with your buddy."

"Austin?" he said. He sounded shocked.

I laughed. "You wish. She's fucking Jason. Basically everyone is getting fucked today except me."

"Oh," he said.

"Is that funny?"

"No," he said. He let his head drop. "Please give me the benefit of the doubt for a second."

"Why?"

"I don't know," he said. "Because I'm asking you to."

I drooped backward on the bed. "My shoes hurt."

He looked down at them. "They do?"

"Yes, they do."

He hesitated. "Did you—or—"

"Fine, I'll do it," I said. I sat up again and pulled them off and then a tide of nausea rose in my throat. "Oh God."

He ventured toward me. "Are you— Do you want, like, a garbage can or—"

I waved him away with one hand and massaged my forehead with the other. "I'm fine."

He came a little closer, and when I didn't wave him off again, he came closer still, until he was crouching next to me. I was too busy trying to calm my stomach to care.

"I'm really—I'm really sorry," he said. "I don't know how to make you believe me, but I am."

"Please don't do this," I said quietly.

"Why not?"

I closed my eyes so I wouldn't have to look at him. "I don't want pity." But that wasn't exactly true. It was more that I didn't want him to know I wanted pity.

"It's not pity," he said.

I opened my eyes and looked at him through the net of my hair.

"Austin—we met in middle school; I was new and he was the only friend I had. I liked being friends with someone who got attention. You must know what that's like. And, you know, his life hasn't been that easy. He's had some—"

"No," I said. "Don't try to make it a . . . like some kind of justification. I don't want to hear about how mean his dad is. It doesn't excuse anything."

"Okay," he said.

"I'm not going to feel sorry for him. And I'm not going to forgive him either."

"It was just a thought." He scrubbed his hands through his hair. "Man, you're putting me through my paces here."

My stomach had reeled back into place. I looked down at him. He was still crouching next to me.

I sighed. "Sit," I said. "That can't be comfortable."

He collapsed cross-legged on the carpet without looking at me.

I laughed. "I meant on the bed, you moron."

When he saw I was smiling, the corner of his mouth turned up. "Are you— I'm not—"

"Get up," I said.

He stood clumsily; his sneakers caught on the frayed bottoms of his jeans. The bed sloped when he sat down. He was close enough that I could feel how warm he was.

"So were you trying to say I should feel sorry for Austin?" I asked.

"No," he said. "I was just trying to— I don't know. I thought if I could explain it, it would . . ."

"Why should *I* have to try to understand *him*?" I said. "Why doesn't he . . ."

"I don't know, Charlie," he said. I was surprised to hear him use my name. "It sucks."

"And you're friends with him because no one else likes you?"

I'd hurt him with that one, I could see. "Thanks," he said, "for pointing that out."

"Sorry," I said.

He shook his head. "How do you explain why you're friends with someone? He's funny sometimes and things are more exciting with him and I guess I . . . liked that. Or at least I used to like it. I'm just—I'm sorry, and I don't think you're ugly."

I looked at him until he looked back at me. He was closer now—I could smell the tang of beer on his breath.

"Turning eighteen is shit," I said. "I don't recommend it."

He laughed a little. "I'll be sure not to do it."

"What were those people by the pool doing, anyway? They sounded like a science experiment."

He smiled. "I guess that's what people do at parties," he said.

"Mm," I said. "You know, you should be less of a coward. You're not that bad underneath."

He smiled shyly. Was he blushing? His eyes were blue, I noticed. Bright blue.

"I don't know about that," he said, and I kissed him.

It lasted only a second—long enough for me to get the impression of warm skin and alcohol—and then he pulled back. For an instant my thoughts coalesced in a paranoid whirl: this had all been an elaborate game; he'd been setting me up; Austin was going to burst in. But he looked shocked, genuinely shocked, and he seemed to search my face to see if I was laughing.

"I think there's been a—a misunderstanding . . . ," he said.

"I'm sorry," I said. "This was a mistake. This is just—" I scrambled back on the bed, trying to get purchase on the slippery bedspread.

"It's okay," he said. "I just wasn't expecting, uh . . ."

"I need to go," I said. "I'm really sorry. This day has been . . ." I shoved my shoes on and didn't do up the laces.

"I didn't mean to— You don't have to—" he said.

"Thanks for coming to my party," I said, and left.

"Hey!" I heard Lila shout as I ran across her front lawn. I could still hear music coming from inside the house, warped and wobbly and mournful-sounding. "Charlie! Where are you going?"

I hesitated before I turned. I was too far away from

the car; she'd catch up before I could leave. "I need to— I have to go—"

She jogged across the buzz-cut grass in her bare feet. It was wet from the automatic sprinklers and it glistened in the floodlights. "You're seriously leaving already?"

"Yes," I said. "No lectures, please."

She looked taken aback. "I wasn't— I was just worried."

"Everything's fine," I said.

"Okay," she said. "Then why are you leaving?"

"For one, you invited Austin and Mike, who I expressly told you not to invite. For another, you were obviously a little"—I scanned her body up and down so she could see me doing it: her mussed hair, her crumpled shirt, her swollen lips—"preoccupied."

She half grinned like she was smiling at the memory. "Oh, well, look, that was—"

"You fucked him, didn't you?"

She looked like she'd tasted something sour at the word *fuck*. "I didn't—yes, but—"

"On my birthday."

She frowned. "What does that matter?"

"During my party!"

"Okay," she said, "I'm sorry about that, but—"

"How dare you have sex on my birthday?" I said. It came out louder than I'd meant it to and echoed down the quiet street.

Lila laughed and then, seeing how angry I was, tried to compose herself. "What does that have to do with anything?"

"It's— You're not allowed—" I suddenly felt like I was choking back a torrent of sobs.

"Are you jealous or something?"

"No!"

She moved in closer. "You're jealous," she said. She was laughing again. "I can't believe it."

"Yeah, I'm incredibly jealous of you getting to bone Jason. What a treat that must be for, like, forty seconds," I said. "You know, Lila, when people get angry at you, it's not always because they're jealous. Sometimes it's because you're being a dick."

She retreated a little. "Harsh. I know you only have eyes for dorky English teachers, but—"

"That's not true," I said.

"Really? What was he wearing today?"

"It was a—" I stopped. "That's not the point. You hurt me deliberately."

Her forehead creased. "You're just upset because he couldn't give a shit about you, aren't you? You think he's your only shot."

I recoiled. "You seemed pretty into him until he rejected you. Besides, I'd rather he didn't care about me than have to be fucked by Jason."

"At least someone's fucking me," she said.

"Well," I said, "congratulations on being a slut."

The word hit her like a slap. She stepped forward and lowered her voice. "Better than being a dog."

"Fuck you," I whispered, shaking my head as if that could get the words out. "Don't ever talk to me again."

chapter 37

I pulled up outside his condo with the confidence of a frequent visitor, although I'd only passed by it once before, and at the time I'd told myself I was just taking a more scenic route home. The street itself was narrow and winding and wooded, and the condo building looked shoved in and out of place, hulking and blocky against the feathered green trees. The walls were cinder block like our English classroom's—not a color so much as a lack of one—and they were spotlit at regular distances so the pools of light looked like eyes with tired gray smudges underneath.

I knew what number he lived at—24—but not where it was. Most of the front doors were well maintained, the concrete expanses larded with welcome mats and hanging plants, but a few of them looked anonymous. His was one of the vacant-looking ones—on the upper floor, in a unit that looked unoccupied except that the light by the door was on. I ran up the stairs two at a time and knocked, panting, before I could change my mind.

There was a hellish pause, and I imagined either that no one would come to the door—he was out, or worse, he had looked through the peephole and turned back, trying not to make a telltale noise—or that some stranger would—a babysitter with children barnacled to her legs, or an annoyed businessman with a folded paper in his hand and reading glasses askew on his neck, or a young woman tying a robe and giving me a puzzled expression before turning back to see if her lover knew who was at the door, and smirking when she realized it was his student.

But the door opened, and it was him. He was wearing red plaid pajama bottoms and an old gray T-shirt, like those ones that are imprinted with a team name and logo in faded lettering, except this one had DICKENS EST 1812 in place of the team and a list of book titles underneath. It was pulled taut across his chest like he was too big for it rather than it being too small for him.

"Charlie," he said. He didn't sound annoyed this time. He didn't look annoyed either. "I thought you—" Then he saw my face, and his forehead creased into a ladder of worry lines. "What's wrong?"

I didn't know where to start. "It's my birthday," I said finally. My voice cracked and it came out pathetically, like a moan. Hearing how stupid it sounded aloud uncorked everything and I started sobbing, hard.

"Oh, sweetheart," he said. He strode forward, over the threshold, and I rushed toward him too, and we collided with the smack of a ball into the seat of a glove. Sometimes when people hugged you it was tentative, like they were trying to give you an impression of contact without having to touch you—homeopathic affection—but he was big and male and he enveloped me completely. I sank into him as I cried. His clothes were soft, and his shirt smelled like detergent. My heart was pounding so hard I was sure he could feel it. I felt loose at the seams, like I was going to shake myself apart. He murmured "It's okay" over and over again, until the words lost any meaning and I just listened to the steady vibration of his voice. Eventually the sobs slowed and I sagged against him, not ready to let go. My face felt humid against his neck.

"I like your shirt," I said when I could speak.

He pulled back gently and looked down at it like he was seeing it for the first time. "Oh," he said. "It was a gift. I get a lot of literature-themed presents."

I nodded and tried to laugh. "I'm sorry I got snot on it."

He waved his hand. "It'll complement the gravy stains," he said. He gestured toward the door. "Come in."

I stepped into his living room, which was mostly bare, except for a TV and a sofa and a coffee table. The sofa was covered in stacks of books, which he shoved out of the way. They spilled onto the floor, their pages lolling open like tongues.

The room was dark, but I could see he hadn't bothered decorating much. All the pieces of furniture were functional and looked like old self-assembly stuff, maybe leftovers from college. The only things that seemed personal, like he'd put effort into them, were the bookcases, which slumped heavily against every wall. Their shelves were crooked with books like mouths crammed full of teeth.

He had obviously been grading papers when I arrived; there was music playing softly in the background, and a half-marked paper was spread-eagled on the table. He sat down where the books had been and I sat where he'd been.

"What happened?" he said.

"I just . . . I had a bad day."

"Start with the worst thing," he said.

"My mom—no—Lila—" I gulped loudly and then laughed. "Sorry. She thinks I'm . . ." I trailed off. My ugliness had always existed as a negative; it was the absence of compliments, the awkward silences, the appraising stares. To voice it meant admitting it was true. "She said I'm . . ." I gestured toward my face. "This whole situation is bad." I tried to laugh and hiccuped a sob instead.

"I'm sorry," he said. "Come here."

I curled up against him and he wrapped his arms around me. It felt so good to give in and touch him, to know that he wanted to touch me. I felt warm and heavy, like my eyelids didn't want to stay open.

"I provoked her," I said. It felt easier to admit it when I wasn't looking at him, now that he had tacitly taken my side.

"Nothing you could have said would've justified that."

"I called her a slut."

He paused. "That's pretty bad."

"I didn't mean it."

"I'm sure Lila didn't mean it either," he said. His voice seemed deeper this close. It vibrated in my skull with the resonance of an organ.

"You know none of what she said is true, right?" he asked after a minute.

"It's true," I said.

"It's not," he said. He turned me around and put his hands on my arms as if to clamp them down. "It's not true. Didn't you see what you did to Dev today?"

I looked at him. "You noticed that?"

"I have eyes," he said.

"He doesn't count."

"Why not?"

I didn't answer. Then I said, "But you—that night in the classroom—you told me I wasn't pretty then."

"No, I didn't," he said. "I never said anything like that."

I was so nervous my jaw was vibrating. "You never said I was pretty either."

He went silent. "It wasn't because I didn't want to," he said finally. "I couldn't."

"You could," I said. "In the hotel, you told me you— It seemed like you told me that you . . . that you had feelings for me but you couldn't . . . you know."

"I was drunk," he said. "I never should have said what I said then."

My tongue stuck to my teeth. "But you meant it."

He didn't answer.

"Please," I whispered.

He wouldn't look at me. "I can't."

"Why not?"

He shook his head.

"You think I'm hideous," I said. "Just like Lila." I felt a sob well up in my chest.

"Oh, Charlie, no," he said. He hugged me again, tightly, as if he were trying to hold me together. He smelled like sweat and soap. His heart was pounding.

"I'm disgusting," I said into the hot damp hollow of his neck.

"You're not." He pressed his mouth against my temple, once and then again.

"You hate me." I pushed myself against him, my cheek against his cheek, my throat against his throat.

"I don't." He took my hand and interlaced his fingers with mine. Our palms were sweaty. His heartbeat was even faster now.

I breathed in sharply. "Tell me."

"I can't," he whispered. His lips brushed my ear.

"Tell me," I said again.

"Oh God," he said. He groaned and slid his mouth along my jaw. He pulled me in tighter.

"Tell me," I said.

"No," he said.

"Then show me," I said.

He kissed me. I felt like the sea was crashing inside my head and I couldn't hear anything else. It was the opposite of how it had been with Mike. It was more intimate than I'd imagined; I felt exposed like a nerve, as if kissing him transmitted my thoughts and now he knew that he'd taken me over completely. His lips were chapped and warm and pliable. Now that I could touch him, I ran my hands everywhere I could: down his arms, so I could feel his muscles ripple underneath like the choppy surface of a lake, across the confident span of his shoulders, to the arch of his back to where his body tapered to the center. I felt greedy, like I wanted to catalog every part of him.

I was dizzy with happiness. I grabbed his hands and tugged him forward, and he let himself fall on top of me.

"You have nice arms," I said.

He chuckled softly. I could feel his breath on my neck, his low laugh. "Thank you," he said. "But don't the kids call them guns these days?" He kissed my throat and then my jaw. When I didn't reply, he raised himself and looked at me. "Well?"

"You're kind of distracting me," I said.

He laughed. "Sorry," he said. "I'll give you a pass this time."

"So do you only do this for your top students?" I was joking, but he looked hurt for a moment, his face like a TV signal flickering into static. Then he said, "Just you so far. Kind of a one-off special."

"Good," I said. "I was worried I was Frank's sloppy seconds."

He laughed. "You're a little preoccupied with my supposed flirtation with Frank."

"I don't like the competition," I said. "Anyway, you flirt with everyone."

"Oh yeah?" he said, and started kissing me again. "Like who?"

"You flirt with the whole class."

He stopped and looked at me. "Really?"

I realized I was distracting him. "Kind of." I drew him down and he kissed me and then lifted himself up again. I thought of him pulling himself out of the pool.

"I don't mean to," he said.

"I know," I said, though that wasn't true. I waited until he'd lowered himself again. "Were you jealous I was flirting with Dev?"

He laughed. "No comment."

"Can I take that as a yes?"

"You can take it that I'd prefer not to comment."

I sat up and pushed him back against the sofa so I was straddling his lap. "Tell me you were."

"You're forceful today," he said.

"You were, though, weren't you?"

He sighed like he knew arguing was futile. "You wouldn't keep asking if you knew you were wrong."

I wriggled happily. "Then say it."

"Yes," he said. "I was."

I had expected to be delighted by this admission, but instead I felt a stab of embarrassment for him. I decided I just needed to hear more. He leaned toward me, but I held myself back.

"Tell me you want me," I said.

"Since when are you a dom?" he said.

"What's a dom?"

"Doesn't matter. Charlie, I want you, okay? We wouldn't be in this particular position if I didn't." He squeezed my legs playfully and moved to kiss me again.

"That's not what you're supposed to say," I said.

He laughed. "What am I supposed to say?"

"It ruins it if I have to tell you," I said. I hesitated, and then I leaned in close and brushed my lips down his jaw. I stopped just before I reached his mouth. "Tell me again."

I was terrified he'd burst into laughter, but instead his breath caught. "I want you," he whispered. "Charlie . . ."

I shivered. "Tell me you don't want anyone else," I said.

"I don't," he said.

I let out a breath. "Tell me I'm pretty."

He looked at me. His eyes were so blue. "You're beautiful," he said.

I swallowed. I wanted to enjoy that he'd said it, finally, chew it over until it was gone, but the words wouldn't go in; they drifted against a door that wouldn't open. He looked so nakedly happy that for a second it struck me as pathetic. Was he really as small and predictable as that? Had I actually figured him out? I thought of him in our class, laughing at something, his head buried in his hands.

"What's that face?" he asked.

"Nothing," I said. "Come here." I tugged on his shirt and pulled him to me. We kissed. My thoughts began to cloud over almost immediately, and I pulled away again. "Tell me you've been in agony," I said.

He looked up at me. "Agony seems a bit—"

I narrowed my eyes at him.

"All right, all right." He looked off to the side. I could see the part in his hair, the dark roots that looked like a doll's plastic scalp. I had to stop myself from running my fingers against it just because I could. "You remember how you caught me smoking?"

"That was me?"

He looked back at me. "Mm."

"Was I the existential crisis?"

He nodded.

"The beard? The hollow eyes?"

"Some of that was just teaching," he said. "But generally, yes."

I sat back and put my hands on his chest. "Why did you tell me you had feelings for me and then not do anything about it?"

He fiddled with my shirt collar. "You know why," he said.

"It was cruel," I said. "To do that and then leave me hanging." I said it in a teasing voice, but I meant it.

"I'm sorry," he said. "Can I make it up to you?"

That struck me as an impressively adult thing to say. I smiled.

"Yes," I said.

He kissed me again. It felt like the sun coming out. We kissed more and more, until I couldn't think, until it wasn't enough. Desire ripped through me like I was a seam splitting open. He pushed against me as if he was dying of thirst and I was the only thing that could slake it.

I ran my hands down his shirt, farther and farther, until I reached his waistband. For a moment he hesitated; he took my hands in his and I thought he would push me away. But he tugged his shirt up and I helped him pull it over his head. His hair frayed out in a halo. I'd seen his body from a distance, but up close I could feel the small creases in his belly and trace my fingers down the veins on his arms. He radiated heat like a furnace.

I don't know how long we kissed, but it was breathless, unthinking; I felt like a freight train unable to brake. His stubble burned my chin but I barely noticed. His hands went lower. He hesitated as he reached my waist, and looked at me. I took his hand and guided it down. I unzipped my fly and slipped his hand under my jeans, and he said, "Are you sure?"

I nodded. Slowly, slowly, he slid his hand down lower. He watched me as he did it. I felt that ache again as he touched me, a warm red point that spread outward like the distant glow of the sun rising. I tried to move closer to his lap, to put my hands on him, but he shook his head and took my wrist and interlocked our fingers again.

The ache grew stronger, until my thoughts went blurry. I laid my other hand on his chest. He felt reassuringly solid. He was breathing hard too, and he looked serious—so serious that I wanted to laugh at him.

I closed my eyes and rested my forehead against his; I thought of him in the pool, cutting a clean arc through the water, and then in the meadow at the hotel, with the sun behind him, smiling at me. I braced myself against him as the glow got warmer and redder, and his fingers were steady and sure, and then it crested through me in a sunburst and I could only think in images: clean, sharp, vivid ones, reds and greens and yellows, expanding and contracting.

After a minute I came back to myself and opened my eyes. He was looking at me.

"Was that good?" he said.

I laughed softly. "That was good. I just need a minute," I said. I laid my head against his chest and slumped into him. He stroked my hair and kissed the top of my head. I pressed myself closer to him, and then I felt something.

I looked up at him and he said, "Oh, that. Sorry."

I felt my pulse speeding up again. I'd done that—I'd turned him on. "I can take care of it if you want," I said, trying to sound sultry.

"No, no, no," he said. "I'm fine, really. Just relax."

"Come on," I said. I slid closer to him and reached my hand down.

He shifted uncomfortably and caught my hand. "Seriously, kid, it's okay. I'm happy just to have made you happy."

Suddenly I felt like I was going to cry. "Please," I said.

His expression changed as if he'd heard a catch in my voice. He took his hand off mine. "I guess if it's *that* important to you . . ."

I laughed and blinked a few times. "It is," I said.

I reached down again, wishing I knew what I was doing. My hand fumbled against his clothing; I was sitting so close to him that I couldn't see anything, and for a second it seemed like there were reams of fabric, all empty seams and bulges, and I flushed, thinking he would have to take my hand and guide me to it. Then I heard his breath hitch.

"Feel good?" I said, reasonably sure I was touching the right place.

"Not bad," he said, sounding out of breath.

I shivered and kissed him. Then I moved back so I could see what I was doing. I could see it now, looking different under the fabric than I had imagined. I'd thought it would just stand straight out in a huge proud tent, but the fabric was tight, and at a certain angle I would have assumed it was just a bulge where the seams had bunched oddly. I ran my hand up the fly experimentally.

"Jesus," he said. He was breathing hard again now.

I laughed, delighted that I'd given him pleasure. I fumbled again, trying to find his waistband.

"Are you sure about this?" he said as he watched me.

I looked at him and ran my hand up the fly.

His breath hitched again. "You make a good argument," he said. Then his own hands went to his waist and he pulled the fabric down, but the elastic on his pants stuck and I laughed and helped him. "Thanks," he whispered. He kissed my neck. "That always happens."

I stopped for a second—it looked much bigger under his boxers—and thought of the other people who'd done this to him, the other times he'd said something like that, whispered and laughed and kissed their necks. *Rachel, Rachel, Rachel.*

"You don't have to," he said.

"Oh, no," I said. "I was just, uh . . ."

"Anything I supply here will make me sound bad," he said.

I smiled. "I was just admiring your incredible, um, taste in boxer shorts."

"Don't be too impressed, but they come in packs of five."

Finally, slowly, I pulled his boxers down. I touched it experimentally; it was warm and firm but not rock-hard, as I had imagined it would be. It wasn't angry-looking or alien. He hadn't taken it out for me to service. It looked hot—like a physical manifestation of how much he wanted me. But I thought suddenly of him in our classroom, teasing Lila, and fear shuddered over me.

I paused only a second before I kissed him again. I shucked off my jeans before I could tell myself I shouldn't. His hands were under my bra, gentle at first and then with more assurance the longer we kissed. He knew exactly where to touch me. I moved myself closer and closer until he was against me and a layer of cotton was the only thing separating us. We were so close now that I felt slightly desperate. I started to pull down my underwear.

"Whoa," he said, his voice hoarse, which only turned me on more. "Are you sure about this?"

"You seem sure," I said.

He laughed softly. "That's not really a good barometer. Parts of me are always sure."

I didn't know how to take that. I tried to kiss him again, but he turned at the last second. I leaned back and looked at him, my heart sinking.

"I don't think—" he said.

"You don't want me."

"Charlie, of course I want you. It's taken me this long to stop myself because I want you so much. But it's—" He rubbed his hands over his face. "What the hell am I doing?"

"Let's just— We've already gone this far," I said. "Why not just keep going and worry about the rest later?"

I expected him to laugh but he didn't. I leaned next to his neck and kissed him gently on his jawline, up to his ear. I'd read in *Cosmo* that earlobes were an erogenous zone. Goose bumps stiffened on his arm. So *Cosmo* had proved to be good for something.

"Oh God," he said in a sort of guttural groan, and he turned and kissed me again, hard. His hands went lower and lower and mine did too, and all I could feel was how much I wanted him. I had to say it. It expanded inside me until I felt like it would burst out.

I leaned against his ear again. "Tell me you love me," I said.

The instant I said it, we both froze. I moved back. We stared at each other for a few seconds, and then he covered his face with his hands and said, "Oh, shit."

"I'm sorry," I said. "Forget I said that. That was stupid."

He didn't say anything; he just made that noise between a sigh and a whimper that I'd loved before.

I felt humiliated. "I'm sorry," I said again, uselessly.

"It's not you," he said, but he didn't look at me. "I just can't believe I did this."

"Oh," I said. I slid off his lap and he didn't stop me. I leaned against him but he didn't respond; where his body had been warm and concave it was now stiff and unwelcoming.

"You okay?" I said when he hadn't spoken for a few minutes.

He sighed and finally took his hands off his eyes. He still didn't look at me. "Not really." He pulled his pants up, and then he stood and retrieved his shirt from the floor. He pulled it over his head, and his hair frayed out again as if he'd rubbed a balloon over it.

Finally he looked at me, my shirt rucked up and my jeans tossed onto the floor. He picked them up and handed them to me. "You should get home," he said quietly.

"Oh," I said again. Tears clouded my vision so he looked warped and far away.

He was moving around the room, gathering up the books he'd spilled, and he didn't notice me crying for a few moments. When he did, he said, "Oh, Charlie, I'm sorry," and sat down next to me on the couch. That made me cry harder.

He hugged me again, but there was no sex behind it this time. It still made my heart speed up. "You don't deserve this," he said. "I've been so stupid. It isn't your fault I've been so stupid."

"I was stupid," I said.

"No," he said. "You're not the one who needs to regret this."

I'd thought I couldn't feel worse. "You're going to regret this?"

"No, not because— I worded that badly. How do I say this?" He put his forehead against mine and I sighed. "I don't regret *you*. I regret what I've done to you. I hurt you. I broke your trust. This was a violation. It would've been a violation with anyone, but especially with you."

I flinched. If it was wrong, then somehow I was wrong too; everything I'd done and thought and wanted was wrong. "But I wanted you to," I said. "I wanted it all year."

"But you needed me not to," he said.

I shook my head. "That doesn't mean anything."

"It does," he said.

"But I know what I need better than you do."

He blew out a long breath. "Normally I wouldn't disagree with you," he said. "It's just that this is . . ." He shook his head.

I leaned forward again and he put his hand on my head, as if by reflex, and gently ran it through my hair, combing it back. "You deserve better than me," he said. "That night in the classroom—I should have stopped it then, at the start, because I knew it would only get worse. I don't know, maybe it was too late by then anyway." He sighed. "Listen to me acting like it was something outside of us—me—that I couldn't control. I thought . . . I tried to tell myself it wasn't getting worse, that I had it under control, but you were so— I couldn't get you out of my head. You wouldn't believe the things I made up to excuse it."

I ducked my head so I wouldn't have to look him in the

eye. "Maybe it was so bad because we're supposed to be together."

His hand stopped moving. Finally he said, "I just wanted to . . . I wanted to protect you." He looked down at the books that were still strewn across the floor. "It's funny the stories you'll tell yourself to pretend things are different." Then his hand dropped. "I'm not a good person," he said quietly.

I was terrified he would start crying. I had sometimes imagined him vulnerable and weeping, but faced with the reality of it, I didn't know what to do. "Don't say that," I said. "Please don't say that."

He was silent for a long time. "Why did you have to be so . . ."

I moved toward him, but he flinched. "Sorry," I said.

He shook his head and said, "I shouldn't be— Ugh, I'm just making it worse. What I'm trying to say is that ultimately it doesn't matter how I feel about you. I have to be the adult here."

"I'm an adult too," I said. "Technically."

"I'm still your teacher," he said.

"Doesn't that kind of make it hotter?" I said.

He smiled sadly but didn't say anything. A silence stretched out.

"Will I see you tomorrow?" I said finally.

He paused, then nodded. "Probably."

I looked down. "You're leaving."

"I don't know yet," he said. "That's the truth."

I tried to ignore the pressure rising in my chest. "Okay."

"I don't know how to make this better," he said.

"Run away with me," I said. I tried to smile so it would seem like a joke.

He smiled a little too. "You're going to do so well without me," he said. "In a year this will just be an embarrassing story you'll tell your boyfriend to make him laugh. How you got off with your loser of a teacher and he made an idiot of himself."

"No, it won't," I said.

He watched me for a moment. Then he said, "Come here, Charlie," and I embraced him desperately. I couldn't relax. I was shaking so hard I knew he must feel it.

"Promise me you'll be okay," he said.

I nodded. He kissed my cheek. I hoped it would start up again, the desperate kissing, but this was soft and sweet. Then he pulled back and got up, and that was it. I knew I wasn't allowed to touch him again. I watched him, thinking how odd it was that a few minutes earlier I'd had my hands all over him and now I couldn't so much as touch his shoulder.

I stood up once I'd gotten ready.

"I can't quite believe I managed to make your birthday worse," he said. "These are my talents."

"You made it better," I said.

He shook his head. "I wish that were true."

When I got home, I stood in the bathroom and looked in the mirror until I had studied my face for so long that I couldn't tell whether I was attractive or ugly anymore. It was like saying a word over and over again until it became a meaningless jumble of letters. I tried every expression I could think of, but none of them fit.

"You slut," I said to my reflection. "You seduced your teacher." I touched my chin, which was bubble gum pink from his stubble.

There was a knock at the door. I opened it reluctantly. It was my dad.

"Hi," I said.

"Hi," he said. "Where have you been?"

I pursed my lips. "Lots of places. Are you mad at me?"

He sighed and rubbed his hand over his beard. "You took your mom's car. And you missed . . ." He leaned in closer to me. "Have you been drinking?"

I blushed. "A little."

"And you drove home?"

I blushed more. "Yes."

He massaged his forehead as if I were physically hurting him. "You realize you're lucky you didn't kill someone."

"I know," I said quietly.

"Or get yourself killed."

I sat down on the toilet lid. "I know," I said again.

"Or wreck your mom's car."

"I'm sorry," I said.

"And you won't do it again," he said. "Ever."

"I won't," I said. I felt like I was about to cry again. "Am I in trouble?"

"You're eighteen now, Charlie," he said. He sounded tired. "I'm not going to punish you."

"You're not going to punish me?" I said.

"No."

"Why not?"

He tilted his head to one side. "Do you *want* me to punish you?"

I paused, and then I heaved a breath that hitched into a sob, and then I was crying again. I was sick of crying. "I'm sorry, Daddy," I said.

"Oh, kiddo," he said. He knelt down in front of me and put his hand on my knee. "I'm sorry about this morning. That had to be traumatic."

I half laughed, half sobbed. "You have no idea."

"I'll pay for the therapy if you want," he said.

"Okay," I said. "I might take you up on that."

He pulled the end of the toilet paper so it spooled out, more and more of it until it mounded in my lap like whipped cream, until I laughed, and then he delicately dabbed it at my eyes. "Come on," he said. "Let's get you some cake."

chapter 38

He did show up the next day. I didn't look at him, so I couldn't tell whether he was avoiding me too. I'd considered not coming in—it was the day after my birthday and I was entitled to a hangover—but I'd decided to prove how little he and Lila had affected me.

"Uh, right," he said after the bell rang. "Where did we leave off the day before yesterday?"

"Deciding whether *Persuasion* is crap next to *Pride and Prejudice*," Asha said.

"Oh, yes, okay," he said. "I did have a passage I wanted to read out loud to see if I could—pardon the wordplay—persuade you, Asha." He glanced back at his desk. "But I don't seem to have my copy. Where is . . . ?" He got up—his chair squealed—and started rummaging through his brown leather bag. "Nowhere," he muttered. I thought of the pile of books on his couch, the ones he'd scattered everywhere so I could sit next to him. Had that been one of them? He ran his hand through his hair. "Can I borrow someone's copy for a minute?"

I looked down at the book I had, the one my mother had given me. I wished I could hide it, but it was too late now; it stuck out, large and regal, among the tattered used copies everyone else had.

I looked up again. He was watching me, his eyebrows raised, his expression tentative. I nodded slightly.

He moved toward me like he was afraid I'd run if he came over too quickly. "Thanks, Charlie," he said softly as I held it out by the edge, to make sure our fingers wouldn't touch.

"Okay," he said as he walked back to his chair. "I know a lot of you think Austen is just a social comedian, but I think she was more self-aware than you're giving her credit for. You remember when Anne is arguing with Captain Harville about the nature of men and women?"

There was a general murmur of assent.

"All right." He gently eased open my book and then turned it over, admiring it. "Nice edition," he said. He flipped to the section he wanted, letting his fingers slide over the pages. "Here it is. Captain Harville is being a blowhard, as usual, and he says, 'I do not think I ever opened a book in my life which had not something to say upon woman's inconstancy. Songs and proverbs, all talk of woman's fickleness. But perhaps, you will say, these were all written by men.' "

A couple of people booed, and Drummond smiled a little without raising his head. "Yes, sure," he said. "Okay, but listen to Anne's response. 'Yes, yes, if you please, no reference to examples in books. Men have had every advantage of us in telling their own story. Education has been theirs in so much higher a degree; the pen has been in their hands. I will not allow books to prove anything.' "

The same kids laughed. Everyone was in a good mood that day; it was nearly the weekend and no one could sit still. Drummond glanced at me, and for a second I felt so punishingly lonely that I couldn't look back.

"Asha," he said, "what do you think?"

"I think Austen's talking about her own book," Asha said. "She wrote her own story. *Persuasion* refutes his argument."

"I think you have a point," he said. He paused, still staring down at the book. He flipped through the pages and then put his palm against the cover with his fingers spread out. "All right," he said eventually, "enough talk. Who wants to watch the movie?" Everyone cheered this time. "Frank, can you set it up?"

The class started chattering as Frank got up. After a minute, I could feel Drummond come over. He slid the book back to me, but he didn't say anything. I put my hand on the cover where his fingers had been. When I raised my head, he was watching me again. We looked at each other for a long time, and I looked down at the book, and I knew he wasn't coming back.

The next day, Dr. Crowley announced that he'd had a family emergency and wouldn't be returning for the rest of the school year.

may

chapter 39

One weekend I found my mother in her study. I didn't know what I wanted from her, but I couldn't stand being alone in my room crying anymore.

"Charlie," she said when she saw me. "What are you doing in here?"

I sat down on the sofa. "I can't visit my loving mother just because I want to?" I said.

"You generally don't, no." She took off her reading glasses and folded them carefully. "What's going on?"

I inhaled shakily. "You think I'm pretty, right?"

She got up and sat down next to me. "You're beautiful, sweetheart. What is this about?"

"I don't—" My voice cracked. "Do you really think so or are you just saying that because you have to?"

"Because I think so," she said. "I think if you'd just let me—"

I shook my head. "No, no qualifications."

"I'm sorry," she said. "You are beautiful. No qualifications."

I looked away. I didn't believe her. She was beautiful herself and had the luxury of bestowing compliments on others, knowing they would be returned. I had to jealously guard every compliment I got and worry it until it was gone.

"What happened?" she said.

"Nothing."

"So you're asking me these questions for no particular reason?"

"Yes."

She put her hand on mine. "I'm not going to pry, but I want you to know I love you no matter what."

"Even if I did something really bad?"

"Even then."

"Even if I totaled Dad's car?"

"You wh—" She stopped when she saw I was smiling. "That wasn't funny."

"Sorry," I said. I got up and wandered around the room, running my fingers over her books. "Did you have a boyfriend in high school?"

"Yes," she said. "It wasn't serious, but we dated for a while."

"Did you have sex with him?"

She looked startled. "Uh, no, I didn't."

"Yes, then?"

She smiled a little. "None of your business."

"We're a little bit past you pretending that you've never had sex."

I could see her reddening. "Yes, I had sex with my boyfriend," she said. "Where's this going? Are you having sex with someone?"

"No," I said automatically, though my mind flashed back to that night with him, the warm, solid feeling of knowing how much he wanted me. I'd been alone for so long it was hard to think of myself as anything other than chaste.

"Are you pregnant?"

"No! This isn't . . . Sorry, I think I need to go to bed."

"Charlie," she said. "Please talk to me."

I sat down. "I just wish . . ." I had to force the words out. "I just wish I were beautiful."

I waited for her to try to argue me out of it, but she didn't.

Finally she said, "It's not fair."

Suddenly I was crying. It felt better for her to acknowledge it than it would have for her to reassure me.

"Oh, honey," she said. "I didn't mean—"

"No, it's not— They're good tears," I said. "Thank you for being honest with me. And for not telling me it's just as hard being pretty."

She was silent as I cried. Then she said, "I wish I understood you better."

I wanted to tell her she did, but we both knew that wasn't true.

"Thank you for trying," I said.

chapter 40

Lila's mother always greeted me with a smile. I couldn't tell whether Lila had told her anything about our fight. "Hi, hon," she said. "Come on in."

"Hi," I said. "Is she in?"

Her mother gestured to the stairs. "She's in her room."

"Thanks," I said, and went up to the second floor. Lila's door was open and she was lying on her bed with her bulky headphones on. I could hear tinny music leaking from them.

I waved to get her attention, and she looked over and then reluctantly turned off her music.

"Hey," I said. Our argument felt so long ago that I could barely remember why I'd been angry at her. I sat down on her bed.

"I thought I wasn't supposed to speak to you ever again." She played with the headphone cord, not looking up.

"Something happened with Drummond. I have to tell someone or I'll go crazy."

She looked up sharply, then away again when she realized she'd betrayed her interest. "I thought maybe something had," she said.

"What an idiot."

She readjusted herself on the bed so she was sitting up. "You or him?"

"Both, I guess. Do you think anyone else suspects?"

Lila shook her head. "Nah. I mean, there are always rumors, but I haven't heard any about you."

"I'm kind of offended," I said.

She smiled, but she looked tired. "So what happened?"

"You're not going to believe me."

"I will."

I hesitated. "We almost had sex."

"Motherfucker!" She put her hand to her mouth. "Sorry. I just wasn't expecting that."

"I told you," I said. We both started giggling.

"Oh my God, Charlie," she said, looking horrified and delighted. "Start from the top. Don't skip anything."

I told her. When I was finished, she leaned back against the wall and said, "Is it incredibly wrong of me to find this hot?" She laughed. "You are so red right now."

I hit her. "It's embarrassing."

"It's really not," she said. She sighed. "All that bullshit about feminism and then he gets it out as soon as he sees an opportunity with his jailbait student."

"I'm legal now, all right?" I said. "And you're one to talk. You tried to kiss him."

"That was months ago," she said. "I've matured. Plus he turned me down."

I snorted softly. "I know he should have turned me down too. But . . ."

"Dude, I don't blame you. I would have done it too."

"Bet he wouldn't have fled with shame after he had sex with you," I said.

"Charlie," she said. "He was a coward to do that. It wasn't because of you."

"I guess," I said.

"Anyway," she said, "you made a grown man give up his job for you. That's power."

I shook my head. "I don't want that kind of power. I want something more . . . I don't know . . . permanent."

She fiddled with the headphone cord again. "So you haven't heard from him?"

"No," I said. "Nothing."

"He could be in love with you, you know. Pining away tragically."

My throat tightened. "He isn't."

She glanced at me but didn't press for details. "So was he good?"

I looked at her out of the corner of my eye. "Yes."

"Yeah, but better than my toothbrush?"

I laughed. "Well, it didn't vibrate."

"Shame. They need to fix that."

We were quiet for a few minutes. It had started to rain outside.

"So, uh, I had something I needed to tell you too," Lila said.

"You broke up with Jason, didn't you?"

She laughed. "No, but—I got into Stanford. So probably yes."

I stared at her. Then I realized I needed to speak. "You're kidding! That's amazing!" I said. I wasn't sure whether she wanted me to hug her, so I put my hand on her shoulder. She looked down at it but didn't move away. "When did you find out?"

She was trying not to smile. "A few weeks ago."

"Oh," I said. I realized how big a gap had opened

between us in so little time: she'd been celebrating for weeks and I hadn't even known. Was that what it would be like from now on? "Well, congratulations. Chatham Valley is going to be crushed."

She smiled. "I'm keeping them as a safety in case this falls through."

"Lila—" I said. I hugged my knees to my chest. "I'm . . ."

"I know," she said. "I am too."

I laughed. Then I said, "Why are all our fights over guys?"

"Not all of them," she said. "Sometimes we fought over Asha too."

"That's true. You know it's because women are subjected to—"

"Please don't try to make a feminist argument when you've still got stubble burns from your English teacher on your tits."

My jaw dropped in mock indignation and I hit her with her pillow. She laughed and pulled me to her, and I let her.

"Your bosom is soft," I said. "And stubble-burn-free."

"I use protection."

"I missed you."

"I know."

"Can we please never fight again?"

"As long as you're able to never be wrong again."

"Promise."

chapter 41

After he left, *Truth Bomb* was covered by a rotating cast of substitute teachers. One day when Asha and I walked in, Ms. Anders was sitting behind his desk, rummaging through her bag.

"Hi," I said. "Are you covering today?"

She looked up, startled. She was still as nervous as a bird. "Oh, hi, Charlotte. I didn't realize you'd be here. Yes, I'm covering. Though I'm not sure why this activity wasn't canceled."

"Ah," I said. "I think it's because we haven't actually produced an issue all year."

Ms. Anders frowned. "You haven't produced an issue?"

Asha sat on a table and I slid down next to her. "We were close," she said, "and then Drummond left and we haven't been sure what to do."

Ms. Anders's frown deepened, folding her forehead up like a concertina. "But why hadn't you produced any issues up to—" She sighed. "But you kids loved him. Never mind. Where are we, then? Is it just you two?"

Dev and Frank appeared at the door.

"These guys sometimes," I said, "when there's food."

Ms. Anders heaved her bag onto Drummond's desk. "I think there might be mints in there if you desperately feel the need."

Frank looked at her bag and then raised his eyebrows at us. Asha shrugged.

"All right," Ms. Anders said. "Let's press on. Can one of you show me where you are?" She stood up and moved toward the bank of computers.

We watched her for a minute, no one moving, and then Frank said, "I'll go. I like brusque women."

"Thanks, Frank," I said, and he saluted me as he walked off.

Dev sat down next to Asha without looking at me.

"Don't get too comfortable," Ms. Anders said, craning around to look at us. "You'll need to come help in a minute."

"Okay," I said. I turned back to Asha. "I'm failing trig."

She laughed. "I almost miss Drummond."

I winced. I hated discussing him, but that was all anyone had wanted to talk about for weeks.

"I definitely miss him," Dev said.

"I know *you* do," Asha said. "I still think he got fired."

"Why would they fire him? What did he do?"

"He never actually finished an issue of the paper. He was relentlessly smug. He didn't teach us anything we couldn't have figured out on our own—"

"Okay, okay," Dev said. He glanced at me and away again. "Don't cross Asha."

I smiled at Dev. He'd been different around me ever since my birthday, and I didn't know how to apologize for how I'd acted.

"I thought you had come around on him," I said to Asha.

"Well," she said, "let's not overstate it."

"Be grateful," I said. "If he hadn't left, you'd have nothing to complain about."

Asha laughed and hit my hand gently. "I'd find something," she said.

I glanced up to see Dev watching us. He looked away when I caught his eye. Asha noticed and said, "Him, probably."

"What?" I asked.

"I'd complain about Dev."

"You do that anyway," Dev said.

"True," she said. "But you give me a sort of focus point."

He rolled his eyes at me. I grinned.

"I saw that," Asha said.

"That was the idea," he said.

I looked at him. He didn't look away. Asha watched us carefully. Then she smiled.

Ms. Anders kept me behind after everyone else had left. I didn't think there was any way she could know about me and Drummond, but I was still nervous as she closed the door.

"So, Charlotte," she said, crossing her legs as she sat down. I noticed there was a run in her stocking that jagged halfway up her thigh like a long skeletal finger and disappeared obscenely into her skirt. The skin underneath was so white it was almost blue. "I know you and Tom were close."

"Uh," I said.

"Sorry—Mr. Drummond," she said. "See? I've gotten better about that."

"I guess," I said.

"So you know what happened?"

My breath caught. "What?"

"You know why he left?"

"A family emergency?" I said.

"No, I mean specifically," she said.

"I, um . . ." I was suddenly sure she knew and was trying to tease it out of me. "No, I don't think . . . Do you know?"

"Dr. Crowley said his mother was sick," she said. "But we're not supposed to tell the students, so please don't pass it around."

"Ah," I said. It took a few moments for my heartbeat to slow down. "Okay. I won't."

"I just wanted you to know in case you were worried," she said.

"Oh," I said. "Thank you."

"I've tried to get in touch, but his phone just goes to voice mail," she said. "No forwarding address either."

"I'm sure they'll give you that information eventually," I said.

"I wouldn't count on that."

When I gave her a quizzical look, she said, "They're hiring someone else permanently for my position next year."

"Oh," I said. "I'm sorry."

"It's fine," she said. "I just—I just thought I had longer, I guess."

I didn't know what to say. "Do you have any plans?"

She shook her head. "We'll see what happens. Couldn't be more of an adventure than this year, right?"

"Yeah," I said. "Right."

She didn't say anything. She ran her hand down her thigh and her nails snagged at the tear. "Oh, great," she said. "Was this there the whole time?" She covered it up with her hand. "Just two more weeks, right?"

"Yep," I said. "Then we're free."

june

chapter 42

The day we graduated was bright and clear, the sky so blue it looked endless.

Everyone looked incredibly young in the sunshine. As I stood there listening to Dr. Crowley speak, I felt a silly, sentimental swell of love for them. I heard my parents cheer as I clutched my diploma.

I couldn't help searching the bleachers, but he hadn't come. In a way I was relieved.

Afterward I remembered that I'd left a jacket in my locker, and I ran inside. I couldn't help taking one last look at our English classroom. He had never decorated the walls with posters or charts, and the room had always seemed a little bare. But now his desk was empty; most of his stuff had been gone for weeks, but he had left a few things—extra copies of books, old handouts and outdated syllabi—and someone had come by and cleared those out too. I realized suddenly that he wouldn't get to sign my yearbook, something I had thought about occasionally before everything had happened. It seemed stupid now that I had been looking forward to it so much: so naive of me, hoping for so little.

When I turned back into the hall, he was there. He looked exactly the same as he always had, but something about him had changed.

"Hi," I said, sounding calmer than I felt. "I didn't think you'd come."

He smiled ruefully. "I wasn't sure I would either. But . . ." He shrugged. "It didn't seem right, not seeing you graduate."

I nodded. "Well, thanks for showing up. It's been a nice day."

"You guys looked great out there," he said. "You looked like the future."

"I guess we are," I said.

"A somewhat terrifying thought," he said, "now that I've spent a year with Frank."

I smiled a little. "True."

"You know, I realized the other day I never got you an internship for the summer."

"Oh," I said. "I actually . . . I found something on my own." I hadn't, but I knew I could. I didn't need his help anymore. "Um, anyway, my parents are expecting me, so . . ."

"Oh," he said. "Of course."

"But it was nice to see you. You know, good luck with everything." I started to turn away and he caught my arm.

"Charlie," he said. He looked sick. "I just came because I wanted to— I know I owe you an apology. I owe you an apology so big that words can't begin to touch it."

"Yeah, you do." My eyes clouded as I said it. I paused, trying to gather my thoughts. "You don't deserve my forgiveness," I said finally.

"I know," he said.

"You don't deserve even getting to ask for it."

"I know," he said again.

"You don't deserve getting to come here."

"I'm sorry," he said.

I glanced into the classroom so I wouldn't have to see his face. "Why are you even here? What do you want?"

He crossed his arms over his chest. "I had to see with my own eyes that they were allowing Sean to graduate."

I tried to frown at him so I wouldn't laugh, but the expression wouldn't stick. I looked up at the ceiling and then down again. "Why did you leave?"

"I had to," he said. He stepped toward me. "If I could change it, I would."

I shook my head. "I don't want you to change it. You don't get to do that. *I* want to— I want to decide how it ends. Okay? I get to write it. I get to decide."

"Okay," he said quietly.

We stood there in silence for a minute. I stared at his hands, his feet, his ears, his mouth, his eyes. He seemed so ordinary now, just some guy I could have passed on the street. I never would have looked at him twice. I felt sad for him then, and all the anger drained away. He was just a person. Nothing more or less.

Suddenly I wanted to give him something, but I only had one thing left.

"Let's pretend," I said finally. "Let's pretend we got married. In a castle in Germany."

He looked startled for a second, and then the corners of his mouth turned down and his eyes became glassy. "You're sure you . . . you want to . . ."

I nodded. He knew how this worked, and what to say, and how I wanted him to lie. He'd taught me.

He uncrossed his arms and cleared his throat. "I protested, but you got your way."

"The food was awful. Bratwurst."

"The DJ played Kraftwerk all night."

"My parents got drunk and made out on the dance floor."

"But you looked radiant," he said. "I could never forget it."

My breath hitched, but I kept going. "You looked ridiculous," I said. "You insisted on wearing lederhosen."

"And the alpine hat," he said. "It looked jaunty." He stepped closer. "*Tirolerhut,* if you want to get technical."

"And afterward we honeymooned in Austria."

"Every morning we were woken by flügelhorns."

"Accordions."

"Whatever."

"We moved to New York."

"For your job at the *Times*. And my residence at NYU."

"We turned them down when they offered you tenure. We couldn't be tied down like that."

"That's right," he said. "Our kids were world travelers."

"They turned out well, though. Rhodes Scholars."

"They had good role models," he said. "We loved each other."

"Married fifty-two years," I said. "And I never once farted on you."

He laughed. "I can't say the same for myself."

I kissed him. As we pulled apart, he whispered, "Bye, Charlotte."

I made a sound between a laugh and a sob. "Bye, Tom," I said.

Then he was gone.

When I stepped outside, I had to shade my eyes from the sun, it was so bright.

Lila appeared out of nowhere. "Hey," she said. "You okay?"

I nodded, my chin shaking. "I will be."

She hooked her arm around mine. "C'mon, Asha wants to take pictures. I'm going to give her my best devil horns." She demonstrated, knowing it would make me laugh, and it did.

"I'm ready," I said.

acknowledgments

Thanks first of all to Phoebe Yeh and David Dunton, my editor and agent—without their enthusiasm and encouragement, this book would have stayed on my laptop forever (so blame them).

Phoebe, thank you for your editorial brilliance, which improved the book in uncountable ways; your dedication (I am still convinced you don't sleep); and your incredible, passionate, dynamo-like backing of this book and me, which I would be suspicious of if it weren't so genuine. David, thank you for your steadiness and your kindness, and for putting up with my incessant emails about pizza. I wanted to find an agent I liked and instead I got you, who I adore. I still owe you a Hot Dog Johnny's (even now), but not until you get me Louis C.K.'s number.

Thanks also to the people who I asked to read this thing before I even knew what I was going to do with it: Alice Swan (enthusiasm I knew was real because you do not lie, and advice on what word to lose in a crucial scene), Sung Woo (lots of excellent structural guidance), Harriet "baggy" Reuter "Hopsgobble" Hapgood (twenty-paragraph emails, bucketloads of "WHAT are they CRAZY?" reassurance, Teacher Gave Me the D, general lols, and endless supplies of apposite gifs). And thank you to the people at Random House who've made the book better than I ever could have alone: Rachel Weinick (Bridgewater Commons forever), Alison Kolani, Jennifer Black, Courtney Code, Jocelyn Lange, and Alison Impey for a (third) fantastic cover.

Thanks also to: Vicki and Lindsay for not killing me, Nikki for general awesomeness, Gen and Zoe for keeping my secret, Bon for everything, my family generally for all your support and occasional sassing, Dee for all the incredible ways you've helped us over the years and (not) for the story about Liam Neeson, and Mom for your love and for pretending you hadn't read the sex scenes.

Thanks to everyone who read this far for tolerating all the in-jokes.

Finally, to John, who was my first and best reader, who cries at everything, who has talked me down from more ledges than I can count, who is kind and thoughtful and curious, who always makes me laugh even when I don't want to, and who cannot pull off a hat JUST STOP TRYING: I love you.